THE NEWS FROM IRELAND

WILLIAM TREVOR

The News from Ireland

OTHER STORIES

THE BODLEY HEAD
LONDON

British Library Cataloguing
in Publication Data
Trevor, William
The News from Ireland
and other stories
I. Title
823'.914[F]   PR6070.R4
ISBN 0-370-30695-3
© William Trevor 1986
Printed in Great Britain for
The Bodley Head Ltd
30 Bedford Square
London WC1B 3RP
by Redwood Burn Ltd, Trowbridge

First published 1986

CONTENTS

The News from Ireland, 9

On the Zattere, 47

Lunch in Winter, 69

The Property of Colette Nervi, 85

Running Away, 107

Cocktails at Doney's, 129

Bodily Secrets, 147

Virgins, 173

Her Mother's Daughter, 205

Music, 226

Two More Gallants, 250

The Wedding in the Garden, 262

Acknowledgments. These stories first appeared in the *Atlantic Encounter, Good Housekeeping, Grand Street,* the *Irish Times, James Joyce and Modern Literature,* the *New Yorker, Atlantic Monthly* and the *Listener.*

THE NEWS FROM IRELAND

The News from Ireland

Poor Irish Protestants is what the Fogartys are: butler and cook. They have church connections, and conversing with Miss Fogarty people are occasionally left with the impression that their father was a rural dean who suffered some misfortune: in fact he was a sexton. Fogarty is the younger and the smaller of the pair, brought up by Miss Fogarty, their mother dying young. His life was saved by his sister's nursing the time he caught scarlatina, when he was only eight.

Dapper in his butler's clothes, a slight and unimposing man with a hazelnut face, Fogarty is at present fascinated by the newly arrived governess: Anna Maria Heddoe, from somewhere in England, a young woman of principle and sensibility, stranger and visitor to Ireland. Fogarty is an educated man, and thinks of other visitors there have been: the Celts, whose ramshackle gipsy empire expired in this same landscape, St Patrick with his holy shamrock, the outrageous Vikings preceding the wily Normans, the adventurers of the Virgin Queen. His present employers arrived here also, eight years ago, in 1839. The Pulvertafts of Ipswich, as Fogarty thinks of them, and wishes they had not bothered to make the journey after old Hugh Pulvertaft died. House and estate fell away under the old man, and in Fogarty's opinion it is a pity the process didn't continue until everything was driven back into the clay it came from. Instead of which along had come the Pulvertafts of Ipswich, taking on more staff, clearing the

(9)

brambles from the garden in their endeavour to make the place what it had been in the past, long before the old man's time. The Pulvertafts of Ipswich belong here now. They make allowances for the natives, they come to terms, they learn to live with things. Fogarty has watched surprise and dismay fade from their faces. He has watched these people becoming important locally, and calling the place they have come to 'home'. Serving them in the dining-room, holding for them a plate of chops or hurrying to them a gravy dish, he wishes he might speak the truth as it appears to him: that their fresh, decent blood is the blood of the invader though they are not themselves invaders, that they perpetrate theft without being thieves. He does not dislike the Pulvertafts of Ipswich, he has nothing against them beyond the fact that they did not stay where they were. He and his sister might alone have attended the mouldering of the place, urging it back to the clay.

The governess is interesting to Fogarty because she is another of the strangers whom the new Pulvertafts have trailed behind them in their advent. Such visitors, in the present and in the past, obsess the butler. He observes Miss Heddoe daily; he studies her closely and from a distance, but he does not reveal his obsession to his sister, who would consider it peculiar. He carries Miss Heddoe's meals to her room when normally this duty would be Cready's or Brigid's; he reads the letters she receives, and the diary she intermittently keeps.

*

October 15th, 1847. I look out of the window of my attic room, and in the early morning the men are already labouring on the road that is to encircle the estate. The estate manager, the one-armed Mr Erskine, oversees them from his horse. Mr Pulvertaft rides up, gesturing about some immediate necessity—how a particular shrub must be avoided, so his gestures suggest, or where best to construct a bridge. The estate manager listens and assents, his men do not cease in their work. Beyond the trees, beyond the high stone walls of the estate, women and children die of the hunger that God has seen fit to visit upon them. In my prayers I ask for mercy.

October 17th, 1847. Fogarty came in with my dinner on a tray and said that the marks of the stigmata had been discovered on a child.

'Is the child alive?' I demanded when he returned a half-hour later for the tray.

'Oh yes, miss. No doubt on that. The living child was brought to Father Horan.'

I was amazed but he seemed hardly surprised. I questioned him but he was vague; and the conversation continuing because he lingered, I told him the Legend of the True Cross, with which he was unfamiliar. He was delighted to hear of its elaborations, and said he would recount these in the kitchen. The stigmata on the child have been revealed on feet and hands only, but the priest has said that other parts of the body must be watched. The priest has cautiously given an opinion: that so clearly marked a stigma has never before been known in Ireland. The people consider it a miracle, a sign from God in these distressful times.

October 20th, 1847. I am not happy here. I do not understand this household, neither the family nor the servants. This is the middle of my third week, yet I am still in all ways at a loss. Yesterday, in the afternoon, I was for the first time summoned to the drawing-room to hear Adelaide play her pieces, and George Arthur's lessons being over for the day he sat by me, as naturally he should. Charlotte and her mother occupied the sofa, Emily a chair in a recess. Mr Pulvertaft stood toasting his back at the fire, his riding-crop tapping time on the side of his polished boot. They made a handsome family picture—Emily beautiful, Charlotte petite and pretty, the plump motherliness of Mrs Pulvertaft, her husband's ruddy presence. I could not see George Arthur's features, for he was a little in front of me, but I knew them well from the hours I have surveyed them across our lessons-table. He is sharp-faced, and dark like all the family except Mrs Pulvertaft, whose hair I would guess was red before becoming grey. Only Adelaide, bespectacled and seeming heavy for her age, does not share the family's gift of grace. Poor Adelaide is cumbersome; her movements are awkward at the piano and she really plays it most inelegantly.

Yet in the drawing-room no frown or wince betrayed the listeners' ennui. As though engrossed in a performance given by a fine musician, Mr Pulvertaft slightly raised and dropped his riding-crop, as he might a baton; similarly expressing absorption, his wife's lips were parted, the hurry and worry of her nature laid aside, her little eyes delighted. And Emily and Charlotte sat as girls more graciously endowed than a plain sister should, neither pouting nor otherwise recoiling from the halting cacophony. I too—I hope successfully—forced delight into an expression that constantly sought to betray me, while surreptitiously examining my surroundings. (I cannot be certain of what passed, or did not pass, over George Arthur's features: in the nursery, certainly, he is not slow to display displeasure.)

The drawing-room is lofty and more than usually spacious, with pleasant recesses, and French windows curving along a single wall. Two smaller windows flank the fire-place, which is of white marble that reflects, both in colour and in the pattern of its carving, the white plasterwork of the ceiling. Walls are of an apricot shade, crowded with landscape scenes and portraits of the Pulvertafts who belong to the past. Silks and velvets are mainly green; escritoires and occasional tables are cluttered with ornaments and porcelain pieces—too many for my own taste, but these are family heirlooms which it would be impolite to hide away. So Mrs Pulvertaft has explained, for the same degree of overcrowding obtains in the hall and dining-room, and on the day of my arrival she remarked upon it.

'*Most* charmingly rendered,' her husband pronounced when the music ceased. 'What fingers Adelaide is blessed with!'

Hands in the drawing-room were delicately clapped. Mr Pulvertaft applauded with his riding-crop. I pursed my lips at the back of George Arthur's head, for he was perhaps a little rumbustious in his response.

'Is not Adelaide talented, Miss Heddoe?' Mrs Pulvertaft suggested.

'Indeed, ma'am.'

Two maids, Cready and Brigid, brought in tea. I rose to go, imagining my visit to the drawing-room must surely now be concluded. But Mrs Pulvertaft begged me to remain.

'We must get to know you, Miss Heddoe,' she insisted in her bustling manner. (It is from his mother, I believe, that George Arthur inherits his occasional boisterousness). 'And you,' she added, 'us.'

I felt, to tell the truth, that I knew the Pulvertafts fairly well already. I was not long here before I observed that families and events are often seen historically in Ireland—more so, for some reason, than in England. It surprised me when Mrs Pulvertaft went into details soon after I arrived, informing me that on the death of a distant relative Mr Pulvertaft had found himself the inheritor of this overseas estate. Though at first he had apparently resisted the move to another country, he ended by feeling it his bounden duty to accept the responsibility. 'It was a change of circumstances for us, I can tell you that,' Mrs Pulvertaft confessed. 'But had we remained in Ipswich these many acres would have continued to lose heart. There have been Pulvertafts here, you know, since Queen Elizabeth first granted them the land.' I thought, but did not remark, that when Mr Pulvertaft first looked upon drawings of the house and gardens his unexpected inheritance must have seemed like a gift from heaven, which in a sense it was, for the distant relative had been by all accounts a good man.

'Much undergrowth has yet to be cleared and burnt,' Mr Pulvertaft was saying now, with reference to the estate road that was being built. 'The merry fires along the route will continue for a while to come. Next, stones must be chipped and laid, and by the lakeside the ground raised and strengthened. Here and there we must have ornamental seats.'

Cake was offered to us by Cready and by Brigid. It was not my place in the drawing-room to check the manners of George Arthur, but they do leave much to be desired. Old Miss Larvey, who was my predecessor and governess to all four children, had clearly become slack before her death. I smiled a little at George Arthur, and was unable to resist moving my fingers slightly in his direction, a gesture to indicate that a more delicate consuming of the cake would not be amiss. He pretended, mischievously, not to notice.

'Will the road go round Bright Purple Hill?' Emily enquired. 'It would be beautiful if it did.'

It could be made to do so, her father agreed. Yes, certainly it could go round the northern slopes at least. He would speak to Erskine.

'Now, what could be nicer,' he resumed, 'than a picnic of lunch by the lake, then a drive through the silver birches, another pause by the abbey, continuing by the river for a mile, and home by Bright Purple Hill? This road, Miss Heddoe, has become my pride.'

I smiled and nodded, acknowledging this attention in silence. I knew that there was more to the road than that: its construction was an act of charity, a way of employing the men for miles around, since the failure of their potato crops had again reduced them to poverty and idleness. In years to come the road would stand as a memorial to this awful time, and Mr Pulvertaft's magnanimity would be recalled with gratitude.

'Might copper beech trees mark the route?' suggested Adelaide, her dumpling countenance freshened by the excitement this thought induced. Her eyes bulged behind her spectacles and I noticed that her mother, in glancing at her, resisted the impulse to sigh.

'Beech trees indeed! Quite splendid!' enthused Mr Pulvertaft. 'And in future Pulvertaft generations they shall arch a roof, shading our road when need be. Yes, indeed there must be copper beech trees.'

The maids had left the drawing-room and returned now with lamps. They fastened the shutters and drew the curtains over. The velvets and silks changed colour in the lamplight, the faces of the portraits became as they truly were, the faces of ghosts.

A silence gathered after the talk of beech trees, and I found myself surprised at no one mentioning the wonder Fogarty had told me of, the marks of Christ on a peasant child. It seemed so strange and so remarkable, an occurrence of such import and magnitude, that I would hardly have believed it possible that any conversation could take place in the house without some astonished reference to it. Yet none had been made, and the faces and the voices in the drawing-room seemed as untouched by this visitation of the miraculous as they had been by Adelaide's labouring on the piano. In the silence I excused myself and left, taking George Arthur with me, for my time to do so had come.

October 23rd, 1847. I am homesick, I make no bones about it. I cannot help dwelling on all that I have left behind, on familiar sounds and places. First thing when I awake

I still imagine I am in England: reality comes most harshly then.

While I write, Emily and George Arthur are conversing in a corner of the nursery. She has come here, as she does from time to time, to persuade him against a military career. I wish she would not do so in this manner, wandering in and standing by the window to await the end of a lesson. It is distracting for George Arthur, and after all this is my domain.

'What I mean, George Arthur, is that it is an uncomfortable life in a general sort of way.'

'Captain Roche does not seem uncomfortable. When you look at him he doesn't give that impression in the least.'

'Captain Roche hasn't lived in a barracks in India. That leaves a mark, so people say.'

'I should not mind a barracks. And India I should love.'

'I doubt it, actually. Flies carry disease in India, the water you drink is putrid. And you would mind a barracks because they're rough and ready places.'

'You'd drink something else if the water was putrid. You'd keep well away from the flies.'

'You cannot in India. No, George Arthur, I assure you you enjoy your creature comforts. You'd find the uniform rough on your skin and the food unappetising. Besides, you have a family duty here.'

The nursery is a long, low-ceilinged room, with a fire at one end, close to which I sit as I write, for the weather has turned bitter. The big, square lessons-table occupies the centre of the room, and when Fogarty brings my tray he places it on the smaller table at which I'm writing now. There are pictures on the walls which I must say I find drab: one, in shades of brown, of St George and the Dragon; another of a tower; others of farmyard scenes. The nursery's two armchairs, occupied now by George Arthur and Emily, are at the other end with a rug between them. The floor is otherwise of polished board.

'Well, the truth is, George Arthur, I cannot bear the thought of your being killed.'

With that, Emily left the nursery. She smiled in her graceful manner at me, her head a little to one side, her dark, coiled hair gleaming for a moment in a shaft of afternoon sun. I had not thought a governess's position was difficult in a household, but somehow I am finding it so. I belong neither with the family nor the servants. Fogarty, in spite of calling me 'miss', addresses me more casually than he does the Pulvertafts; his sister is scarcely civil.

'Do they eat their babies, like in the South Seas?' George Arthur startled me by asking. He had crossed to where I sat and in a manner reminiscent of his father stood with his back to the fire, thereby blocking its warmth from me.

'Do who eat their babies, George Arthur?'

'The poor people.'

'Of course they don't.'

'But they are hungry. They have been hungry for ever so long. My mother and sisters give out soup at the back gate-lodge.'

'Hungry people do not eat their babies. And I think, you know, it's enemies, not babies, who are eaten in the South Seas.'

'But suppose a family's baby *did* die and suppose the family was hungry—'

'No, George Arthur, you must not talk like that.'

'Fogarty says he would not be surprised.'

*

'Well, she has settled down, I think,' Mrs Pulvertaft remarks to her husband in their bedroom, and when he asks her whom she refers to she says the governess.

'Pleasant enough, she seems,' he replies. 'I do prefer, you know, an English governess.'

'Oh yes, indeed.'

*

George Arthur's sisters have developed no thoughts about Miss Heddoe. They neither like nor dislike her; they do not know her; their days of assessing governesses are over.

But George Arthur's aren't. She is not as pretty as Emily or Charlotte, George Arthur considers, and she is very serious. When she smiles her smile is serious. The way she eats her food is serious, carefully cutting everything, carefully and slowly chewing. Often he comes into the nursery to find her eating from the tray that Fogarty carries up the back staircase for her, sitting all alone on one side of the fire-place, seeming very serious indeed. Miss Larvey had been different somehow, although she'd eaten her meals in much the same position, seated at the very same table, by the fire. Miss Larvey was untidy, her grey hair often working loose from its coils, her whole face untidy sometimes, her tray untidily left.

'Now it is transcription time,' Miss Heddoe says, interrupting all these reflections. 'Carefully and slowly, please.'

*

Fogarty thinks about the governess, but hides such thoughts from his sister. Miss Heddoe will surely make a scene, exclaiming and protesting, saying to the Pulvertafts all the things a butler cannot. She will stand in the drawing-room or the hall, smacking out the truth at them, putting in a nutshell all that must be said. She will bring up the matter of the stigmata found on the child, and the useless folly of the road, and the wisdom of old Hugh Pulvertaft. She will be the voice of reason. Fogarty dwells upon these thoughts while conversing with his sister, adept at dividing his mind. All his faith is in the governess.

'Declare to God,' remarks Miss Fogarty, 'Brigid'll be the death of me. Did you ever know a stupider girl?'

'There was a girl we had once who was stupider,' Fogarty replies. 'Fidelma was she called?'

They sit at the wide wooden table that is the pivot of kitchen activities. The preparation of food, the polishing of brass and silver, the stacking of dishes, the disposal of remains, the eating and drinking, all card-playing and ironing, all cutting out of patterns and cloth, the trimming of lamps: the table has as many uses as the people of the kitchen can devise. Tears have soaked into its grain, and blood from meat and accidents; the grease of generations polishes it, not quite scrubbed out by the efforts made, twice every day, with soap and water.

The Fogartys sit with their chairs turned a little away from the table, so that they partly face the range and in anticipation of the benefit they will shortly receive from the glow of dampened slack. It is their early evening pose, daily the same from October to May. In summer the sunlight penetrates to the kitchen in a way that at first seems alien but later is welcomed. It spreads over the surface of the table, drying it out. It warms the Fogartys, who move their chairs to catch its rays when they rest in the early evening.

'You would not credit,' remarks Miss Fogarty, 'that Brigid has been three years in this kitchen. More like three seconds.'

'There are some that are untrainable.' His teeth are less well preserved than his sister's. She is the thinner of the two, razorlike in face and figure.

'I said at the time I would prefer a man. A man is more trainable in my opinion. A man would be more use to yourself.'

'Ah, Cready knows the dining-room by now. I wouldn't want a change made there.'

'It's Cready we have to thank for Brigid. Wasn't it Cready who had you blackguarded until you took her on?'

'We had to take someone. To give Cready her due she said we'd find her slow.'

'I'll tell you this: Cready's no racehorse herself.'

'The slowness is in that family.'

'Whatever He did He forgot to put brains in them.'

'We live with His mistakes.'

Miss Fogarty frowns. She does not care for that remark. Her brother is sometimes indiscreet in his speech. It is his nature, it is part of his cleverness; but whenever she feels uneasy she draws his attention to the source of her uneasiness, as she does now. It is a dangerous remark, she says, better it had not been made.

Fogarty nods, knowing the nod will soothe her. He has no wish to have her flurried.

'The road is going great guns,' he says, deeming a change of subject wise. 'They were on about it in the dining-room.'

'Did they mention the ground-rice pudding?'

'They ate it. Isn't it extraordinary, a road that goes round in a circle, not leading anywhere?'

'Heddoe left her ground rice. A pudding's good enough for the dining-room but not for Madam.'

'Was there an egg in it? Her stomach can't accept eggs.'

'Don't I know the woman can't take eggs? Isn't she on about it the entire time? There were four good turkey eggs in that pudding, and what harm did a turkey egg do anyone? Did eggs harm Larvey?'

'Oh true enough, Larvey ate anything. If you'd took a gate off its hinges she'd have ate it while you'd wink.'

'Larvey was a saint from heaven.'

Again Fogarty nods. In his wish not to cause flurry in his sister he refrains from saying that once upon a time Miss

Larvey had been condemned as roundly as Miss Heddoe is now. When she'd been cold in her room she'd sent down to the kitchen for hot-water jars, a request that had not been popular. But when she died, as if to compensate for all this troublesomeness, Miss Larvey left the Fogartys a remembrance in her will.

'A while back I told Heddoe about that child. To see what she'd say for herself.'

Miss Fogarty's peaked face registers interest. Her eyes have narrowed into the slits that all his life have reminded Fogarty of cracks in a plate or a teacup.

'And what did the woman say?'

'She was struck silent, then she asked me questions. After that she told me an extraordinary thing: the Legend of the True Cross.'

As Fogarty speaks, the two maids enter the kitchen. Miss Fogarty regards them with asperity, telling Brigid she looks disgraceful and Cready that her cap is dirty. 'Get down to your work,' she snappishly commands. 'Brigid, push that kettle over the heat and stir a saucepan of milk for me.'

She is badly out of sorts because of Heddoe and the ground rice, Fogarty says to himself, and thinks to ease the atmosphere by relating the legend the governess has told him.

'Listen to me, girls,' he says, 'while I tell you the Legend of the True Cross.'

Cready, who is not a girl, appreciates the euphemism and displays appropriate pleasure as she sets to at the sink, washing parsnips. She is a woman of sixty-one, carelessly stout. Brigid, distantly related to her and thirty or so years younger, is of the same proportions.

'The Legend of the True Cross,' says Fogarty, 'has to do with a seed falling into Adam's mouth, some say his ear. It lay there until he died, and when the body decomposed a tree grew from the seed, which in time was felled to give timber for the beams of a bridge.'

'Well, I never heard that,' exclaims Cready in a loud, shrill voice, so fascinated by the revelation that she cannot continue with the parsnips.

'The Queen of Sheba crossed that bridge in her majesty. Later—well, you can guess—the cross to which Our Lord was fastened was constructed from those very beams.'

'Is it true, Mr Fogarty?' cries Cready, her voice becoming still shriller in her excitement, her mouth hanging open.

'Control yourself, Cready,' Miss Fogarty admonishes her. 'You look ridiculous.'

'It's only I was never told it before, miss. I never knew the Cross grew out of Adam's ear. Did ever you hear it, Brigid?'

'I did not.'

'It's a legend,' Fogarty explains. 'It illustrates the truth. It does not tell it, Miss Fogarty and myself would say. Your own religion might take it differently.'

'Don't you live and learn?' says Cready.

There is a silence for some moments in the kitchen. Then Brigid, stirring the saucepan of milk on the range as Miss Fogarty has instructed her, says:

'I wonder does Father Horan know that?'

'God, I'd say he would all right.' Cready wags her head, lending emphasis to this opinion. There isn't much relating to theological matters that eludes Father Horan, she says.

'Oh, right enough,' agrees Fogarty. 'The priests will run this country yet. If it's not one crowd it's another.' He explains to the maids that the Legend of the True Cross has come into the house by way of the governess. It is a typical thing, he says, that a Protestant English woman would pass the like of that on. Old Hugh wouldn't have considered it suitable; and the present Pulvertafts have been long enough away from England to consider it unsuitable also. He'd guess they have anyway; he'd consider that true.

Miss Fogarty, still idle in her chair by the range, nods her agreement. She states that, legend or not, she does not care for stuff like that. In lower tones, and privately to her brother, she says she is surprised that he repeated it.

'It's of interest to the girls,' he apologises. 'To tell the truth, you could have knocked me down when she told me in the nursery.'

*

'The boulders from the ridge may be used for walls and chipping?' enquires Mr Pulvertaft of his estate manager.

'It is a distance to carry boulders, sir.'

'So it is, but we must continue to occupy these men, Erskine. Time is standing still for them.'

'Yes, sir.'

The two men pace together on a lawn in front of the house, walking from one circular rosebed to the next, then turning and reversing the procedure. It is here that Mr Pulvertaft likes to discuss the estate with Erskine, strolling on the short grass in the mid-morning. When it rains or is too bitterly cold they converse instead in the great open porch of the house, both of them gazing out into the garden. The eyes of Mr Pulvertaft and Erksine never meet, as if by unspoken agreement. Mr Pulvertaft, though speaking warmly of Erskine's virtues, fears him; and Erskine does not trust his eye to meet his master's in case that conjunction, however brief, should reveal too much. Mr Pulvertaft has been a painless inheritor, in Erskine's view; his life has been without hardship, he takes too easily for granted the good fortune that came his way.

'The road,' he is saying now, seeming to Erskine to make his point for him, 'is our generation's contribution to the estate.

You understand me, Erskine? A Pulvertaft planted Abbey Wood, another laid out these gardens. Swift came here, did you know that, Erskine? The Mad Dean assisted in the planning of all these lawns and shrubberies.'

'So you told me, sir.'

It is Erskine's left arm that is missing but he considers the loss as serious as if it had been his right. He is an Englishman, stoutly made and once of renowned strength, still in his middle age. His temper is short, his disposition unsentimental, his soldier's manner abrupt; nor is there, beneath that vigorous exterior, a gentler core. Leading nowhere, without a real purpose, the estate road is unnecessary and absurd, but he accepts his part in its creation. It is ill fortune that people have starved because a law of nature has failed them, it is ill fortune that he has lost a limb and seen a military career destroyed: all that must be accepted also. To be the manager of an estate of such size and importance is hardly recompense for the glories that might have been. He has ended up in a country that is not his own, employing men whose speech he at first found difficult to understand, collecting rents from tenants he does not trust, as he feels he might trust the people of Worcestershire or Durham. The Pulvertaft family—with the exception of Mr Pulvertaft himself—rarely seek to hold with him any kind of conversation beyond the formalities of greeting and leave-taking. Stoically he occupies his position, ashamed because he is a one-armed man, yet never indulging in melancholy, for this he would condemn as weakness.

'There is something concerning the men, sir.'

'Poor fellows, there is indeed.'

'Something other, sir. They have turned ungrateful, sir.'

'Ungrateful?'

'As well to keep an eye open for disaffection, sir.'

'Good God, those men are hardly fit for that.'

'They bite the hand that feeds them, sir. They're reared on it.'

He speaks in a matter-of-fact voice. It is the truth as he recognises it; he sees no point in dissembling for politeness' sake. He watches while Mr Pulvertaft nods his reluctant agreement. He does not need to remind himself that this is a landowner who would have his estate a realm of heaven, who would have his family and his servants, his tenants and all who work for him, angels of goodness. This is a landowner who expects his own generosity of spirit to beget such generosity in others, his unstinted patronage to find a reflection in unstinted gratitude. But reality, as Erskine daily experiences, keeps shattering the dream, and may shatter it irrevocably in the end.

They speak of other matters, of immediate practicalities. Expert and informed on all the subjects raised, Erskine gives the conversation only part of his attention, devoting the greater part to the recently arrived governess. He has examined her in church on the four occasions there have been since she joined the household. Twenty-five or -six years old, he reckons, not pretty yet not as plain as the plain one among the Pulvertaft girls. Hair too severely done, features too nervous, clothes too dowdy; but all that might be altered. The hands that hold the hymn book open before her are pale as marble, the fingers slender; the lips that open and close have a hint of voluptuousness kept in check; the breast that rises and falls has caused him, once or twice, briefly to close his eyes. He would marry her if she would have him, and why should she not, despite the absence of an arm? As the estate manager's wife she would have a more significant life than as a governess for ever.

'Well, I must not detain you longer,' Mr Pulvertaft says. 'The men are simple people, remember, rough in their ways. They may find gratitude difficult and, you know, I do not expect it. I only wish to do what can be done.'

Erskine, who intends to permit no nonsense, does not say so. He strides off to where his horse is tethered in the paddocks, wondering again about the governess.

*

Stout and round, Mrs Pulvertaft lies on her bed with her eyes closed. She feels a familiar discomfort low down in her stomach, on the left side, a touch of indigestion. It is very slight, something she has become used to, arriving as it does every day in the afternoon and then going away.

Charlotte will accept Captain Roche; Adelaide will not marry; Emily wishes to travel. Perhaps if she travels she will meet someone suitable; she is most particular. Mrs Pulvertaft cannot understand her eldest daughter's desire to visit France and Austria and Italy. They are dangerous places, where war is waged when offence is taken. Only England is not like that: dear, safe, uncomplicated England, thinks Mrs Pulvertaft, and for a moment is nostalgic.

The afternoon discomfort departs from her stomach, but she does not notice because gradually it has become scarcely anything at all. George Arthur must learn the ways of the estate so that he can sensibly inherit when his own time comes. Emily is right: it would be far better if he did not seek a commission. After all, except to satisfy his romantic inclination, there is no need.

Mrs Pulvertaft sighs. She hopes Charlotte will be sensible. An officer's wife commands a considerable position when allied with means, and she has been assured that Captain Roche's family, established for generations in Meath, leave nothing whatsoever to be desired socially. It is most unlikely that Charlotte will be silly since everything between her and

Captain Roche appears to be going swimmingly, but then you never know: girls, being girls, are naturally inexperienced.

Mrs Pulvertaft dozes, and wakes a moment later. The faces of the women who beg on Sundays have haunted a brief dream. She has heard the chiming of the church bell and in some confused way the Reverend Poole's cherub face was among the women's, his surplice flapping in the wind. She stepped from the carriage and went towards the church. 'Give something to the beggars,' her husband's voice commanded, as it does every Sunday while the bell still rings. The bell ceases only when the family are in their pew, with Mr Erskine in the Pulvertaft pew behind them and the Fogartys and Miss Heddoe in the estate pew in the south transept.

It is nobody's fault, Mrs Pulvertaft reflects, that for the second season the potatoes have rotted in the ground. No one can be blamed. It is a horror that so many families have died, that so many bloated, poisoned bodies are piled into the shared graves. But what more can be done than is already being done? Soup is given away in the yard of the gate-lodge; the estate road gives work; the Distress Board is greatly pleased. Just and sensible laws prevent the wholesale distribution of corn, for to flood the country with corn would have consequences as disastrous as the hunger itself: that has been explained to her. Every Sunday, led by the Reverend Poole, they repeat the prayer that takes precedence over all other prayers: that God's love should extend to the hungry at this time, that His wrath may be lifted.

Again Mrs Pulvertaft drifts into a doze. She dreams that she runs through unfamiliar landscape, although she has not run anywhere for many years. There are sand dunes and a flat expanse which is empty, except for tiny white shells, crackling beneath her feet. She seems to be naked, which is alarming, and worries her in her dream. Then everything changes and she is in the drawing-room, listening to Adelaide playing her pieces. Tea is brought in, and there is ordinary conversation.

*

Emily, alone, walks among the abbey ruins on the lake-shore. It is her favourite place. She imagines the chanting of the monks once upon a time and the simple life they led, transcribing Latin and worshipping God. They built where the landscape was beautiful; their view of Bright Purple Hill had been perfect.

There is a stillness among the ruins, the air is mild for late October. The monks would have fished from the shore, they would have cultivated a garden and induced bees to make honey for them. For many generations they would have buried their dead here, but their graveyards have been lost in the time that has passed.

Evening sun bronzes the heathery purple of the hill. In the spring, Emily reflects, she will begin her journeys. She will stay with her Aunt Margery in Bath and her Aunt Tabby in Ipswich. Already she has persuaded her Aunt Margery that it would be beneficial to both of them to visit Florence, and Vienna and Paris. She has persuaded her father that the expense of all the journeys would be money profitably spent, an education that would extend the education he has expended money on already. Emily believes this to be true; she is not prevaricating. She believes that after she has seen again the architecture of England—which she can scarcely remember—and visited the great cities of Europe some anxious spirit within her will be assuaged. She will return to Ireland and accept a husband, as Charlotte is about to do; or not accept a husband and be content to live her life in her brother's house, as Adelaide's fate seems certainly to be. She will bear children; or walk among the abbey ruins a spinster, composing verse about the ancient times and the monks who fished in the lake.

A bird swoops over the water and comes to rest on the pebbled shore, not far from where Emily stands. It rises on spindly legs, stretches out its wings and pecks at itself. Then it staggers uncomfortably on the pebbles before settling into an attitude that pleases it, head drawn into its body, wings wrapped around like a cloak. Such creatures would not have changed since the time of the monks, and Emily imagines a cowled and roughly bearded figure admiring the bird from a window of the once gracious abbey. He whispers as he does so and Emily remembers enough from her lessons with Miss Larvey to know that the language he speaks is not known to her.

It is a pleasant fancy, one for verse or drawing, to be stored away and one day in the future dwelt upon, and in one way or the other transcribed to paper. She turns her back on the lake and walks slowly through the ruins, past the posts which mark the route of the estate road, by the birchwood and over the stone bridge where Jonathan Swift is said to have stood and ordered the felling of three elms that obscured the panorama which has the great house as its centre. In the far distance she can see the line of men labouring on the road, and the figure of Erskine on his horse. She passes on, following a track that is familiar to her, which skirts the estate beneath its high boundary wall. Beyond the wall lie the Pulvertaft acres of farmland, but they have no interest for Emily, being for the most part flat, a territory that is tediously passed over every Sunday on the journey to and from church.

She reaches the yard of a gate-lodge and speaks to the woman who lives there, reminding her that soup and bread will be brought again tomorrow, that the utensils left last week must be ready by eleven o'clock on the trestle tables. Everything will be waiting, the woman promises, and a high fire alight in the kitchen.

*

October 31st, 1847. Fogarty told me. He stood beside me while I ate my dinner by the fire: stew and rice, with cabbage; a baked apple, and sago pudding. The child with the stigmata has died and been buried.

'And who will know now,' he questioned, himself as much as me, 'exactly what was what?'

There is a kind of cunning in Fogarty's nutlike face. The eyes narrow, and the lips narrow, and he then looks like his sister. But he is more intelligent, I would say.

'And what *is* what, Mr Fogarty?' I enquired.

'The people are edgy, miss. At the soup canteen they are edgy, I'm to understand. And likewise on the road. There is a feeling among them that the child should not have died. It is unpleasant superstition, of course, but there is a feeling that Our Lord has been crucified again.'

'But that's ridiculous!'

'I am saying so, miss. Coolly ridiculous, everything back to front. The trouble is that starvation causes a lightness in the head.'

'Do the Pulvertafts know of this? No one but you has mentioned this child to me.'

'I heard the matter mentioned at the dinner table. Mr Pulvertaft said that Mr Erskine had passed on to him the news that there was some superstition about. "D'you know its nature, Fogarty?" Mr Pulvertaft said, and I replied that it was to do with the marks of Our Lord's stigmata being noticed on the feet and hands of a child.'

'And what did anyone say then?'

' "Well, what's the secret of it, Fogarty?" Mr Pulvertaft said, and I passed on to him the opinion of Miss Fogarty and myself: that the markings were inflicted at the time of birth. They had all of them reached that conclusion also: Mrs Pulvertaft and Miss Emily and Miss Charlotte and Miss Adelaide, even Master George Arthur, no doubt, although he was not present then. As soon as ever they heard the news they had come to that assumption. Same with Mr Erskine.'

I stared, astonished, at the butler. I could not believe what he was telling me, that all these people had independently dismissed, so calmly and so finally, what the people who were closer to the event took to be a miracle. I had known, from the manner in which Fogarty spoke after his introduction of the subject, that he was in some way dubious. But I had concluded that he doubted the existence of the marks, that he doubted the reliability of the priest. I had never seen Father Horan, so did not know what kind of man he was even in appearance, or what age. Fogarty had told me he'd never seen him either, but from what he gathered through the maids the priest was of advanced years. Fogarty said now:

'My sister and I only decided that that was the truth of it after Cready and Brigid had gone on about the thing for a long time, how the priest was giving out sermons on it, how the bishop had come on a special journey and how a letter had been sent to Rome. Our first view was that the old priest had been presented with the child after he'd had a good couple of glasses. And then oiled up again and shown the child a second time. He's half blind, I've heard it said, and if enough people raved over marks that didn't exist, sure wouldn't he agree instead of admitting he was drunk and couldn't see properly? But as soon as Miss Fogarty and myself heard that the bishop had stirred his stumps and a letter had gone to Rome we realised the affair was wearing a different pair of shoes. They're as wily as cockroaches, these old priests, and there isn't one among them who'd run a chance of showing himself up by giving out sermons and summoning his bishop. He'd have let the matter rest, he'd have kept it local if he was flummoxed. "No doubt at all," Miss Fogarty said. "They've put marks on the baby." '

I couldn't eat. I shivered even though I was warm from the fire. I found it difficult to speak, but in the end I said:

'But why on earth would this cruel and blasphemous thing be done? Surely it could have been real, truly there, as stigmata have occurred in the past?'

'I would doubt that, miss. And hunger would give cruelty and blasphemy a different look. That's all I'd say. Seven other children have been buried in that family, and the two sets of grandparents. There was only the father and the mother with the baby left. "Sure, didn't they see the way things was turning?" was how Miss Fogarty put it. "Didn't they see an RIP all ready for them, and wouldn't they be a holy family with the baby the way they'd made it, and wouldn't they be sure of preservation because of it?" '

In his dark butler's clothes, the excitement that enlivened his small face lending him a faintly sinister look, Fogarty smiled at me. The smile was grisly; I did not forgive it, and from that moment I liked the butler as little as I liked his sister. His smile, revealing sharp, discoloured teeth, was related to the tragedy of a peasant family that had been almost extinguished, as, one by one, lamps are in a house at night. It was related to the desperation of survival, to an act so barbarous that one could not pass it by.

'A nine days' wonder,' Fogarty said. 'I'd say it wasn't a bad thing the child was buried. Imagine walking round with a lie like that on you for all your mortal days.'

He took the tray and went away. I heard him in the lavatory off the nursery landing, flushing the food I hadn't eaten down the WC so that he wouldn't have to listen to his sister's abuse of me. I sat until the fire sank low, without the heart to put more coal on it even though the coal was there. I kept seeing that faceless couple and their just-born child, the woman exhausted, in pain, tormented by hunger, with no milk to give her baby. Had they touched the tiny feet and hands with a hot coal? Had they torn the skin open, as Christ's had been on the Cross? Had either of them in that moment been even faintly sane? I saw the old priest, gazing in wonder at what they later showed him. I saw the Pulvertafts in their dining-room, accepting what had occurred as part of their existence in this house. Must not life go on lest all life cease? A confusion ran wildly in my head, a jumble without a pattern, all sense befogged. In a civilised manner nobody protested at the cacophony in the drawing-room when the piano was played, and nobody spoke to me of the stigmata because the subject was too terrible for conversation.

I wept before I went to bed. I wept again when I lay there, hating more than ever the place I am in, where people are driven back to savagery.

*

'The men have not arrived this morning,' Erskine reports. 'I suspected they might not from their demeanour last evening. They attach some omen to this death.'

'But surely to heavens they see the whole thing was a fraud?'

'They do not think so, sir. Any more than they believe that the worship of the Virgin Mary is a fraud perpetrated by the priests. Or that the Body and the Blood is. Fraud is grist to their mill.'

Mr Pulvertaft thanks Erskine for reporting the development to him. The men will return to their senses in time, the estate manager assures him. What has happened is only a little thing. Hunger is the master.

*

Emily packs for her travels, and vows she will not forget the lake, or the shadows and echoes of the monks. In Bath and Florence, in Vienna and Paris she will keep faith with her special corner, where the spirit of a gentler age lingers.

*

Mrs Pulvertaft dreams that the Reverend Poole ascends to the pulpit with a bath towel over his shoulder. From this day forth we must all carry bath towels wherever we go, and the feet of Jesus must be dried as well as washed. 'And the woman anointed the feet,' proclaims the Reverend Poole, 'and Jesus thanked her and blessed her and went upon his way.' But Mrs Pulvertaft is unhappy because she does not know which of the men is Jesus. They work with shovels on the estate road, and when she asks them they tell her, in a most unlikely manner, to go away.

*

Alone in front of the drawing-room piano, Adelaide sits stiffly upright, not wishing to play because she is not in the mood. Again, only minutes ago, Captain Roche has not noticed her. He did not notice her at lunch; he did not address a single word to her, he evaded her glance as if he could not bear to catch it. Charlotte thinks him dull; she has said so, yet she never spurns his attentions. And he isn't dull. His handsome face, surmounting his sturdily handsome body, twinkles with vigour and with life. He has done so much and when he talks about the places he has been he is so interesting she could listen to him for ages.

Adelaide's spectacles have misted. She takes them off and wipes them with her handkerchief. She must not go red when he comes again, or when his name is mentioned. Going red will give away her secret and Emily and Charlotte will guess and feel sorry for her, which she could not bear.

*

'Very well,' Charlotte says by the sundial in the fuchsia garden.

Captain Roche blinks his eyes in an ecstasy of delight, and Charlotte thinks that yes, it probably will be nice, knowing devotion like this for ever.

*

'Heddoe's gone broody,' Fogarty reports in the kitchen.

'Not sickness in the house! One thing you could say about Larvey, she was never sick for an hour.'

'I think Heddoe'll maybe leave.' Fogarty speaks with satisfaction. The governess might leave because she finds it too much that such a thing should happen to a baby, and that her employers do not remark on it because they expect no better of these people. Erskine might be knocked from his horse by the men in a fit of anger because the death has not been honoured in the house or by the family. Erskine might lie dead himself on the day of the governess's departure, and the two events, combining, would cause these Pulvertafts of Ipswich to see the error of their ways and return to their native land.

The china rattles on the tea-trays which the maids carry to the draining-boards, and Fogarty lights the lamps which he has arrayed on the table, as he does every afternoon at this time in winter. He inspects each flame before satisfying himself that the trimming of the wick is precisely right, then one after another places the glasses in their brass supports and finally adjusts each light.

The maids unburden the trays at the sink, Miss Fogarty places a damp cloth around a fruitcake and lays aside sandwiches and scones, later to be eaten in the kitchen. Then the maids take the lamps that are ready and begin another journey through the house.

*

In the nursery Miss Heddoe reads from the history book Miss Larvey has used before her: 'In this manner the monasteries were lawfully dissolved, for the King believed they harboured vile and treacherous plots and were the breeding grounds for future disaffection. The King was privy, through counsellors and advisers, of the vengeance that was daily planned, but was wise and bade his time.'

George Arthur does not listen. He is thinking about the savages of the South Sea islands who eat their enemies. He has always thought it was their babies they ate, and wonders if he has misunderstood something Miss Larvey said on the subject. He wonders then if Emily could possibly be right in what she says about the discomfort of the regimental life. It is true that he enjoys being close to the fire, and likes the cosiness of the nursery in the evenings; and it is true that he doesn't much care for rough material next to his skin. He knows that in spite of what Emily says officers like Captain Roche would not be made to drink putrid water, and that flies can't kill you, but the real thing is that he is expected to stay here because he is the only son, because somebody will have to look after the place when his father isn't able to any more. 'Duty,' Emily says, and it is that in the end that will steal from him his dream of military glory. Itchy and uneasy, like the bite of an insect, this duty already nags him.

*

January 12th, 1848. Today it snowed. The fall began after breakfast and continued until it was almost dark. Great drifts have piled up in the garden, and from my window the scene is beautiful. George Arthur has a cold and so remained in bed; he was too feverish for lessons.

January 18th, 1848. The snow is high on the ground. In the garden we break the ice on pools and urns so that the birds may drink. Scraps are thrown out of the scullery doors for them.

February 4th, 1848. It is five months since I arrived here, and all that I have learnt is distressing. There is nothing that is not so. Last night I could not sleep again. I lay there thinking of the starvation, of the faces of the silent women when they come to the gate-lodge for food. There is a yellow-greyness in the flesh of their faces, they are themselves like obedient animals. Their babies die when they feed them grass and roots; in their arms at the gate-lodge the babies who survive are silent also, too weak to cry until the sustenance they receive revives them. Last night I lay thinking of the men who are turned away from the work on the road because they have not the strength that is necessary. I thought of the darkness in the cottages, of dawn bringing with it the glaring eyes of death. I thought of the graves again clawed open, the earth still loose, another carcass pushed on to the rotting heap. I thought of an infant tortured with Our Saviour's wounds.

The famine-fever descends like a rain of further retribution, and I wonder—for I cannot help it—what in His name these people have done to displease God so? It is true they have not been an easy people to govern; they have not abided by the laws which the rest of us must observe; their superstitious worship is a sin. But God is a forgiving God. I pray to understand His will.

February 5th, 1848. Charlotte Pulvertaft is not to be married until her sister's return, so the engagement will of necessity be lengthy. 'Will you still be with us for the wedding?' Fogarty impertinently enquired last night, for he knows the age of George Arthur and unless I am dismissed I must of course still be here. The work continues on the road, it having been abandoned during the period of snow.

March 6th, 1848. A singular thing has happened. Walking alone in the grounds, I was hailed by Mr Erskine from his horse. I paused, and watched while he dismounted. I thought he had some message for me from the house, but in this I was wrong. Mr Erskine walked beside me, his horse trailing obediently behind. He spoke of the sunshine we were enjoying, and of the estate road. Beyond saluting me at church on Sundays he has never before paid me any attention whatsoever. My surprise must have shown in my face, for he laughed at something that was displayed there. 'I have always liked you, Miss Heddoe,' he said to my astonishment.

I reddened, as any girl would, and felt extremely awkward. I made no attempt at a reply.

'And have you settled, Miss Heddoe?' he next enquired. 'Do you care for it here?'

No one has asked me that before: why should they? My inclination was to smile and with vague politeness to nod. I did so, for to have said that I did not care for this place would have seemed ill-mannered and offensive. Mr Erskine, after all, is part of it.

'Well, that is good.' He paused and then resumed: 'If ever on your walks, Miss Heddoe, you pass near my house you would be welcome to stroll about the garden.'

I thanked him.

'It is the house at the southernmost point of the estate. The only large house there is, nearly hidden in summer by sycamore trees.'

'That is very kind of you, Mr Erskine.'

'I reclaimed the little garden, as the estate was reclaimed.'

'I see.'

The subject of conversation changed. We spoke again of the time of year and the progress that was being achieved on the estate road. Mr Erskine told me something of his history, how a military career had been cut short before it had properly begun. In return, and because the subjects seemed related, I passed on the ambition George Arthur had had in this direction.

'He is reconciled now,' I said, and soon after that the estate manager and I parted company, he riding back along the way we'd walked, I turning toward the house.

*

The estate road is completed on June 9th, 1848. Soon after that a letter arrives for Mr Pulvertaft from the Distress Board, thanking him for supplying so many months of work for the impoverished men. Since the beginning of the year the families of the area—some of them tenants of Mr Pulvertaft, some not—have been moving away to the harbour towns, to fill the exile ships bound for America. At least, Fogarty overhears Mr Pulvertaft remark in the dining-room, there is somewhere for them to go.

*

In August of that year there is champagne at Charlotte's wedding. Guests arrive from miles around. Emily, returned from her travels, is a bridesmaid.

At the celebrations, which take place in the hall and the

drawing-room and the dining-room, and spill over into the garden, Fogarty watches Miss Heddoe, even though he is constantly busy. She wears a dress he has not seen before, in light-blue material, with lace at the collar and the wrists, and little pearl buttons. Wherever she is, she is in the company of George Arthur in his sailor suit. They whisper together and seem, as always nowadays, to be the best of friends. Occasionally Miss Heddoe chides him because an observation he has made oversteps the mark or is delivered indiscreetly. When Mr Erskine arrives he goes straight to where they are.

*

September 24th, 1848. I have been here a year. The potatoes are not good this year but at least the crop has not failed as completely as hitherto. I have not given Mr Erskine his answer, but he is kind and displays no impatience. I am very silly in the matter, I know I am, but sometimes I lie awake at night and pretend I am already his wife. I repeat the name and title; I say it aloud. I think of the house, hidden among the sycamores. I think of sitting with him in church, in the pew behind the Pulvertafts, not at the side with the Fogartys.

September 25th, 1848. A Mr Ogilvie comes regularly to take tea, and often strolls with Emily to the ruined abbey. Emily has made some drawings of it, which show it as it used to be. 'Well?' Mr Erskine said quietly this afternoon, riding up when I was out on my walk. But I begged, again, for more time to consider.

November 1st, 1848. All Saints' Day. Fogarty frightened me tonight. He leaned against the mantelpiece and said:

'I would advise you not to take the step you are considering, miss.'

'What step, Fogarty?'

'To marry or not to marry Mr Erskine.'

I was flabbergasted at this. I felt myself colouring and stammered when I spoke, asking him what he meant.

'I mean only what I say, miss. I would say to you not to marry him.'

'Are you drunk, Fogarty?'

'No, miss. I am not drunk. Or if I am it is only slight. You have been going through in your mind whether or not to marry Mr Erskine. A while ago you said you could never settle in this troubled place. You said that to yourself, miss. You could not become, as the saying goes, more Irish than the Irish.'

'Fogarty—'

'I thought you would go. When I told you about the child I thought you would pack your bags. There is wickedness here: I thought you sensed it, miss.'

'I cannot have you speaking to me like this, Fogarty.'

'Because I am a servant? Well, you are right, of course. In the evenings, miss, I have always indulged myself with port: that has always been my way. I have enjoyed our conversations, but I am disappointed now.'

'You have been reading my diary.'

'I have, miss. I have been reading your diary and your letters, and I have been observing you. Since they came here I have observed the Pulvertafts of Ipswich also, and Mr Erskine, who has done such wonders all around. I have watched his big square head going about its business; I have listened when I could.'

'You had no right to read what was private. If I mentioned this to Mr Pulvertaft—'

'If you did, miss, my sister and I would be sent packing. Mr Pulvertaft is a fair and decent man and it is only just that disloyal servants should be dismissed. But you would have it on your conscience. I had hoped we might keep a secret between us.'

'I have no wish to share secrets with you, Fogarty.'

'A blind eye was turned, miss, you know that. The hunger was a plague: what use a few spoonfuls of soup, and a road that leads nowhere and only insults the pride of the men who built it? The hunger might have been halted, miss, you know that. The people were allowed to die: you said that to yourself. A man and his wife were driven to commit a barbarous act of cruelty: blasphemy you called it, miss.'

'What I called it is my own affair. I should be grateful, Fogarty, if you left me now.'

'If the estate had continued in its honest decline, if these Pulvertafts had not arrived, the people outside the walls would have travelled here from miles around. They would have eaten the wild raspberries and the apples from the trees, the peaches that still thrived on the brick-lined walls, the grapes and plums and greengages, the blackberries and mulberries. They would have fished the lake and snared the rabbits on Bright Purple Hill. There is pheasant and woodcock grown tame in the old man's time. There was his little herd of cows they might have had. I am not putting forth an argument, miss; I am not a humanitarian; I am only telling you.'

'You are taking liberties, Fogarty. If you do not go now I will most certainly mention this.'

'That was the picture, miss, that might have been. Instead we had to hear of Charlotte's marrying and of Emily's travelling, and of George Arthur's brave decision to follow in the foosteps of his father. Adelaide sulks in the drawing-room and is jealous of her sisters. Mrs Pulvertaft, good soul, lies harmlessly down in the afternoon, and you have put it well in calling her husband a fair and decent man.'

'I did not call him that.'

'You thought it long before I said it.'

'You are drunker than you think, Fogarty.'

'No, miss, I am not. The wickedness here is not intentional, miss. Well, you know about the wickedness, for you have acutely sensed it. So did Mr Pulvertaft at first, so did his wife. Charlotte did not, nor Adelaide, nor did the boy. Emily sensed it until a while ago. Emily would linger down by the old abbey, knowing that the men who lie dead there have never been dispossessed by all the visitors and the strangers there have been since. But now the old abbey is a lady's folly, a pretty ruin that pleases and amuses. Well, of course you know all this.'

'I know nothing of the sort. I would ask you to leave me now.'

'You have thought it would be better for the boy to have his military life, to perish for Queen and empire, and so extinguish this line. Listening to talk of the boy's romance, you have thought that would not be bad. So many perish anyway, all about us.'

'That is a wicked thing to say,' I cried, made furious by this. 'And it is quite untrue.'

'It is wicked, miss, but not untrue. It is wicked because it comes from wickedness, you know that. Your sharp fresh eye has needled all that out.'

'I do not know these things.' My voice was quieter now, even, and empty of emotion. 'I would ask you to leave this room at once.'

But Fogarty went on talking until I thought in the end he must surely be insane. He spoke again of Charlotte's marriage to Captain Roche, of Emily and Adelaide, of George Arthur taking the place of his father. He spoke again of the hungry passing without hindrance through the gates of the estate, to feed off what its trees and bushes offered. He spoke of his sister and himself left after the old man's death, he glad to see the decay continue, his sister persuaded that they must always remain.

'The past would have withered away, miss. Instead of which it is the future that's withering now.'

Did he mean the hunger and the endless death, the exile ships of those who had survived? I did not ask him. He frightened me more than ever, standing there, his eyes as dead as ice. He was no humanitarian, he repeated, he was no scholar. All he said came from a feeling he had, a servant's feeling which he'd always had in this house during the years the old man had let everything decline. Poor Protestants as they were, he and his sister belonged neither outside the estate gates with the people who had starved nor with a family as renowned as the Pulvertafts. They were servants in their very bones.

'You have felt you have no place either, miss. You can see more clearly for that.'

'Please go, Fogarty.'

He told me of a dream he'd had the night before or last week, I was too upset to note which. The descendants of the people who had been hungry were in the dream, and the son of George Arthur Pulvertaft was shot in the hall of the house, and no Pulvertaft lived in the place again. The road that had been laid in charity was overgrown through neglect, and the gardens were as they had been at the time of old Hugh Pulvertaft, their beauty strangled as they returned to wildness. Fogarty's voice quivered as his rigmarole ridiculously rambled on; an institution for corrected girls the house became, without carpets on the floors. The bones of the dogs that generations of Pulvertafts had buried in the grounds were dug up by the corrected girls when they were ordered by a Mother Superior to make vegetable beds. They threw the bones about, pretending to be frightened by them, pretending they were the bones of people.

'I don't wish to hear your dreams, Fogarty.'

'I have told you only the one, miss. It is a single dream I had.

(44)

The house of the estate manager was burnt to the ground, and people burnt with it. The stone walls of the estate were broken down, pulled apart in places by the ivy that was let grow. In a continuation of the dream I was standing here talking to you like I'm talking now. I said to you not to perpetuate what has troubled you.'

He took my tray from me and went away. A moment later I heard him in the lavatory, flushing away the food I had not eaten.

*

'Not a bad soul,' Miss Fogarty remarks, 'when you come to know her.'

'Her father was a solicitor's clerk.'

'Oh granted, there's not a pennyworth of background to the creature. But I'd hardly say she wasn't good enough for Erskine.'

Fogarty does not comment. His sister resumes:

'I would expect to be invited to the house for late tea. I would expect her to say: "Why not walk over on Wednesday, Miss Fogarty, if you have a fancy for it?" I would expect the both of us to walk over for cards with the Erskines of an evening.'

'She has pulled herself up by marrying him. She is hardly going to drop down again by playing cards with servants.'

'Friends,' corrects Miss Fogarty. 'I would prefer to say friends.'

'When a bit of time goes by they'll dine with the Pulvertafts, she and Erskine. You'll cook the food at the range, I'll serve it at the table.'

'Oh, I hardly believe that'll be the order of it.'

Fogarty considers it unwise to pursue his argument and so is silent. Anna Maria Heddoe, he thinks, who was outraged when two guileful peasants tried on a trick. Well, he did his best. It is she, not he, who is the scholar and humanitarian. It is she, not he, who came from England and was distressed. She has wept into her pillow, she has been sick at heart. Stranger and visitor, she has written in her diary the news from Ireland. Stranger and visitor, she has learnt to live with things.

On the Zattere

Without meaning to, Verity had taken her mother's place. Six months after her mother's death she had given up her flat and moved back to the house where she and her two brothers— both of them now married—had grown up. She had pretended, even to herself at times, that she was concerned about her father's loneliness but the true reason was that she wished to make a change on her own account, to break a pattern in her life. She became, as her mother had been, her father's chief companion and was in time exposed to traits in his nature she had not known existed. Preserving within the family the exterior of a bluff and genial man, good-hearted, knowledgeable and wise, her father had successfully disguised the worst of himself; and had been assisted by his wife's loyalty. It was different for a daughter, and Verity found herself watching the old man in a way she would once not have believed possible, impatient with his weaknesses, judging him.

Mr Unwill, unaware of this development in his daughter, was greatly pleased with the turn events had taken. He was touched when Verity gave up her flat and returned to the family home, and he was proud to be seen in her company, believing that strangers might not take her for his daughter but assume instead that he was an older man to whom this beautiful woman was sentimentally attached. He dressed the part when they went on their first holiday together—to Venice, which every autumn in her lifetime he had visited with his wife. In swirls of green and red, a paisley scarf was knotted at his throat and matched the handkerchief that spilt from the top pocket of his navy-blue blazer. There was no reason why they should be taken as father and daughter, he argued to himself, since they were so very different in appearance. Verity, who was neither small nor tall, gave an impression of slightness because she was slim and was delicately made. The nearly perfect features of her face were set on the suspicion of a slant, turning ordinary beauty into the unusual and causing people who saw it for the first time to glance again. Her hair, clinging smoothly around the contours of classically high cheekbones, was the brown of chestnuts; her eyes, almost strangely, matched it. She dressed and made up with care, as if believing that beauty should be honoured.

In contrast, Mr Unwill was a large man in his advanced sixties, with a ruddy complexion and a freckled bald head. People who knew him quite well had difficulty remembering, when no longer in his presence, if he had a moustache or not. The lingering impression of his face—the ruddiness, the tortoiseshell spectacles—seemed somehow to suggest another, taken-for-granted characteristic, and in fact there was one: a grey growth of bristle on his upper lip, unnoticeable because it so easily became one with the similar greyness that flanked the freckled dome.

'Well, what shall you do today?' he asked in the pensione dining-room when they had finished breakfast on their third day. 'I'll be all right, you know. Don't spare a worry for me.'

'I thought I'd go to the Church of San Zaccaria.'

'Why not? You trot along, my dear. I'll sit and watch the boats go by.'

They were alone in the dining-room: in early November the pensione was not full. The American family had not come in to breakfast, presumably having it in their rooms. The German girls had been and gone; so had the French threesome and the lone Italian lady in her purple hat.

'Nice, those German girls,' Mr Unwill said. 'The pretty one made a most interesting observation last night.' He paused, tobacco-stained teeth bared, his eyes ruminative behind his spectacles. 'She said she wondered where waiters go between meals. *Most* unGermanic, I thought.'

Verity, who was thirty-eight and had recently come to believe that life was going to pass her by, reached across the table and took one of her father's cigarettes from the packet that was open beside his coffee cup. She acknowledged the observation of the German girl by briefly nodding. She lit her cigarette from the flame of a small, gold lighter, given to her by the man she'd been in Venice with before.

'The pretty one's from Munich,' her father said. 'The other—now, where on earth did they tell me the fat one came from?' Furrows of thought appeared on his forehead, then he gave up. Slowly he removed his spectacles and in the same unhurried manner proceeded to wipe them with his paisley handkerchief. It was a way of his, a hobby almost. The frames were polished first, then each lens; sometimes he went to work with his Swiss penknife, tightening the screws of the hinges with the screwdriver that was incorporated in one of the blades. 'The pretty one's a laboratory assistant,' he said, 'the other one works in a shop or something.'

The penknife had not, this morning, been taken from his blazer pocket. He held the spectacles up to the light. 'I'll probably sit outside at the Cucciolo,' he said.

'The coffee's better at Nico's. And cheaper.'

It was he—years ago, so he said— who had established that, and yesterday it had been confirmed. She'd sat outside the Cucciolo by mistake, forgetting what he'd told her, obliging him to join her when he emerged from the pensione after his afternoon sleep. He'd later pointed out that a cappucino at the Cucciolo was fifteen hundred but only eleven at Nico's or Aldo's. Her father was mean about spending small sums of money, Verity had discovered since becoming his companion. He didn't like it when she reached out and helped herself to one of his cigarettes, but he hadn't yet learnt to put the packet away quickly.

'Oh, I don't know that I'm up to the walk to Nico's this morning,' he said.

It took less than a minute to stroll along the Zattere to Nico's, and he was never not up to things. She had discovered also that whenever he felt like it he told petty, unimportant lies, and as they left the dining-room she wondered what this latest one was all about.

*

Straining a white jacket, beads of perspiration glistening on his forehead, the pensione's bearded waiter used a battery-powered gadget to sweep the crumbs from the tablecloths in the dining-room. His colleague, similarly attired and resembling Fred Astaire, laid two tables for the guests who had chosen to have lunch rather than dinner.

The dining-room was low-ceilinged, with mirrors and sideboards set against the fawn silk on the walls, and windows of round green panes. The breathing of the bearded waiter and the slurping of the canal just outside these windows were the only sounds after the crumbs had been cleared and the tables laid. The waiters glanced over their domain and went away to spend their time mysteriously, justifying the German girl's curiosity.

In the hall of the pensione guests who were never seen in the dining-room, choosing to take no meals, awaited the attention of the smart receptionist, this morning all in red. A kitten played on her desk while patiently she gave directions to the Church of the Frari. She told the Italian lady with the purple hat that there was a dry cleaner's less than a minute away. '*Pronto?*' she said, picking up her telephone. The hall, which was not large, featured in the glass door of the telephone-box and the doors that led outside the same round green panes as the dining-room. There were faded prints on the walls, and by the reception desk a map of Venice and a list of the pensione's credit-card facilities. A second cat, grey and gross and bearing the marks of a lifetime's disputes, lay sleeping on the stairs.

'Enjoy yourself, my dear,' Mr Unwill said to his daughter, stepping over this animal. She didn't appear to hear so he said it again when they had passed through the round-paned doors and stood together for a moment on the quayside.

'Yes,' she said. 'I'll probably wander a bit after I've been to San Zaccaria.'

'Why not, old girl? I'll be as happy as a sandboy, you know.'

The fog that had earlier obscured the houses of Giudecca on the other side of the canal was lifting; already the sun evaporated the dankness in the air. Verity wore a flecked suit of pinkish-orange, with a scarf that matched it loosely tied over a cream blouse. In one lapel there was a tiny amber brooch, another gift from the man she'd been in Venice with before.

She turned into the *fondamenta* that ran along one side of the pensione. It was cold there, untouched by the November sunshine. She shivered, but felt it was not from this chilliness. She wished she was not alone, for an irony in her present circumstance was that she found the company of other people both tiresome and of use. She walked more quickly, endeavouring to keep certain insistent thoughts out of her mind. At the Accademia she bought her ticket for the vaporetto and waited on the landing-stage. Other people, no matter who they were, disrupted such thoughts, which was something she welcomed. The attention other people demanded, the conversations they began, their faces and their voices, clogged her communication with herself; and yet, so much of the time while in the company of other people, she wished she was not.

Odd, to have taken her mother's place in this old-fashioned way: on the vaporetto she saw again the tortoiseshell spectacles in her father's hands, his square, wide fingers working the paisley silk over the lens. Repetition had etched this image in some corner of her mind: she heard his early-morning cough, and then the lowered tone he used when talking to himself. Had it been panic that had caused her to use his loneliness as an excuse, to break the pattern she found so merciless? Love-making had been easy in the convenient flat, too much had been taken for granted. But even so, giving up the flat might have struck some people as extreme.

On the vaporetto the Italians glanced at her, women assessing her in some Italian way, the men desirous. Venice was different in November, less of a bauble than the summer city she remembered. The tourist crowds had gone, with the mosquitoes and the cruel Italian heat. The orchestras had ceased to play in the Piazza San Marco, the Riva degli Schiavoni was again the property of the Venetians. She imagined her parents walking arm in arm on the Riva, or going to Torcello and Burano. Had the warmth of their companionship been a pretence on his part? For if he'd loved his wife how could he so easily come back to the city he and she had discovered together and had affectionately made their own? Eleven months had passed since her death and already in the pensione they had come to know so well he was striking up acquaintanceships as though nothing of importance had occurred since last he'd been there. There had been a moment in the hall when he mumblingly spoke to the smartly dressed receptionist, who said that everyone at the pensione sympathised. The elderly maid who welcomed him upstairs had murmured in Italian, and in the dining-room the waiters' voices had been low at first. It was he himself who subsequently set the mood, his matter-of-fact manner brushing sentiment aside, summarily dismissing death. Had her mother loved him or had their companionship in this city been, on her part also, a pretence? Marriage was riddled with such falsity, Verity reflected, dressed up as loyalty or keeping faith.

Palaces loomed majestically on either side of her, the lion of St Mark disdainful on his column, St Theodore modest on his. Carpaccio would still have recognised his city in the tranquillity of November, the Virgins of Cima still crossed the city's bridges. It was her mother who had said all that to her, translating emotions she had felt. Verity went on thinking about her parents, not wishing to think about herself, not wishing to catch a glimpse of herself in the summer dresses she had worn when she'd been in Venice before. There had been many weekends spent faithfully with the same companion in many beautiful cities, but Venice that July had left behind a special meaning because hope had died there.

*

Mr Unwill settled himself on one of the Cucciolo Bar's orange plastic seats. Verity was right: the Cucciolo wasn't a patch on Nico's or Aldo's. Fewer people passed by for a start, and the one cappucino he'd been served yesterday by the Cucciolo's dour waiter had tasted of the last person's sugar. But the trouble with sitting outside Nico's or Aldo's was that people often turned off the Zattere before they reached them, and he happened to know that the pretty little German girl was still in the pensione because he'd seen the fat one striding off on her own half an hour ago. Of course it could be that the pretty one had preceded her friend, in which case he'd be four hundred lire down, which would be annoying.

'*Prego, signore?*'

He ordered his coffee. He wished he spoke Italian so that he might draw the waiter's attention to the inadequately washed cup he'd been presented with yesterday. He'd have done so in England: one of the few good things about being old was that you could make a fuss. Another was that you could drop into conversation with people without their thinking it was peculiar of you. Last night he'd wandered in from his stroll after Verity had gone to her room, and had noticed the two girls in the lounge. He'd leafed through a pile of magazines that had to do with the work of the Venetian police, and then the girls had begun to giggle unrestrainedly. By way of a polite explanation, the pretty one had spoken to him in English, explaining that it was the remark about where waiters go between meals which had caused their merriment. After that the conversation had drifted on. He'd told them a thing or two about Venice, which he knew quite well in a professional way.

Mr Unwill was retired, having been employed for all his adult life in a shipping office. Ships and their cargoes, the building, sale and insuring of ships, were what he was most familiar with. It was this interest that had first brought him to Venice, as it had to many other great ports. While his three children were still growing up it had been necessary to limit such travel to the British Isles, but later he and his wife had travelled as far and as adventurously as funds permitted, always economising so that journeys might be extended or prolonged. Venice had become their favourite.

'Hullo there!' he called out to the German girl as she stepped around the corner, shading her eyes against the sun. She was wearing a short dress that was almost the same colour as her very blonde hair.

'What a day!' Mr Unwill said, standing up so that she could not easily just walk by. 'Now, how about a coffee?'

Her teeth, when she smiled her appreciation of this invitation, glistened damply, large white teeth, each one perfectly shaped. But to his disappointment, while smiling she also shook her head. She was late already, she explained: she was to meet her friend at the Rialto Bridge.

He watched her hurrying along the Zattere, her sturdy legs nicely bronzed, a camera slung across her shoulder. She turned the corner by the Church of the Gesuati and Mr Unwill sighed.

*

In the Church of San Zaccaria Verity gazed at the Bellini altarpiece her mother had sent her postcards of. Perfectly, she still contained her thoughts, conjecturing again. Had her mother stood on this very spot? Had her father accompanied her to the churches she liked so much or in all their visits had he been concerned only with duller interests? Verity didn't know; it had never seemed important.

The lights that illuminated the picture abruptly went out. Verity felt in her purse for two hundred lire, but before she found the coins a man stepped forward and dropped his through the slot of the little grey box on one side of the altar. The Virgin and her saints, in sacred conversation, were there again. Verity looked for a few moments longer and then moved away.

She hadn't looked at pictures that July. For a second she saw herself and heard her laughter: in a dress with primroses on it, wearing sunglasses and laughing, although she had not felt like laughing. In the church she felt again the effort of that laughter and was angry because for a single second her concentration had faltered. She dropped some money into a poor-box by the door. She hadn't realised how fond she'd been of her mother

(55)

until the very last moment, until the coffin had soundlessly slipped away behind a beige curtain in the chapel of the crematorium. The soundlessness was eerie and unpleasant; Verity had hated that moment.

She left the church and walked back to the Riva. Metal trestles supported planks of wood, like crude table tops, on which people might walk if the tides rose and the floods of autumn began. These improvised bridges were called *passerelle*, her father had told her, pointing them out to her on the Zattere. 'Oh heavens, of course I'll manage,' he'd kept repeating on the afternoon of the funeral and all of them, her brothers and her sisters-in-law, she herself, had admired his urbanity and his resolve not to be a nuisance.

She rose and walked slowly along the Riva towards the Arsenale. Already the quayside hotels had a deserted look; the pink Gabrielli-Sandwirth had put up its shutters. 'No, absolutely not,' her father had said on some later occasion. 'You have your own life, Verity.' And of course she had: her own life, her own job, her own flat in which love might be made.

A fun-fair was being erected further along the quay, dodgem cars and a tunnel of fear, swing-boats and fruit machines. 'American Games' a garish announcement read; 'Central Park' proclaimed another. Two bespectacled old women washed down a rifle-range; hobby-horses were unloaded. Outside the Pensione Bucintoro a shirt-sleeved waiter smoked a cigarette and watched.

In the Via Garibaldi children with satchels or schoolbooks chased one another on their journey home from morning school; women jostled and pushed at the vegetable stalls. In the public park, tatty and forgotten in the low season, cats swarmed or huddled—mangy tomcats with ravenous eyes, pitiful kittens that seemed resentful of their recent birth, leanly slinking mothers. All of them were dirty; two weakly fought, a hissing, clawing ball of different-coloured fur. Verity bent down and tried to attract a dusty marmalade-coloured kitten, but alarmed by her attentions it darted off. She walked on, still determinedly dwelling upon her father's heartlessness in so casually returning to this city, to the pensione, to the Zattere. She dwelt again upon her mother's misplaced loyalty, which had kept the marriage going. But she herself, in her primrose-yellow dress and her sunglasses, crept through these irrelevant reflections so crudely forced upon her consciousness. Her parents arm-in-arm in Venice, loving or not loving, vanished into wisps of mist, and were replaced by the sound of her own ersatz laughter. There was an image of her face, strained with a smile that choked away the hopelessness she was frightened to surrender to. The ice tinkled in her well-chilled Soave; the orchestras played in the great, romantic square. 'Oh, I am happy!' came the echo of her lying voice, and in the dingy public park her beauty fled as swiftly as the marmalade kitten had leapt from her grasp. She wept, but it did not matter because no one was about.

*

Mr Unwill, deprived of a conversation with the German girl, left the Cucciolo Bar and strolled down the Zattere in the direction of the western Stazione Marittima. It was an interesting place, this particular Stazione Marittima, and he would like one day to find someone who would show him round it. He often loitered by the bridge that led almost directly into it, hoping to catch the eye of some official with an hour or two on his hands who would welcome the interest of an Englishman who had been concerned with maritime commerce for a lifetime. But the officials were always in a hurry, and usually in groups of three or four, which made matters difficult. Clerks of course they'd be, not quite right anyway. Once he'd noticed a

(57)

man with gold braid on his cap and his uniform, but when Mr Unwill smilingly approached him the man expostulated wildly, alarmed presumably by the sound of a language he did not understand. Mr Unwill had thought it a strange reaction in a seafaring man, who should surely be used to the world's tongues.

A cargo boat called the *Allemagna Express*, registered in Venice in spite of its German-sounding name, and flying the Italian flag, was being painted. On planks suspended along the side of its hull men dipped long-handled rollers into giant paint-containers which dangled at a convenient drop below each man. A single painter used a brush, touching in the red outline on the letters of *Allemagna Express*. Cautiously he moved back and forth on his plank, often calling up to his colleagues on the deck to work one of the ropes or pulleys. A yellow stripe extended the length of the hull, separating the white of the ship's upper reaches from the brown beneath. The old girl was certainly beginning to look smart, Mr Unwill considered, and wondered if they'd still be in Venice when the job was completed. There was nothing as rewarding as a well painted ship, nothing as satisfying even if your own contribution had only been to watch the men at work. Mr Unwill sat for a long time on a stone bench on the quayside, content in this unexacting role. He wondered why *Express* was spelt with an 'x' since the vessel was Italian. That morning from his bedroom window he'd noticed the *Espresso Egitto* chugging by.

At half-past eleven he rose and walked to Nico's, where he bought a banana ice-cream and ate it sitting on a *passerella*.

*

'There was a time, you know, when the Venetians could build a warship in a day.'

For dinner they sat at a round table in a corner of the low-ceilinged dining-room of the pensione. The bearded waiter doled out salad on to side plates and the one who looked like Fred Astaire went round with platters of chicken and fried potatoes.

'I passed near the Arsenale today,' Verity said, remembering that that was where such warships had been built. '*Grazie.*'

'*Prego, signorina.*'

'You called in at the Naval Museum, did you?'

'No, actually I didn't.'

Apart from the German girls, the people who'd been in the dining-room the night before were there again. The American woman, with a blue-and-white bow-tie, sat with her husband and her daughter at the table closest to the Unwills'. The two thin Frenchwomen and the frail man were beside the screen that prevented draughts. The solitary Italian woman in the purple hat was by the door. Other Italians, a couple who had not been in the dining-room last night, were at a table next to the German girls.

'I remember going to the Naval Museum,' Mr Unwill said. 'Oh, years ago. When I was first in Venice with your mother.'

'Did she go too?'

'Your mother always liked to accompany me to places. Most interesting she found the Naval Museum. Well, anyone would.'

He went on talking, telling her about the Naval Museum; she didn't listen. That afternoon she'd gone across to the Lido because it was a part of Venice they hadn't visited that July. But instead of the escape she'd hoped for she'd caught a melancholy mood from its windswept, shuttered emptiness and its dead casino. She'd sat in a bar drinking brandy she didn't like the taste of, and when she returned to the pensione she found herself not wanting to change out of the clothes she'd worn all day. She'd seen her father glancing in surprise at her tired

(59)

orange suit and she'd felt, ridiculously, that she was letting him down.

'Ah, here they are!' he exclaimed, making a sudden noise as the German girls entered. '*Buona sera!*' he shouted at them eagerly.

The girls smiled, and Verity wondered what on earth they thought of him. One of the Frenchwomen was complaining that her gnocchi was cold. The waiter who resembled Fred Astaire looked worried. She could not eat cold gnocchi, the woman protested, throwing her fork down, marking the white tablecloth.

'Where have you been today?' Mr Unwill called across the dining-room to the German girls. 'Done something nice?'

'*Ja*,' the fat girl replied. 'We have been in a glass factory.'

'Very sensible,' said Mr Unwill.

Another plate of gnocchi replaced the cold one at the French table. The American woman told her daughter that on her wedding day in Nevada she had thrown a cushion out of a window because she'd felt joyful. 'I guess your momma'd been drinking,' the father said, laughing very noisily. The Italian couple talked about the Feast of St Martin.

There had been only one love-making weekend since she'd moved back to the family house: she'd told her father some lie, not caring if he guessed.

'It's an interesting thing,' he was saying to her now, 'this St Martin business. They have a week of it, you know. Old people and children get gifts. Have you seen the confections in the shop windows? San Martino on horseback?'

'Yes, I've noticed them.' Made of biscuit, she had presumed, sometimes chocolate-coated, sometimes not, icing decorated with sweets.

'And *cotognata*,' he went on. 'Have you seen the *cotognata*? Centuries old, that St Martin's sweetmeat is, far nicer than Turkish delight.'

She smiled, and nodded. She'd noticed the *cotognata* also. She often wondered how he came by his information, and guessed he was for ever dropping into conversation with strangers in the hope that they spoke English.

'The first ghetto was in Venice,' he said. 'Did you know that? It's an Italian word, called after the place where the Jewish settlement was.'

'No, I didn't know that.'

'Well, there you are. Something every day.'

The bearded waiter cleared their plates away and brought them each a bowl of fruit.

'I thought we might wander down the Zattere after dinner,' her father suggested, 'and take a glass of mandarinetto and perhaps a slice of cake. Feel up to that, old girl?'

If she didn't accompany him he'd bother the German girls. She said a glass of mandarinetto would be nice.

'They're painting the *Allemagna Express*. Fine-looking vessel.'

In her bedroom she tied a different scarf around her neck, and put her coat on because the nights were cold. When she returned to the hall her father was not there and when he did appear he came from the dining-room, not from upstairs. 'I told them we were going for a drink,' he said. 'They'll join us in a moment. You all right, old girl?'

He was smoking a cigarette and, like her, he had gone to his room for his overcoat. On the Zattere he put his hat on at a jaunty angle. There was a smell of creosote because they'd been repainting the rafts that afternoon. Sheets of newspaper were suspended from strings that were looped along the quayside to draw attention to the newly treated timbers. A terrier settled down for the night among the rubble on a builder's barge. Cats crept about. It was extraordinary, she suddenly thought, that just because she'd given up her flat she should find herself in Venice with this old man.

'Nice here, eh?' he said in the café, surveying the amber-coloured cloths on the tables, the busyness behind the bar. He took his hat and overcoat off, and sat down. He stubbed his cigarette out and lit a fresh one. 'Mandarinetto,' he said to the waiter who came up. '*Due.*'

'*Sì, signore. Subito.*'

She lit a cigarette herself, caressing her lighter with her fingers, then feeling angry and ashamed that she had done so.

'Ah, here they are!' Her father was on his feet, exclaiming like a schoolboy, waving his hat at the German girls. He shouted after the waiter, ordering two more mandarinettos. 'I really recommend it here,' he informed the German girls, flashing his tobacco-stained smile about and offering them cigarettes. He went on talking, telling them about the *Allemagna Express.* He mentioned the Stazione Marittima and asked them if they had noticed the biscuit horsemen and the *cotognata.* 'By the weekend the Votive Bridge will be complete,' he said. 'A temporary timber bridge, you know, erected as a token of thanksgiving. Every year, for three days, Venetians celebrate the passing of the Plague by making a pilgrimage across it, their children waving balloons about. Then it's taken down again.'

Verity smiled at the fatter German, who was receiving less attention than her friend. And a bridge of boats, her father continued, was temporarily established every summer. 'Again to give thanks. Another tradition since the Plague.'

The Americans who had been in the pensione came in and sat not far away. They ordered ice-creams, taking a long time about it, questioning the waiter in English as to whether they would come with added cream.

'Oh, I remember Venice forty years ago,' Mr Unwill said.

'Of course, it's greatly changed. The Yugoslavs come now, you know, in busloads.' He issued a polite little laugh. 'Not to mention the natives of your own fair land.'

'Too many, I think,' the prettier girl responded, grimacing.

'Ah, *ja*, too many,' agreed her companion.

'No, no, no. You Germans travel well, I always say. Besides, to the Venetian a tourist's a tourist, and tourists mean money. The trouble with the Yugoslavs, they apparently won't be parted from it.'

It wasn't usually his opinion that Germans travelled well; rather the opposite. He told the girls that at one time the Venetians had been capable of building a warship in a day. He explained about ghettoes, and said that in Venice it was the cats who feared the pigeons. He laughed in his genial way. He said:

'That was a very clever remark you made last night, Ingrid. About waiters.'

'It was Brigitta who said it first, I think.'

'Oh, was it? Well, it's quite amusing anyway. Now, what we really want to know is how long you're staying at the pensione?'

'*Ja*, just today,' Ingrid said. 'Tomorrow we have gone.'

'Oh dear me, now that's very sad.'

He would not, when the moment came, pay for the mandarinettos or the cake he was now pressing upon his guests. He would discover that he had left his wallet in some other pocket.

'You must not spoil your looks, eh?' he said when Ingrid refused the cake. His smile nudged her in a way he might have thought was intimate, but which Verity observed the girl registering as elderly. Brigitta had already been biting into a slice of cake when the remark was made about the losing of looks. Hastily she put it down. They must go, she said.

'Go? Oh, surely not? No, please don't go.'

But both girls were adamant. They had been too tired last

night to see the Bridge of Sighs by lamplight and they must see that before they left. Each held out a hand, to Verity and then to her father. When they had gone Verity realised she hadn't addressed a single word to either of them. A silence followed their departure, then Mr Unwill said in a whisper:

'Those Americans seem rather nice, eh?'

He would hold forth to the Americans, as he had to the German girls, concentrating his attention on the daughter because she was the most attractive of the three. The mother was vulgarly dressed, the father shouted. In the presence of these people everything would be repeated, the painting of the *Allemagna Express*, the St Martin's confections, the temporary bridges.

'No,' Verity said. 'No, I don't want to become involved with those Americans.'

He was taken aback. His mouth remained open after he'd begun to say something. He stared at her, slowly overcoming his bewilderment. For the second time that evening, he asked her if she felt all right. She didn't reply. Time of the month, he supposed, this obvious explanation abruptly dawning on him, wretched for women. And then, to his very great surprise, he was aware that his daughter was talking about her decision, some months ago, to return to the family home.

' "My father's on his own now," I told him, "so I have given up the flat." As soon as I had spoken I felt afraid. "We must be together," is what I thought he'd say. He'd be alarmed and upset, I thought, because I'd broken the pattern of our love affair by causing this hiatus. But all he said was that he understood.'

They'd known, of course, about the wretched affair. Her mother had been depressed by it; so much time passing by, no sign of a resolution in whatever it was, no sign of marriage. Verity had steered all conversation away from it; when the subject was discreetly approached by her mother or her brothers she made it clear that they were trespassing on private property; he himself had made no forays in that direction, it not being his way. Astonishing it was, that she should wish to speak of it now.

'I didn't in the least,' she said, 'feel sorry for your loneliness. I felt sorry for myself. I couldn't bear for a moment longer the routine love-making in that convenient flat.'

Feeling himself becoming hot, Mr Unwill removed his glasses and searched in the pockets of his blazer for his handkerchief. He didn't know what to say, so he said nothing. He listened while Verity more or less repeated what she had said already. There had been sixteen years of routine love-making, ever since she was twenty-two. Her love affair had become her life, the routine punctuated by generous gifts and weekends in beautiful cities.

There was a silence. He polished one lens and then the other. He tightened the screws of the hinges with the useful little screwdriver in his penknife. Since the silence continued, eventually he said:

'If you made an error in coming back to the house it can easily be rectified, old girl.'

'Surely, I thought, those brief weekends would never be enough? Surely we would have to talk about everything again, now that there was no flat to go to?' She spoke of the cities where the weekends had been spent: Bruges, Berlin, Paris, Amsterdam, Venice. Bruges had been the first. In Bruges she had assumed, although he had not said so, that he would leave his wife. They had walked through chilly squares, they had sat for hours over dinner in the Hotel Duc du Bourgogne. In Paris, some time later, she had made the same assumption. He did not love his wife; when the children grew up he would leave her. By the time they visited Venice, the children had grown up.

'Only just grown up,' she said. 'The last one only just, that summer.'

He did not say anything; the conversation was beyond his reach. He saw his daughter as an infant, a nurse holding a bundle towards him, the screwed-up face and tiny hands. She'd been a happy child, happy at school, happy with her friends. Young men had hung about the house; she'd gone to tennis-club dances and winter parties. 'Love's a disease sometimes,' her mother had said, angrily, a year or so ago. Her mother had been cross because Verity always smiled so, pretending the happiness that was no longer there, determinedly optimistic. Because of the love affair, her mother had said also, Verity's beauty had been wasted, seeming to have been uselessly visited upon her.

'It wasn't just a dirty weekend, you know, here in Venice. It's never just that.'

'Please, Verity. Please, now . . .'

'He can't bring himself to be unkind to his wife. He couldn't be bad to a woman if he tried. I promise you, he's a remarkable man.'

He began to expostulate but changed his mind. Everything he tried to say, even everything he felt, seemed clumsy. She stared beyond him, through the smoke from her cigarette, causing him to feel a stranger. Her silliness in love had made her carelessly harsh, selfish and insensitive because she had to think so much about herself. In a daughter who was not naturally silly, who had been gentle as a child, these qualities were painful to observe. Once she could have imagined what it was like for him to hear her refer so casually to dirty weekends; now she didn't care if that hurt him or not. It was insulting to expect him to accept that the man was remarkable. It dismissed his intellect and his sense.

'It was ridiculous,' she said eventually, 'to give up my flat.'

He made some protest when she asked the waiter for the bill, but she didn't listen, paying the bill instead. He felt exhausted. He had sat in this very café with a woman who was dead; the man his daughter spoke of was still alive. It almost seemed the other way round. He would not have claimed a great deal for the marriage there had been: two people rubbing along, forgiving each other for this and that, one left alone to miss the nourishment of affection. Yet when the coffin had slipped away behind the beige curtain his grief had been unbearable and had remained so afterwards, for weeks and months, each day a hell.

'I'm sorry for being a nuisance,' she said before they rose from the table, and he wanted to explain to her that melancholy would have become too much if he allowed a city and its holiday memories to defeat him, that memories were insidious. But he didn't say anything because he knew she would not listen to him properly. She could not help thinking badly of him; the harshness that had been bred in her prevented the allowances that old age demanded. Nor could he, because of anger, make allowances for her.

'Hi!' one of the Americans whom he'd thought it might be quite nice to know called out. They had finished their ice-creams and were preparing to leave also. All of them smiled but it was Verity, not he, who returned their greeting.

'It's I who should be sorry,' he said on the Zattere. He'd been more gently treated than she: you knew where you were with death, in no way was it a confidence trick. He began to say that but changed his mind, knowing she would not wish to hear.

'Heavens, how cold it has become!' She hurried through the gathering fog, and so did he. The conversation was over, its loose ends hanging; each knew they would never be picked up. '*Buona notte,*' the smart receptionist, all in green now, murmured in the hall of the pensione, and they bade her good-night in their different ways.

They lifted their keys from the rack beside the stairs and stepped over the sleeping cat on the bottom step. On the first-floor landing they said good-night, were briefly awkward because of what had passed between them, then entered their separate rooms. Slowly he prepared himself for bed, slowly undressing, slowly washing, folding his clothes with an old man's care. She sat by her window, staring at the lights across the water, until the fog thickened and there was nothing left to see.

Lunch in Winter

Mrs Nancy Simpson—who did not at all care for that name and would have wished to be Nancy le Puys or Nancy du Maurier—awoke on a December morning. She had been dreaming of a time long past in her life, when her name had been Nancy Dawes, before she'd been married to anyone. The band had been playing *You are my Honeysuckle* and in the wings of the Old Gaiety they had all been in line, smiles ready, waiting to come on. *You are my honey-honeysuckle, I am the bee* . . . Was it called something else, known by some other title? *Smoke Gets in your Eyes* had once been called something else, so Laurie Henderson had said, although, God knows, if Laurie'd said it it probably wasn't true. You could never tell with songs. *If You were the Only Girl in the World,* for instance: was that the full title or was it *If You were the Only Girl in the World and I was the Only Boy?* She'd had an argument with Laurie about that, a ridiculous all-night argument in Mrs Tomer's digs, Maccles-field, 1949 or '50. '50 probably because soon afterwards Laurie went down to London, doing something—barman probably—for the Festival of Britain thing. He'd walked out of Mrs Tomer's and she hadn't seen him for nine years. '51 actually it must have been. Definitely the Festival had been 1951.

She rose, and before she did anything else applied make-up to her face with very great care. She often thought there was nothing she liked better than sitting in her petticoat in front of a looking-glass, putting another face on. She powdered her lipstick, then smiled at herself. She thought about Fitz because today was Thursday and they'd drifted into the way of having lunch on Thursdays. 'My God, it's Nancy!' he'd said when by extraordinary chance he'd come upon her six months ago gazing into the windows of Dickins and Jones. They'd had a cup of tea, and had told one another this and that. 'Of course, why ever not?' she'd said when he'd suggested that they might occasionally see one another. 'Old times' sake,' she'd probably said: she couldn't remember now.

Her flat in Putney was high in a red-brick Victorian block, overlooking the river. Near by was the big, old-fashioned Sceptre Hotel, where drinkers from the flats spent a few evening hours, where foreign commercial travellers stayed. During Wimbledon some of the up-and-coming players stayed there also, with the has-beens. She liked to sit in the Bayeux Lounge and watch them passing through the reception area, pausing for their keys. That German who'd got into the Final about ten years ago she'd noticed once, and she liked to think that McEnroe had stayed in the Sceptre before he'd got going, but she hadn't actually seen him. Every year from the windows of her tiny flat she watched the Boat Race going by, but really had no interest in it. Nice, though, the way it always brought the crowds to Putney. Nice that Putney in the springtime, one Saturday in the year, was not forgotten.

Fitz would be on his train, she thought as she crossed Putney Bridge on her way to the Underground. The bridge was where Christie, who'd murdered so many prostitutes, had been arrested. He'd just had a meal in the Lacy Dining Rooms and perhaps he'd even been thinking of murdering another that very night when the plain clothes had scooped him up. He'd gone, apparently, without a word of protest.

'My, you're a romantic, Fitz!' she'd said all those years ago, and really he hadn't changed. Typical of him to want to make it a regular Thursday rendezvous. Typical to come up specially from the Coast, catching a train and then another train back. During the War they'd been married for four years.

She sang for a moment, remembering that; and then wanting to forget it. His family had thought he was mad, you could see that immediately. He'd led her into a huge drawing-room in Warwickshire, with a grand piano in one corner, and his mother and sister had actually recoiled. 'But for God's sake, you can't!' she'd heard his sister's shrill, unpleasant voice exclaiming in the middle of that same night. 'You can't marry a chorus girl!' But he had married her; they'd had to stomach her in the end.

She'd been a sunflower on the stage of the Old Gaiety when he'd first picked her out; after that he'd come night after night. He'd said she had a flimsy quality and needed looking after. When they met again six months ago in Regent Street he'd said in just the same kind of way that she was far too thin. She'd seen him eyeing her hair, which had been light and fair and was a yellowish colour now, not as pretty as it had been. But he didn't remark on it because he was the kind to remark only on the good things, saying instead she hadn't changed a bit. He seemed boyishly delighted that she still laughed the way she always had, and often remarked that she still held the stem of a glass and her cigarette in her own particular way. 'You're cold,' he'd said a week ago, reminding her of how he'd always gone on in the past about her not wearing enough clothes. He'd never understood that heavy things didn't suit her.

In other ways he hadn't changed, either. Still with a military bearing and hardly grey at all, he had a sunburnt look about the face, as always he'd had. He had not run to fat or slackness, and the sunburnt look extended over his forehead and beyond where his hair had receded. He was all of a piece, his careful suits, his soldier's walk. He'd married someone else, but after twenty-three years she'd gone and died on him.

*

'Good week?' he enquired in the Trattoria San Michele. 'What have you got up to, Nancy?'

She smiled and shrugged her lean, narrow shoulders. Nothing much, she didn't say. There'd been a part she'd heard about and had hoped for, but she didn't want to talk about that; it was a long time since she'd had a part.

'The trout with almonds,' he suggested. 'Shall we both have that?'

She smiled again and nodded. She lived on alimony, not his but that of the man she had married last, the one called Simpson. She lit a cigarette; she liked to smoke at meals, sometimes between mouthfuls.

'They've started that thing on the TV again,' she said. 'That Blankety Blank. Hilarious.'

She didn't know why she'd been unfaithful to him. She'd thought he wouldn't guess, but when he'd come back on his first leave he'd known at once. She'd promised it would never happen again, swearing it was due to the topsy-turviness of the War, the worry because he was in danger. Several leaves later, when the War was almost over, she promised again. 'I couldn't love anyone else, Fitz,' she'd whimpered, meaning it, really and truly. But at the beginning of 1948 he divorced her.

She hated to remember that time, especially since he was here and being so nice to her. She wanted to pay him back and asked him if he remembered the theme from *State Fair*. 'Marvellous. And then of course *Spring Fever*, in the same picture.' She sang for a moment. ' . . . *and it isn't even Spring*. 'Member?'

Eventually she had gone to Canada with a man called Eddie

Lush, whom later she had married. She had stayed there, and later in Philadelphia, for thirteen years, but when she returned to England two children who had been born, a boy and a girl, did not accompany her. They'd become more attached to Eddie Lush than to her, which had hurt her at the time, and there'd been accusations of neglect during the court case, which had been hurtful too. Once upon a time they'd written letters to her occasionally, but she wasn't sure now what they were doing.

'And *I'll Be Around.* 'Member *I'll Be Around?*' She sang again, very softly. *'No matter how . . . you treat me now . . .* Who was it sang it, d'you 'member?'

He shook his head. The waiter brought their trout and Nancy smiled at him. The tedium that had just begun to creep into these Thursday lunches had evaporated as soon as she'd set eyes on the Trattoria's new waiter six or so weeks ago. On Thursday evenings, in her corner of the Bayeux Lounge, his courtesy and his handsome face haunted her. Yes, he was a little sad, she often said to herself in the Bayeux Lounge. Was there even a hint of pain in those steady Latin eyes?

'Oh, lovely-looking trout,' she said, continuing to smile. 'Thanks ever so, Cesare.'

The man she had been married to was saying something else, but she didn't hear what it was. She remembered a chap like Cesare during the War, an airman from the base whom she'd longed to be taken out by, although in fact he'd never invited her.

'What?' she murmured, becoming aware that she'd been asked a question. But the question, now repeated, was only the familiar one, so often asked on Thursdays: did she intend to remain in her Putney flat, was she quite settled there? It was asked because once she'd said—she didn't know why—that the flat was temporary, that her existence in Putney had a temporary feel to it. She couldn't tell all the truth, she couldn't—to Fitz of all people—reveal the hope that at long last old Mr Robin Right would come bob-bob-bobbing along. She believed in Mr R.R., always had, and for some reason she'd got it into her head that he might quite easily walk into the Bayeux Lounge of the Sceptre Hotel. In the evenings she watched television in her flat or in the Bayeux Lounge, sometimes feeling bored because she had no particular friend or confidante. But then she'd always had an inclination to feel a bit like that. Boredom was the devil in her, Laurie Henderson used to say.

'Thanks ever so,' she said again because Cesare had skilfully placed a little heap of peas beside the trout. Typical of her, of course, to go falling for a restaurant waiter: you set yourself out on a sensible course, all serious and determined, and the next thing was you were half in love with an unsuitable younger man. Not that she looked fifty-nine, of course, more like forty—even thirty-eight, as a chap in the Bayeux Lounge had said when she'd asked him to guess a month ago. Unfortunately the chap had definitely not been Mr R.R.

'I just wondered,' Fitz was saying.

She smiled and nodded. The waiter was aware of her attention, no doubt about it. There was a little wink she was gifted with, a slight little motion of the lids, nothing suggestive about it. 'Makes me laugh, your wink,' Eddie Lush used to say, and it was probably Simpson who had called it a gift. She couldn't think why she'd ever allowed herself to marry Simpson, irritating face he'd had, irritating ways.

'It's been enjoyable, making the garden, building that wall. I never thought I'd be able to build a wall.'

He'd told her a lot about his house by the sea, a perfect picture it sounded, with flowerbeds all around the edge, and rustic trellising with ivy disguising the outside sanitary arrangements. He was terribly proud of what he'd done, and every right he had to be, the way he'd made the garden out of nothing. Won some kind of award the garden had, best on the South Coast or the world or something.

'I could sell it very well. I've begun to think of that.'

She nodded. Cesare was expertly gathering up the plates four businessmen had eaten from. The men were stout and flushed, all of them married: you could tell a married look at once. At another table a chap who was married also was taking out a girl less than half his age, and next to them a couple looked as though they were planning a dirty weekend. A party of six, men and women, were at the big central table, just beside where the salads and the bowls of fruit were all laid out and where the dessert trolley was. She'd seen that party here a couple of weeks ago; they'd been talking about *En Tout Cas* tennis courts.

'Once you've made something as you want it,' Fitz was saying, 'you tend to lose interest, I suppose.'

The head waiter called out to the other, younger Italian, she didn't know what his name was, lumpy-looking boy. But Cesare, because he was less busy, answered. *'Pronto! Pronto!'*

'You're never selling up, Fitz?'

'Well, I'm wondering about it.'

He had told her about the woman he'd married, a responsible type of woman she sounded, but she'd been ill or something and hadn't been able to have children. Twenty-three years was really a very long time for any two people to keep going. But then the woman had died.

'You get itchy feet,' he said. 'Even when you're passing sixty.'

'My, you don't look it.' Automatically she responded, watching the waiter while he served the party at the central table with T-bone steaks, a San Michele speciality. He said something

(75)

else, but it didn't impinge on her. Then she heard:

'I often think it would be nice to live in London.'

He was eyeing her, to catch her reaction to this. 'You've had a battered life,' he'd said to her, the second time they'd had lunch. He'd looked at her much as he was looking at her now, and had said it twice. That was being an actress, she'd explained: always living on your nerves, hoping for this part or that, the disappointment of don't-call-us. 'Well, I suppose it batters you in the end,' she'd agreed. 'The old Profession.'

He, on the other hand, had appeared to have had quite a cosy time in the intervening years. Certainly, the responsible-sounding woman hadn't battered him, far from it. They'd been as snug as anything in the house by the sea, a heavy type of woman, Nancy imagined she'd been, with this thing wrong with her, whatever it was. It was after she'd dropped off her twig that he'd begun to feel sorry for himself and of course you couldn't blame him, poor Fitz. It had upset him at first that people had led unattached women up to him at cocktail parties, widows and the like, who'd lost their figures or had let their hair go frizzy, or were old. He'd told her all that one lunchtime and on another occasion he'd confessed that after a year or so had passed he'd gone to a bureau place, an introduction agency, where much younger women were fixed up for him. But that hadn't worked either. He had met the first of them for tea in the Ceylon Centre, where she'd told him that her deceased husband had been an important figure in a chemicals firm and that her older daughter was married in Australia, that her son was in the Hong Kong Police and another daughter married to a dentist in Worcester. She had not ceased to talk the entire time she was with him, apparently, telling him that she suffered from the heat, especially her feet. He'd taken another woman to a revival of *Annie Get Your Gun*, and he'd met a third in a bar she had suggested, where she'd begun to slur her speech after half an hour. Poor Fitz! He'd always been a simple soldier. She could have told him a bureau place would be no good, stood to reason you'd only get the down-and-outs.

'Sorry?' she said.

'I don't suppose you'd ever think of giving it another go?'

'Darling Fitz! *Dear* darling Fitz!'

She smiled at him. How typical it was that he didn't know it was impossible to pick up pieces that had been lying about for forty years! The past was full of Simpson and Laurie Henderson and Eddie Lush, and the two children she'd borne, the girl the child of a fertiliser salesman, which was something Eddie Lush had never guessed. You couldn't keep going on journeys down Memory Lane, and the more you did the more you realised that it was just an ugly black tunnel. Time goes by, as the old song had it, a kiss and a sigh and that was that. She smiled again. '*The fundamental things of life,*' she sang softly, smiling again at her ex-husband.

'I just thought—' he began.

'You always said pretty things, Fitz.'

'I always meant them.'

It had been so romantic when he'd said she needed looking after. He'd called her winsome another time. He was far more romantic than any of the others had ever been, but unfortunately when being romantic went on for a while it could become a teeny bit dreary, no other word for it. Not of course that you'd ever call poor Fitz dreary, far from it.

'Where d'you come from, Cesare?' she asked the waiter, thinking it a good idea to cause a diversion—and besides, it was nice to make the waiter linger. He was better looking than the airman from the base. He had a better nose, a nicer chin. She'd never seen such eyes, nor hair she longed so much to touch. Delicate with the coffee flask, his hands were as brown as an Italian fir-cone. She'd been to Italy once, to Sestri Levante

(77)

with a man called Jacob Fynne who'd said he was going to put on *Lilac Time*. She'd collected fir-cones because she'd been bored, because all Jacob Fynne had wanted was her body. The waiter said he came from somewhere she'd never heard of.

'D'you know Sestri Levante?' she asked in order to keep him at their table.

He said he didn't, so she told him about it. Supposing she ran into him on the street, like she'd run into Fitz six months ago? He'd be alone: restaurant waiters in a city that was foreign to them could not know many people. Would it be so strange to walk together for a little while and then maybe to go in somewhere for a drink? 'Are your lodgings adequate, Cesare?' She would ask the question, and he would reply that his lodgings were not good. He'd say so because it stood to reason that the kind of lodgings an Italian waiter would be put into would of course be abominable. 'I'll look out for somewhere for you': would it be so wrong to say that?

'Would you consider it, Nancy? I mean, is it beyond the pale?'

For a moment it seemed that the hand which had seized one of hers was the waiter's, but then she noticed that Cesare was hurrying away with his flask of coffee. The hand that was paying her attention was marked with age, a bigger, squarer hand than Cesare's.

'Oh Fitz, you are a dear!'

'Well . . .'

'D'you think we might be naughty and go for a brandy today?'

'Of course.'

He signalled the waiter back. She lit another cigarette. When the brandy came and more coffee was being poured she said:

'And how do you like England? London?'

'Very nice, *signora*.'

'When you've tired of London you've tired of life, Cesare. That's a famous saying we have.'

'*Sí, signora*.'

'D'you know Berkeley Square, Cesare? There's a famous song we have about a nightingale in Berkeley Square. Whereabouts d'you live, Cesare?'

'Tooting Bec, *signora*.'

'Good heavens! Tooting's miles away.'

'Not too far, *signora*.'

'I'd rather have Naples any day. See Naples and die, eh?'

She sang a little from the song she'd referred to, and then she laughed and slapped Cesare lightly on the wrist, causing him to laugh also. He said the song was very nice.

'I'm sorry,' Fitz was saying. 'It was a silly thing to say.'

'You've never been silly in your life, Fitz.' She laughed again. 'Except when you married me.'

Gallantly, he shook his head.

'Thanks ever so,' she called after the waiter, who had moved with his coffee flask to the table with the business people. She thought of his being in Putney, in the room she'd found for him, much more convenient than Tooting. She thought of his coming to see her in the flat, of their sitting together with the windows open so that they could look out over the river. It was an unusual relationship, they both knew that, but he confessed that he had always liked the company of older women. He said so very quietly, not looking at her, speaking in a solemn tone. Nothing would change between them, he promised while they drank Campari sodas and she explained about the Boat Race.

'I shouldn't have said it. I'm sorry, Nancy.'

She hummed a snatch of something, smiling at him to show it didn't matter in the least. He'd made another proposal, just like he had when she'd been a sunflower at the Old Gaiety. It was a compliment, but she didn't say so because she was still thinking about sitting with the windows open in Putney.

'I must get back. I'll take an earlier train today,' he said.

'Just a teeny 'nother coffee, Fitz? And perhaps . . .' She lifted her empty brandy glass, her head a little on one side, the way he'd so often said he liked. And when the waiter came again she said:

'And have you always been a waiter, Cesare?'

He said he had, leaving a plate with the bill on it on the table. She tried to think of something else to say to him, but could think of nothing.

When they left the restaurant they walked with a bitter wind in their faces and he didn't take her arm, the way he'd done last week and the week before. On a crowded street the hurrying people jostled them, not apologising. Once they were separated and for a moment she couldn't see her ex-husband and thought that he had slipped away from her, punishing her because she had been embarrassing with the waiter. But that was not his way. 'I'm here,' his voice said.

His cold lips touched her cheeks, first one, then the other. His large, square fingers gripped her arm for just a moment. 'Well, goodbye, Nancy,' he said, as always he did on Thursday afternoons, but this time he did not mention next week and he was gone before she could remind him.

*

That evening she sat in her usual corner of the Bayeux Lounge, sipping vodka and tonic and thinking about the day. She'd been terrible; if she knew poor Fitz's number she'd ring him now from the booth in the passage and say she was sorry. 'Wine goes to your head, Nancy,' Laurie Henderson used to say and it was true. A few glasses of red wine in the Trattoria San Michele and she was pawing at a waiter who was young enough to be her son. And Fitz politely sat there, officer and gentleman still written all over him, saying he'd sell his house up and come to London. The waiter'd probably thought she was after his body.

Not that it mattered what he thought, because he and the Trattoria San Michele already belonged in Memory Lane. She'd never been there until that lunchtime six months ago when old Fitz had said, 'Let's turn in here.' No word would come from him, she sensed that also: never again on a Thursday would she hurry along to the Trattoria San Michele and say she was sorry she was late.

I'll be around, no matter how you treat me now . . . She'd seen him first when they'd sung that number, the grand finale; she'd suddenly noticed him, three rows from the front. She'd seen him looking at her and had wondered while she danced if he was Mr R.R. Well, of course, he had been in a way. He'd stood up for her to his awful relations, he'd kissed away her tears, saying he would die for her. And then the first thing she'd done when he'd married her after all that fuss, when he'd gone back after his leave, was to imagine that that stupid boy with a tubercular chest was the be-all and end-all. And when the boy had proved beyond a shadow of doubt that he was no such thing there was the new one they'd taken on for his tap-dancing.

She smiled in the Bayeux Lounge, remembering the laughter and the applause when the back legs of Jack and the Beanstalk's Dobbin surprised everyone by breaking into that elegant tap-dance, and how Jack and his mother had stood there with their mouths comically open. She'd told Fitz about it a few lunches ago because, of course, she hadn't been able to tell him at the time on account of the thing she'd had with the back legs. He had nodded solemnly, poor Fitz, not really amused, you could see, but pleased because she was happy to remember. A right little trouble-maker that tap-dancer had turned out to be, and a right little scrounge, begging every penny he could lay his hands on, with no intention of paying a farthing back.

If she'd run out of hope, she thought, she could have said yes, let's try again. She could have admitted, because it was only fair to, that she'd never be like the responsible woman who'd gone and died on him. She could have pointed out that she'd never acquire the class of his mother and his sister because she wasn't that sort of person. She'd thought all that out a few weeks ago, knowing what he was getting around to. She'd thought it was awful for him to be going to a bureau place and have women telling him about how the heat affected their feet. She'd imagined saying yes and then humming something special, probably *Love is the Sweetest Thing*, and leaning her face towards him across the table, waiting for his kiss again. But of course you couldn't live in fantasies, you couldn't just pretend.

'Ready for your second, Nancy?' the barmaid called across the empty lounge, and she said yes, she thought she was.

You gave up hope if you just agreed because it sounded cosy. When he'd swept her off her feet all those years ago everything had sounded lovely: being with him in some nice place when the War was over, never again being short, the flowers he brought her. 'No need to come to London, Fitz,' she might have said today. 'Let's just go and live in your house by the sea.' And he'd have been delighted and relieved, because he'd only mentioned selling up in order to show her that he would if she wanted him to. But all hope would be gone if she'd agreed.

She sighed, sorry for him, imagining him in the house he talked about. He'd have arrived there by now, and she imagined him turning the lights on and everything coming to life. You could tell from the way he talked that there were memories there for him, that the woman he'd married was still all over the place: it wasn't because he'd finished making a stone wall in the garden that he wanted to move on. He'd probably pour himself a drink and sit down to watch the television; he'd open a tin later on. She imagined him putting a match to the fire and pulling over the curtains. Probably in a drawer somewhere he had a photo of her as a sunflower. He'd maybe sit with it in his hand, with his drink and the television. 'Dear, it's a fantasy,' she murmured. 'It couldn't ever have worked second time round, no more'n it did before.'

'Warm your bones, Nancy,' the barmaid said, placing her second vodka and tonic on a cardboard mat on the table where she sat. 'Freeze you tonight, it would.'

'Yes, it's very cold.'

She hadn't returned to the flat after the visit to the Trattoria San Michele; somehow she hadn't felt like it. She'd walked about during the couple of hours that had to pass before the Bayeux Lounge opened. She'd looked in the shop windows, and looked at the young people with their peculiarly coloured hair. Two boys in Eastern robes, with no hair at all, had tried to sell her a record. She hadn't been keen to go back to the flat because she wanted to save up the hope that something might have come on the second post, an offer of a part. If she saved it up it would still hover in her mind while she sat in the Bayeux Lounge—just a chance in a million but that was how chances always were. It was more likely, when her luck changed, that the telephone would ring, but even so you could never rule out a letter. You never should. You should never rule out anything.

She wished now she'd tried to tell him all that, even though he might not ever have understood. She wished she'd explained that it was all to do with not giving up hope. She'd felt the same when Eddie had got the children, even though one of them wasn't his, and when they'd gone on so about neglect. All she'd been doing was hoping then too, not wanting to be defeated, not wanting to give in to what they demanded where the children were concerned. Eddie had married someone else, some woman who probably thought she was an awful kind of person because she'd let her children go. But one day the children would write, she knew that inside her somewhere; one day there'd be that letter waiting for her, too.

She sipped more vodka and tonic. She knew as well that one day Mr R.R. would suddenly be there, to make up for every single thing. He'd make up for all the disappointment, for Simpson and Eddie and Laurie Henderson, for treating badly the one man who'd been good to you. He'd make up for scrounging tap-dancers and waiters you wanted to be with because there was sadness in their faces, and the dear old Trattoria San Michele gone for ever into Memory Lane. You couldn't give up on Mr R.R., might as well walk out and throw yourself down into the river; like giving up on yourself it would be.

'I think of you only,' she murmured in her soft whisper, feeling much better now because of the vodka and tonic, 'only wishing, wishing you were by my side.' When she'd come in at half-past five she'd noticed a chap booking in at the reception, some kind of foreign commercial traveller since the tennis people naturally didn't come in winter; fiftyish, handsome-ish, not badly dressed. She was glad they hadn't turned on the television yet. From the corner where she sat she could see the stairs, where sooner or later the chap would appear. He'd buy a drink and then he'd look around and there she'd be.

The
Property of Colette Nervi

Drumgawnie the crossroads was known as, and for miles around the land was called Drumgawnie also. There was a single shop at the crossroads, next to a pink house with its roof gone. There was an abandoned mill, with tall grain stores no longer used for any purpose. Drumgawnie Rath, a ring of standing stones that predated history, was half a mile across the fields where Odd Garvey grazed his cattle.

It was in 1959, an arbitrary date as far as the people who lived in and around Drumgawnie were concerned, that visitors began to take an interest in the stones, drawing their cars up by the mill and the grain stores. English or French people they usually were, spring or summertime tourists who always called in at the shop to enquire the way. Mrs Mullally, who owned the shop, had thought of erecting a small sign but in the end had abandoned the notion on the grounds that one day, perhaps, a visitor might glance about her premises and purchase something. None ever had.

'You have to cross the little stream,' she informed a French couple in the early summer of 1968. 'Continue on past where you've drawn your car in and then there's rocks you can step on to see you over the bit of water. Go neither right nor left after that until you'll strike the stones standing up in the grass.'

In her bedroom Dolores Mullally, then aged twenty-two, watched from her window, the lacy half-curtain pulled back at the edge. She had heard the car coming to a halt by the mill, and minutes later foreign voices had become louder as the visitors approached the shop. She had pushed herself up from her bed and limped across to the window. The woman was wearing a black leather coat, a thin woman with a smiling, slanted face, strange looking and beautiful. The man had a moustache and a slender pipe.

Dolores imagined these foreign people asking her mother about the standing stones, and her mother telling them, using the same expressions she always did. When her mother wasn't there and Dolores gave the directions herself she never used expressions like 'to see you over the bit of water' or 'you'll strike the stones standing up in the grass'. All that was her mother's old-fashioned way of putting things. Dolores simply said that the visitors must cross the stream at a place they'd see and then keep straight on. Her father, no longer alive, had once carried her to see the standing stones and she hadn't found them much to look at. But a visitor who had spent the whole afternoon examining them and had afterwards returned to the shop to verify the way to the Rossaphin road had stated that they were the most extraordinary stones of their kind in the whole of Europe. 'I think he was maybe drunk,' Dolores's mother had commented, and her father had agreed.

As soon as they left the shop the Frenchman took the woman's arm affectionately, both of them laughing at something or other. Dolores watched them walking on the left-hand side of the road, towards the mill and the towering grain stores. There had been prosperity in the place once, both her father and her mother had said, at the time when the mill operated. Its owner had lived in the pink-distempered house with the fallen-in roof, a man called Mr Hackett, who had grown some special kind of plums in his garden.

The French couple stood for a moment by their car, a small,

bright red vehicle, hired in Dublin, Dolores guessed. A group of English people and an American woman, returning from the stones some years ago, had been unable to start theirs and had telephoned the Dan Ryan car-hire organisation from the shop. It was then, for the first time, that Dolores had realised it was possible for visitors from other countries to hire motor-cars and to drive all over Ireland in them.

The Frenchman removed the pipe from his mouth and knocked it out on the edge of his shoe. He unlocked one of the car doors and took from it two pairs of short green gum-boots, which he and the woman put on. They stowed their shoes in the car and then the man put his arms about his companion. He bent her head backwards, leaning his body against her and pushing his lips on to hers, although Dolores could not quite see that detail of the embrace. He released the woman and she at once placed her hands, fingers splayed out, on his black hair, drawing his face down to hers again. After a moment they separated and set off, hand in hand, their arms stretched across the path they walked along. On either side of them nettles and docks grew in great profusion; daisy-heads and buttercups decorated the grass of the path; ragwort was everywhere. The afternoon was sunny, puffy little clouds were stationary in the sky. On the red roof of the car there was what appeared to be a shadow, small and rectangular and vividly black: it was an object, Dolores realised when she screwed her eyes up, not a shadow at all. Carelessly the two had left it there.

She dropped the edge of the half-curtain and limped back to her bed, where she had been reading *Holster in the Dust* by Tom K. Kane. She picked a cigarette from a packet of Afton Major, open on the candlewick counterpane. She lit it and inhaled. Because of her bad leg she lay down for an hour or so almost every afternoon, unless it was the time of year when the seed potatoes had to be put in on the slope at the back or the later time when the grown potatoes had to be gathered. Years ago, when Dolores was twelve, old Dr Riordan had suggested that a rest in the afternoon might be a relief. The leg, shrivelled to the bone as a result of infantile paralysis, necessitated the use of a crutch, although in making her way across her bedroom or the kitchen, or sometimes moving about in the shop, Dolores could manage without this aid, limping from one steadying surface to the next. *The evening sun-rays reddened the canyon,* she read. *Dust was acrid in One-Draw's nostrils and grimy on his cheeks.* Her father had bought these yellow-backed books of the Wild West Library, which were closely printed on absorbent paper, a perpendicular line down the centre of each page, separating the prose as in a newspaper. Their soft covers were tattered now, creases running through horses and riders and gun-smoke, limp spines bent and split. Her father had bought one in Mackie's the newsagent's every Friday, making the journey to Rossaphin in the horse and cart, taking Dolores with him. He had brought to the town the carrots and cabbages he grew on the slope, turnips and potatoes when he had them, plums from the forgotten garden next door. A waste of time, Dolores's mother had always maintained, because of the small profit there'd been, and when Mr Mullally died the practice had ceased and the horse had been sold. The cart was still in the yard at the back, its faded orange-painted wood just beginning to rot. Even though her father had died fourteen years ago, Dolores still missed those weekly journeys and the feeling of excitement their anticipation had engendered.

The shop, patronised by everyone in the neighbourhood, kept Mrs Mullally and her daughter going. The bus dropped off newspapers there, groceries and confectionery were stocked, and a rudimentary post office maintained. At the time of Drumgawnie's greater prosperity Mrs Mullally's father had run it profitably, with a public house as well. Dolores's own father, once employed in Mr Hackett's milling business, had married into the shop after the closing of the mill. In his lifetime it was still thought that Dolores's affliction might miraculously right itself as she grew up, but this had not happened. He died in the kitchen armchair, having complained for several months of pains in the chest which Dr Riordan had not taken seriously. 'Well, Mother of God, isn't it the most surprising thing in three decades of practising medicine?' Dolores remembered him saying in the kitchen, the body already covered with a bed-sheet. 'Riordan was drunk as a fish,' her mother was afterwards to remark. 'His breath would've knocked you down.' Not used to that particular smell, Dolores had imagined it to be a variation of the disinfectant in Dr Riordan's house in Rossaphin.

One-Draw slid from the saddle. His eyes were slits, measuring the distance. 'Cassidy!' he shouted. 'Reach, Cassidy!' There was no reply, no movement. Not a sound in the canyon.

Dolores folded down the corner of the page to keep her place. She lit another Afton Major. There was never any pain in her leg; it was just the ugliness of it, the difficult, unattractive movement, the crutch she hated so. She'd become used over the years to all the cumbersome arrangements that had to be made for her, the school bus coming specially to the crossroads to take her to the convent in Rossaphin, the Crowleys calling in on a Sunday to take her and her mother to mass in their Ford. Once a year, three weeks before Christmas, she and her mother went for the day to shop in Rossaphin, driven on that occasion also by the Crowleys. They had a meal in Love's Café and didn't return to the crossroads until six o'clock. Her mother had to get special permission to close the post-office counter, which was something Father Deane was able to arrange, just as it was he who persuaded the Crowleys to be kind in the way they were.

Now and again, between one December and the next, Dolores managed to get in to Rossaphin on the bus, but the journey home again had to be arranged carefully and in advance, with the co-operation of one of the drivers who called regularly at the shop. Phelan, who brought the bread, was no good because he came out in the morning, but the Mitchelstown Cheese man always passed through Rossaphin in the late afternoon and then came on to the crossroads, and Jimmy Reilly, who brought the bacon, came in the afternoon also. Having chosen a particular day and made the arrangement to meet one or other of the delivery men at a time and a place, Dolores usually had three hours or a bit more on her own. Her mother didn't like it though; her mother worried in case the van men might forget. Neither of them ever had, but something once did go wrong with Jimmy Reilly's engine and Dolores was left waiting outside the Provincial Bank until five o'clock when she should have been collected at two. A boy had come up to her with a message, and then Father Deane had appeared on his bicycle. He rang the bell of the bank and the manager's wife had allowed Dolores to sit on a chair in the hall until the Crowleys arrived in their Ford. The tears were running down her mother's cheeks when eventually she arrived back at the crossroads, and after that Dolores never again went into Rossaphin on her own.

She squashed her cigarette butt on the ashtray that lay beside *Holster in the Dust* on the candlewick counterpane. The ashtray was made of glass, with green letters advertising 7-Up on it, a free gift from one of the delivery men. She'd easily finish *Holster in the Dust* tonight, Dolores considered, she'd even start *Guns of the Apache Country*. She'd read both of them before, but not recently.

She tidied the counterpane, brushing the wrinkles from it. She paused for a moment by the looking-glass on her dressing-table to smear fresh lipstick on to her lips and to run a comb through her long black hair. Her face was round, her chin a pleasant curve. Her father had told her that her eyes were like a dog's he'd once owned, meaning it as a compliment. They were brown and serious, as if all the time Dolores was intent on thoughts she chose not to share with other people. But mostly what she thought about were the adventures of the Wild West Library.

*

'Are you rested, pet?' her mother enquired in the shop. 'You didn't smoke too much?'

'Only two,' Dolores lied.

'You're better off without, pet.'

Dolores nodded. 'That's a well-dressed pair went up to the stones.'

'Did you see them? You should stay lying down, pet.'

'I'll look after the shop now.'

Her mother said that Mrs Connell hadn't come in for her bread yet, nor Whelan for his *Independent*. 'French those people said they were.'

She sliced a couple of rashers as she spoke and took them away on the palm of her hand, through the small store-room at the back of the shop, into the kitchen. In a moment the smell of frying would drift through the store-room, as it did every evening at this time, and soon afterwards Dolores would put up the wire shutter on the post-office counter and lock the drawer where the postal orders and the stamps and the registration book were kept. She'd take the key into the kitchen with her when eventually she went to sit down to her tea. She would hang it on a hook on the dresser, but the shop itself would remain open and anyone who came into it would rap on the counter for attention, knowing that that was expected.

'Mademoiselle,' the Frenchman said, and went on talking. Dolores couldn't understand him. He wasn't smiling any more, and his thin companion in her leather coat wasn't smiling either. They were agitated: the man kept gesturing, moving his hands about; the woman frowned, muttering in French to herself. Dolores shook her head. '*Je ne sais pas,*' the Frenchman said. '*Peut-être ici.*'

He looked around the shop. The woman looked also, on the counter, on the post-office counter, on the cartons that had arrived yesterday and had not yet been opened, on the floor.

'I didn't catch what you said,' Dolores explained, but the woman continued to speak French.

'*Le sac. Le sac noir.*'

'The handbag of my friend,' the man said. 'We lose the handbag.'

'Lose?'

'I place it,' the woman said. 'It is that I place it.'

Dolores reached for her crutch. She lifted the flap of the counter and helped in the search. She called loudly to her mother and when her mother arrived, wiping her hands on her apron, she explained that a handbag had been lost, that it might have been left in the shop.

'I would have noticed,' Mrs Mullally said quickly.

'*Ah, oui, oui,*' the man agreed.

'She was carrying a handbag,' Mrs Mullally said, a defensive note entering her voice. 'She definitely walked out of the shop with it. A square handbag, under her arm.'

Dolores tried to remember: had the woman had a handbag when they walked together to the car? Had she had it when they'd embraced? And then she did remember: the square dark shadow on the red roof, too vivid to be just a shadow.

'She put it on top of the car,' she said, and as she spoke she seemed to see what at the time had passed unnoticed: the woman's arm raised in the moment just before the embrace, the handbag in her hand and then on the red metal that glittered in the sunlight. Dolores had been too intent on the embrace to have observed this properly, but she was certain it had happened.

'Oh, yes,' she said, nodding to lend emphasis to her claim. 'You put it on the roof of your car.'

'You observe?' the Frenchman asked.

'I saw from a window upstairs.'

'Ah, merci, mademoiselle. Merci beaucoup.' It was the woman who spoke. The man said they were grateful, thanking Dolores in English.

She watched, leaning against the doorway of the shop. Her mother accompanied the French couple across the road and then disappeared from sight because of the incline down to the mill. Dolores had sensed her mother's anxiety, the feeling there'd been in her mother's mind that an accusation was being made. She thought of going upstairs to her bedroom to watch again from the window, and was about to do so when the smell of burning bacon wafted from the kitchen. Hurriedly, she shuffled through the shop and the store-room.

'They never found it,' her mother said, returning ten minutes later. 'They moved the car to see if it had fallen off. They'd been up and down to the stones four times, they said, looking on the path in case she dropped it.'

'She put it on the car, she couldn't have dropped it.'

'Ah, sure, you can't watch them.'

'So it's gone, is it?'

'They wrote down an address for me in case it would surface some day. She was down in the mouth, that woman.'

Dolores saw the beautiful, slanted face pulled further to one side, the mouth dragged into a corner of itself, tears threatening. The man would put his arm around the smartly clad shoulders, so very slight beneath the leather. He would comfort his lover and promise her another handbag because people like that, who could hire a motor-car, who could come all the way from France to see some stones in a field, wouldn't have to bother about the expense.

'Did you tell them to go to the gardai at Rossaphin?'

'I didn't mention the gardai to them.' Mrs Mullally spoke firmly again, and Dolores knew that she hadn't suggested the police because she didn't want it to become known that a handbag had disappeared in this manner at the crossroads. 'Sure, won't they find the thing in their motor-car somewhere?'

Dolores nodded, silently agreeing that somehow or other this would be the outcome of the matter. When they had returned from the stones the woman must have taken the handbag from the roof without noticing what she was doing, and she must have bundled it into the car without noticing either. Dolores cut a piece of fried bread and dipped it into the little mound of salt on the side of her plate. She began to think about One-Draw Hagan and his enemy, Red Cassidy.

'Only Henry Garvey was about,' her mother continued, 'driving in the old man's heifers. He'd have been too far away to catch what was going on.'

Dolores nodded again. Perhaps when the lovers returned to the car there had been another embrace, which had driven everything from their minds—like in *Travellin' Saddles* when Big Daunty found his Indian love and both of them went into a swoon, lost to the world. *Colette Nervi*, it said on the piece of paper the French lovers had given her mother. *10 rue St Just, Toulouse, France.* They had insisted on giving her money also, so that she could send them a letter in case the handbag ever turned up.

*

Henry Garvey was a large, slow man of forty, known in the neighbourhood for his laziness and his easy-going nature. His uncle, Odd Garvey, had outlived both of Henry's parents, and the two lived together in the farmhouse which the whole Garvey family had once occupied. Odd Garvey, small and wizened in his old age, had never married—due to meanness, so it was locally said. He was reputed to be affected in the head, though this impression which he gave was perhaps no more than another reflection of a miserly nature. The farmhouse he occupied with his nephew was in need of considerable repair, its roof leaky, its walls wet with rising damp. Henry spent as little time as he could there, preferring to ride his mother's ancient bicycle into Rossaphin every morning and to remain there until it was time to fetch the heifers in. He laid bets, and drank in a number of selected public houses while waiting for the afternoon's racing to begin. He bet on greyhounds as well as horses, and had been known in one bar or another to offer odds on a variety of propositions, including the year of his uncle's decease. A permanent smile split his sunburned face, the easy, lazy smile of a man who was never in a hurry. Sometimes in the evenings he rode back into Rossaphin again, to drink more stout and to talk about race-horses. His uncle owned the farmhouse and the heifers, Henry the fields and the brood of turkeys he fattened every year for Christmas. He received payment from his uncle for the grazing of the heifers and from two other farmers for the grass he let them have on an annual basis: with his turkey profits, this made him a living of a kind. His four sisters had long ago left the neighbourhood, only one of them remaining in Ireland.

'There was foreign people over at the stones,' he reported to his uncle on the evening the French couple had come. 'Jabbering away.'

'Did you approach them? Did you charge them a price for

going over our fields?'

Henry vaguely wagged his head, and knowing that such a charge had not been made the old man continued to grumble, his empty gums squashing up baked beans before he swallowed them. Because he had difficulty with crusts, he tore pieces of bread from the centre of a slice and dipped the soft white lumps into the sauce that went with the beans. Mumbling through this food, he said that the number of people who nowadays crossed their land was a disgrace. It was a favourite mealtime topic: every day, whether there had been visitors to the standing stones or not, the old man urged Henry to protest to the police or the Board of Works, or somebody at the courthouse in Rossaphin. He was convinced that a substantial sum of money was owing to the Garvey family because no toll had ever been charged on the right of way to Drumgawnie Rath. Now, at eighty-six, he was too old to do anything about it. He hadn't been to mass for ten years, nor spoken to anyone except his nephew for six. No one ever came to the farmhouse.

In Henry's view the old man could have kept himself normal by picking up the groceries and the newspaper every day in Mrs Mullally's shop. In a normal manner he could have whiled away his time with Mrs Mullally or the daughter instead of skulking behind the trees, looking out for visitors. But he wouldn't enter the shop because he couldn't bear to hand over money to anyone, so Henry had to see to everything like that. Not that he particularly minded. He had a basket which he hung from the handlebars of his bicycle and he actually enjoyed loitering in shops, Mrs Mullally's or anyone else's. He would light a cigarette and sometimes in Mullally's might have a bottle of lemonade. He would lean his back against the counter and listen to the Mullally girl going on about the Wild West stories she read. She was a decent enough looking creature in her way, the only pity was the leg she was afflicted with.

'Dressed up to the nines they were,' Henry continued in the kitchen. 'A useless type of person, I'd say.'

His uncle emitted a sucking noise. The footsteps made by the visitors wore the grass down. Another thing was, the Board of Works should be informed that cars were being left without charge on the piece of verge by the mill.

'I don't think it's a matter for the Board of Works.'

'Why wouldn't it be? Didn't the Board man come to see me in 1949? Wasn't it the Board drew attention to the stones before any stranger knew they were there?'

'If it's anyone's concern I'd say it was the County Council's.'

'Go into the courthouse in that case. Go into the head clerk and say we're deprived of grass for the cattle due to footsteps wearing it down.'

Henry promised that he would do as he was asked. He always promised when the subject came up. He ate his beans and bread and drank several cups of tea. He didn't say that there were other ways of charging for the use of the path through the fields. He didn't explain that you could get what was owing to you if you were sharp with your eyes and used the intelligence you were born with.

*

Four years after the Frenchwoman's mishap with her handbag Dolores became aware—in the late summer of 1972—of Henry Garvey's interest in her. During that July and August his manner changed. He no longer stood with his back to her, for instance, smiling through the open door at the roadway outside while she told him the plot of another Wild West novel. Instead he faced her, leaning an elbow on the counter. He even lifted his eyes to her face and scrutinised it. Now and again his glance moved over her long dark hair and over her shoulders. Once she'd noticed him looking at her hands.

It had never occurred to Dolores, twenty-six now, that romance would come her way. One cold January day, ages ago, the Crowleys had driven her and her mother to the cinema in Ballyreddy, sixteen miles beyond Rossaphin, for the Sunday matinee. Father Deane had had a hand in the arrangement—had no doubt said that it would be an act of charity—and the Crowleys, seeking through his good offices a chance of heavenly life, had acceded easily to his wish. *From Here to Eternity* the film had been, and Dolores had never forgotten any of it, far richer in romance than anything in her father's Wild West Library. But that was as close as she had so far come to the world of love and passion, and what neither the intercession of Father Deane nor the kindness of the Crowleys could achieve for her was a place among the Friday-night dancers in Rossaphin. Dolores had never been inside the Electric Dance-hall and she guessed she never would. There would be no point: she knew that and accepted it. Yet sometimes she dreamed that miraculously she danced beneath fairyland lights to the music she'd heard on the radio, and was sad for a moment after she woke up.

'I had him backed both ways,' Henry Garvey said towards the end of that August. 'I was fortunate all right.'

He had been talking about the horse, Wonder Boy, a day or two before. It was running on some English race-course, destined to make him a fortune. He had told her about a greyhound called Trumpeter, which had won at Limerick, and another greyhound called Smasheroo. His uncle had died, nearly two years ago now, and she and her mother had gone to the funeral in Rossaphin, driven by the Crowleys. Afterwards they'd all had a cup of tea in Love's Café and Mrs Mullally had taken the opportunity to purchase some oilcloth in Buckley's.

Even though old Garvey had been poor company, it was apparent enough that Henry had become lonely in the farmhouse. He came more often to the shop and lingered there longer than he used to. And then, one morning when Dolores was in the middle of telling him the plot of *Kid Kelly,* she found him scrutinising her even more closely than before. Her mother was present on that occasion and Dolores knew she had observed, and had understood, Henry Garvey's interest. After he'd gone her mother was beside herself with delight, although she didn't say a word. Dolores heard her humming in the kitchen, and her manner was so sprightly when Jimmy Reilly delivered the bacon in the afternoon that he asked her if she'd won the sweep.

'D'you know what it is,' Henry Garvey said at the beginning of September, 'I'm uncertain what to do with myself.'

As he spoke, he pushed his cigarette packet across the counter at her. She was sitting on the black-topped stool which Father Deane had given her as a present, its legs cut down to just the right height. She could sit on it and lean on the counter, just like Henry Garvey was leaning now, on a level with him.

'The old farmhouse above is shook,' he said.

Her mother was not there. Her mother had taken to slipping out to the potato slope whenever Henry Garvey appeared, even if it was raining. Dolores knew that the news of the courtship had been passed on to the Crowleys and to the van men who called at the shop, to Father Deane and to all the people who came to the crossroads for their groceries. When she rested in the afternoons she could hear the excited tone of her mother's voice in the shop below. She was never able to make out the words but she knew that the latest of Henry Garvey's attentions was being retailed and exaggerated.

'I'm wondering,' he said at the beginning of September, 'would I sell the old fellow's heifers?'

She made a slight gesture with the hand that held the cigarette, a shrug of the fingers intended to imply that Henry

Garvey was his own master, that he alone had the privilege of reaching a decision about his late uncle's heifers.

'I have the acres all right, but sure what use is the old house to me? Isn't it falling down on account of the old fellow wouldn't permit a bit of cement to be applied to it?'

Dolores, who had never seen the farmhouse, made the same gesture again.

'And sure you could hardly call them heifers any more. Wouldn't I be better without the trouble of those lassies?'

He turned his ample smile towards her, the red-brick flesh of his face screwed up into small bulges. She had only once seen him wearing a tie and that was at the funeral of his uncle. On Sundays he went to a later mass than her mother and herself: she supposed he'd put the tie on for that also.

'Another factor is,' he continued, 'I need a new bicycle.'

In the shop, and in the rooms above it and behind it, on the slope out at the back, he could take her father's place. He could occupy the chair in which her father had so abruptly died. He could marry into the shop and the house just as her father had, and he would bring with him the rent for the grazing of his fields. Her father had brought nothing.

'What I'm wondering is,' he said, 'could I learn to drive a car?'

She did not reply. She did not even make the same gesture again. She saw herself stepping out of the car he spoke of, the point of the crutch secure on the pavement. She saw herself limping beside him towards the cinema at Ballyreddy, up the steps and down the long passage with framed photographs of film stars on the walls. She saw herself in Rossaphin, not having to wait outside the Provincial Bank for Jimmy Reilly and his van, but going at her leisure in and out of the shops. On a Sunday, mass would be attended when it was convenient, no need to fit in with the Crowleys. And would there be any harm in going, just once, into the Electric Dance-hall and standing there for a while, looking at the dancers and listening to the music?

'I'm sure you could drive a car,' she said. 'If Phelan can drive that bread van I'd say you could drive a car.'

'The old bike was a good machine in its day, but the mudguards is overtaken by the rust.'

'A car would be handy for you, Henry.'

'There's nothing I like better than talking about matters like that to you.'

He paid the compliment without looking at her, gazing as he used to out into the roadway. He was nearly twenty years older than she was, but no other man would ever come into this shop and say he liked talking to her about bicycles and cars. No other man would examine her hair and her hands—or if he did he'd stop it in a hurry, like the new young conductor on the long-distance bus had when he'd realised she was crippled and misshapen.

Henry Garvey left the shop after he'd paid the compliment, and when her mother came in from the back Dolores told her he was considering buying a car. Her mother would have already said prayers, begging Our Lady to make it all right, begging that a crippled woman should not one day find herself alone at the crossroads. The paralysis had been a shock out of nowhere: the attentions of Henry Garvey were just as unexpected, a surprise that came surely from God.

'A car?' her mother said. 'Ah, wouldn't that be grand, pet?'

*

The crossroads was nearer to the town than the farmhouse was, the journey would be shorter, and easier without the stony track that led down to the farm. Often, lounging in the shop, he'd smelt a bit of cooking going on in the kitchen; he remembered Mullally in his day, selling stamps and weighing out potatoes. He liked it when she told him about Kid Kelly and One-Draw Hagan, and she appeared to be interested when he outlined his chances in a race. When an animal didn't come in she appeared to be sympathetic.

'That's fixed so,' he said to her on the day they arranged the marriage. 'Sure, it'll be suitable for the pair of us.'

He gave her a present, a necklace he'd found in the handbag he'd taken years ago as payment for all the strangers who had walked across the fields. There were little blue jewels in it: twenty-two of them, she told him, because she counted them. A week or so later he pushed the handbag itself across the counter at her. He'd found it with the necklace, he said, among his mother's possessions. Tim Durcan was teaching him to drive a car, he said.

*

Dolores knew when Henry Garvey gave her the necklace that Mrs Garvey had never possessed such a piece of jewellery. Her mother knew also, but did not say anything. It wasn't until the handbag appeared that both of them guessed Henry Garvey had stolen the Frenchwoman's property. They still did not say anything. In the drawer where the postal orders and the registration book were kept there remained the scrap of paper on which Colette Nervi had written down her address. It had been there for all the intervening time, together with the small sum of money for postage in case the handbag ever came to light. Mrs Mullally destroyed the scrap of paper after Dolores had received her presents, and looking in the drawer one day Dolores discovered that she had done so.

*

The wedding was to take place in June. Two girls Dolores had been at the convent with were to be bridesmaids, and one of Henry Garvey's bar-room companions had agreed to act as best man. Everyone for miles around Drumgawnie was invited, all the shop's customers, the same people who'd attended Mr Mullally's funeral nineteen years ago, and Odd Garvey's funeral. The Crowleys were invited, and some Rossaphin people, Jimmy Reilly and Phelan the bread man. Some of the other van-drivers lived too far beyond the district but all of them, without exception, brought gifts for Dolores a week or so before the wedding day.

Father Deane had a crutch painted white and asked Mrs Crowley to cover the arm-support in lace to match the wedding-dress. Dolores thought she'd never seen a crutch look so pretty, and wondered if it was a marriage tradition for crippled brides, but did not ask. Henry Garvey's farmhouse was up for sale, the cattle had already been sold. Mrs Mullally had arranged to move out of her room, into the one that had always been Dolores's. 'The simplest thing,' she said, not dwelling upon the subject.

'I don't know will he ever communicate the knack of it,' Henry Garvey said, referring to Tim Durcan's efforts to teach him to drive a motor-car. The car had a way of jumping about with him, juddering and stalling before he even got it started. He had heavy feet, Tim Durcan explained: a man driving a car needed to be sensitive with the clutch and the accelerator. 'You'd think it would be easy,' Henry said to Dolores, and she softly encouraged him, urging him to persevere. There would be nothing nicer, she continued in the same soft voice, than having a car. The white crutch was in her bedroom, in a corner by the dressing-table, waiting for the day in June. She had covered the lace on the arm-support with a piece of brown paper from the shop in case it got dirty.

On the night before the wedding Dolores wondered what else there had been in the handbag. Money would have been bet on a horse or a greyhound, keys perhaps thrown away; somewhere in the unsold farmhouse there'd be a make-up compact. In a month's time there was to be an auction of the furniture and the few remaining bits of farm machinery: before that happened she would find the compact and hide it carefully away. She would not keep her money in the black handbag, nor her cigarettes and matches; she would not be seen in the shops with it. She would be careful with the gifts of Henry Garvey in case, after all, the lovers from France had reported the loss to the police. Henry Garvey would not notice that the necklace was never seen at her neck because he was not the kind to notice things; nor was he the kind to realise that you had to be careful. She felt drowsily comforted by knowing what she must do, but when she turned the light out and attempted to sleep a chilliness possessed her: what if Henry Garvey rode over in the morning on his mother's bicycle to say he'd made a mistake? What if he stood with his back to the counter the way he used to, gazing with his smile out into the roadway? He would not say that the folly of the marriage had at last been borne in upon him. He would not say that he had seen in his mind's eye the ugliness of his bride's body, the shrivelled limb distorting everything. He would not say it had suddenly occurred to him that the awkward, dragging movement when she walked without her crutch was more than he could look at for the remainder of his life. 'I gave you stolen presents,' he'd say instead. 'I'm too ashamed to marry you.' And then he'd mount the bicycle and ride away like one of the cowboys of the Wild West.

In the darkness she lit another cigarette, calming herself. If he'd rather, he could have this room on his own and she could share her mother's. Being a bachelor for so long, that might be a preference he'd have. She'd hate it, in with her mother, but there was an empty back room, never used, which one day might be fixed up for her. There would be a bed and a wardrobe up at the farm, there might even be a length of linoleum going.

She turned the light on and read. She finished *Silent Prairie* and began one she hadn't read for ages, *King Cann Strikes Gold!* by Chas. D. Wasser. Through a faint dawn the birds eventually began to sing. At half-past six she heard her mother moving.

*

He made a cup of tea in the kitchen. No one would buy the place, the way the roof and the kitchen wall were. The wall would hardly last the winter, the crack had widened suddenly, nearly nine inches it must be now. The old furniture would fetch maybe a hundred pounds.

At the kitchen table he stirred sugar into his tea. He wondered if he'd ever manage the driving. And if he did, he wondered if Mrs Mullally would stand the price of a car. It was a matter he hadn't mentioned yet, but with all the trouble he was going to over the learning wouldn't she tumble to it that he had done his share? The three of them were in it together, with the farmhouse the way it was and the girl the way she was. It was only a pity there hadn't been a ring in the handbag he'd taken as payment for the use of the path across his fields. Still and all, he'd got seven to one on Derby Joan with the money there'd been in the purse, which easily covered the cost of the ring he'd had to buy.

He drank his tea and then moved over to the sink to shave himself. They stocked razor blades in the shop, which would be useful too.

*

In front of the altar she leant on the white crutch, wishing she could manage without it but knowing that the effort would be too much. Father Deane's voice whispered at them, and she could sense the delight in it, the joy that he truly felt. Beside her, Henry Garvey was wearing a tie, as she had known he would. There was a carnation and a few shreds of fern in his buttonhole. He smelt of soap.

She had to kneel, which was always difficult, but in time the ceremony was over and she made her way down the aisle, careful on the tiles, one hand gripping the wooden cross-piece of the crutch, the other holding on to him. Hidden beneath her wedding-dress, the necklace that had been stolen from Colette Nervi was cool on the flesh of her neck, and in those moments on the aisle Dolores recalled the embrace. She saw the lovers as they had been that day, the woman's leather coat, the man knocking out his pipe. Sunlight glimmered on the red, polished car, and enriched the green of the nettles and the docks. The woman's fingers were splayed out on her lover's dark head; the two faces were pressed into each other like the faces of the man and the woman in *From Here to Eternity*.

Running Away

It is, Henrietta considers, ridiculous. Even so she feels sorry for the girl, that slack wan face, the whine in her voice. And as if to add insult to injury, Sharon, as a name, is far from attractive.

'Now, I'm sure,' Henrietta says gently, 'you must simply forget all this. Sharon, why not go away for a little? To . . . to . . . ' Where would a girl like Sharon Tamm want to go? Margate? Benidorm? 'I could help you if you'd like me to. We could call it a little loan.'

The girl shakes her head. Hair, in need of washing, flaps. She doesn't want to go away, her whine protests. She wants to stay since she feels she belongs here.

'It's only, Sharon, that I thought it might be easier. A change of scene for a week or two. I know it's hard for you.'

Again the head is shaken, the lank hair flaps. Granny spectacles are removed and wiped carefully on a patchwork skirt, or perhaps a skirt that is simply patched. Sharon's loose, soiled sandals have been kicked off, and she plays with them as she converses. She is sitting on the floor because she never sits on chairs.

'We understand each other, you see,' Henrietta continues softly. 'My dear, I do want you to realise that.'

'It's all over, the thing I had with the Orange People. I'm not like that any more. I'm perfectly responsible.'

'I know the Orange thing is over. I know you've got your feet quite on the ground, Sharon.'

'It was awful 'smatter of fact, all that.'

The Orange People offer a form of Eastern mysticism about which Henrietta knows very little. Someone once told her that the mysticism is an excuse for sexual licence, but explained no further. The sect is apparently quite different from the Hare Krishna people, who sometimes wear orange also but who eat food of such poor quality that sexual excess is out of the question. The Orange People had camped in a field and upset the locals, but all that was ages ago.

'And I know you're working hard, my dear. I know you've turned over a new leaf.' The trouble is that the leaf has been turned, absurdly, in the direction of Henrietta's husband.

'I just want to stay here,' Sharon repeats. 'Ever since it happened I feel I don't belong anywhere else.'

'Well, strictly speaking, nothing *has* happened, dear.'

'It has to me, though, Henrietta.'

Sharon never smiles. Henrietta can't remember having ever seen a smile enlivening the slack features any more than a hint of make-up has ever freshened the pale skin that stretches over them. Henrietta, who dresses well and maintains with care the considerable good looks she possesses, can understand none of it. Unpresentable Sharon Tamm is certainly no floosie, and hardly a gold-digger. Perhaps such creatures do not exist, Henrietta speculates, one perhaps only reads about them.

'I thought I'd better tell you,' Sharon Tamm says. 'I thought it only fair, Henrietta.'

'Yes, I'm glad you did.'

'*He* never would.'

The girl stands up and puts her sandals on to her grimy feet. There is a little white plastic bow, a kind of clasp, in her hair: Henrietta hasn't noticed it before because the hair has covered it in a way it wasn't meant to. The girl sorts all that out now, shaking her head again, taking the bow out and replacing it.

'He can't hurt people,' she tells Henrietta, speaking of the man to whom Henrietta has been married for more than twenty years.

Sharon Tamm leaves the room then, and Henrietta, who has been sitting in a high-backed chair during the conversation, does not move from it. She is flabbergasted by the last two impertinent statements of the girl's. How dare she say he never would! How dare she imply some knowledge of him by coyly remarking that he cannot hurt people! For a moment she experiences a desire to hurry after the girl, to catch her in the hall and to smack her on the face with the open palm of her hand. But she is so taken aback, so outraged by the whole bizarre conversation, that she cannot move. The girl, at her own request—a whispery whine on the telephone—asked to come to see her 'about something urgent'. And although Henrietta intended to go out that afternoon she at once agreed to remain in, imagining that Sharon Tamm was in some kind of pickle.

The hall-door bangs. Henrietta—forty-three last month, dressed now in a blue jersey and skirt, with a necklace of pink corals at her throat and several rings on the fingers of either hand, her hair touched with a preparation that brings out the reddish brown in it—still does not move. She stares at the place on the carpet where the girl has been crouched. There was a time when Sharon Tamm came quite often to the house, when she talked a lot about her family, when Henrietta first felt sorry for her. She ceased to come rather abruptly, going off to the Orange People instead.

In the garden Henrietta's dog, a cairn called Ka-Ki, touches the glass of the French windows with her nose, asking to be let in. Henrietta's husband, Roy, has trained her to do that, but the training has not been difficult because the dog is intelligent. Henrietta crosses the room to open the French windows, not answering in her usual way the fuss the dog makes of her, scampering at her feet, offering some kind of gratitude. The awful thing is, the girl seemed genuinely to believe in the extraordinary fantasy that possesses her. She would have told Roy of course, and Roy being Roy wouldn't have known what to do.

They had married when Roy was at the very beginning of his career, seven years older than Henrietta, who at the time had been a secretary in the department. She'd been nervous because she didn't belong in the academic world, because she had not had a university education herself. 'Only a typist!' she used bitterly to cry in those early, headstrong quarrels they'd had. 'You can't expect a typist to be bright enough to understand you.' But Roy, urbane and placid even then, had kissed her crossly pouting lips and told her not to be so silly. She was cleverer, and prettier, and more attractive in all sorts of other ways, than one after another of his female colleagues: ever since he has been telling her that, and meaning it. Henrietta cannot accept the 'cleverer', but 'prettier' and 'more attractive' she believes to be true, and isn't ashamed when she admits it to herself. They dress appallingly for a start, most of the women in the department, a kind of arrogance, Henrietta considers.

She clears away the tea things, for she has naturally offered Sharon Tamm tea, and carries them to the kitchen. Only a little less shaky than she was in the sitting-room after the girl's final statements, she prepares a turkey breast for the oven. There isn't much to do to it, but she likes to spike it with herbs and to fold it round a celery heart, a recipe she devised herself. She slices parsnips to roast with it, and peeled potatoes to roast also. It isn't a special meal in any way, but somehow she finds herself taking special care because Roy is going to hate it when she mentions the visit of the girl.

She makes a pineapple pudding he likes. He has schoolboy

tastes, he says himself, and in Henrietta's view he has too great a fondness for dairy products. She has to watch him where cream is concerned, and she insists he does not take too much salt. Not having children of their own has affected their relationship in ways like this. They look after one another, he in turn insisting that she should not Hoover for too long because Hoovering brings on the strain in her back.

She turns the pudding out into a Pyrex dish, ready to go into the oven in twenty minutes. She hears her husband in the hall, her own name called, the welcoming bark of Ka-Ki. 'Let's have a drink,' she calls back. 'Let's take a drink to the garden.'

He is there, by the summerhouse, when she arrives with the tray of sherry and gin and Cinzano. She has done her face again, although she knows it hardly needs it; she has tied a red chiffon scarf into her hair. 'There now,' she says. 'Dinner'll be a while.' He's back earlier than usual.

She pours gin and Cinzano for him, and sherry for herself. 'Well, then?' She smiles at him.

'Oh, nothing much. MacMelanie's being difficult.'

'That man should be shot.'

'I only wish we could find someone to do it.'

There is nothing else to report except that a student called Fosse has been found hallucinating by a park keeper. A pity, apparently, because the boy is bright and has always seemed to be mature and well-balanced.

'Roy, I've something to tell you.'

'Ah?'

He is a man who sprawls over chairs rather than sits in them. He has a sprawling walk, taking up more room than is his due on pavements; he sprawls in cinemas and buses, and over the wheel of his car. His grey hair, of which there is a lot, can never acquire a combed look even though he combs it regularly and in the normal way. His spectacles, thickly rimmed and large, move about on his reddish face and often, in fact, fall off. His suits become tousled as soon as he puts them on, gaps appearing, flesh revealed. The one he wears now is of dark brown corduroy, the suit he likes best. A spotted blue handkerchief cascades out of an upper pocket, matching a loose bow-tie.

'Sharon Tamm was here,' Henrietta says.

'Ah.'

She watches while he gulps his gin and vermouth. His eyes behind the pebbly glass of his spectacles are without expression. His mind does not appear to be associated with what she is saying. She wonders if he is thinking that he is not a success in the department, that he should have left the university years ago. She knows he often thinks that when MacMelanie has been troublesome.

'Now, Roy, you have to listen.'

'Well then, I'm listening.'

'It's embarrassing,' she warns.

'What is?'

'This Sharon Tamm thing.'

'She's really pulled herself together, you know. She's very bright. *Really* bright, I mean.'

'She has developed a fantasy about you.'

He says nothing, as if he has not heard, or has heard and not understood.

'She imagines she's in love with you.'

He drinks a mouthful of his drink, and then another. He reaches out to the tray on the table between them and pours himself some more, mostly gin, she notices. He doesn't gesture towards her sherry. He doesn't say anything.

'It was such an awkward conversation.'

All she wants is that it should be known that the girl arrived and said what she did say, that there should be no secret between them about so absurd a matter.

'I had to tell you, Roy. I couldn't not.'

He drinks again, still gulping at the liquid rather than sipping. He is perturbed: knowing him so well she can see that, and she wonders how exactly it is that MacMelanie has been a nuisance again, or if he is depressed because of the boy, Fosse. His eyes have changed behind the glass of his spectacles, something clouds his expression. He is trying not to frown, an effort she is familiar with, a sign of emotion in him. The vein that comes and goes in his forehead will soon appear.

'Roy.'

'I'm sorry Sharon came.'

Attempting to lighten the atmosphere, she laughs slightly. 'She should wear a bra, you know, for a start.'

She pours herself more sherry since he does not intend to. It didn't work, saying the girl should wear a bra: her voice sounded silly. She has a poor head for alcohol of any kind.

'She said you can't hurt people.'

He pulls the spotted handkerchief out of his pocket and wipes sweat from his chin with it. He runs his tongue over his lips. Vaguely, he shakes his head, as if denying that he can't hurt people, but she knows the gesture doesn't mean that. He is upset by what has happened, as she herself has been. He is thinking, as she did, that Sharon Tamm was once taken under their wing. He brought her back with him one evening, encouraging her, as a stray dog might be encouraged into the warmth. Other students, too, have been like daughters or sons to them and have remained their friends, a surrogate family. It was painful when Sharon Tamm left them for the Orange People.

'Of course I know,' Henrietta says, 'that was something we didn't understand.'

Vaguely he offers her more sherry, not noticing that she has had some. He pours more of his mixture for himself.

'Yes, there was something wrong,' he says.

They have been through all that. They talked about it endlessly, sending themselves to sleep with it, lazing with it on a Sunday morning. Henrietta found it hard to forgive the girl for being ungrateful. Both of them, she considered, had helped her in so very many ways.

'Shall we forget it all now?' she suggests, knowing that her voice has become nervous. 'Everything about the wretched girl?'

'Forget?'

That is impossible, his tone suggests. They cannot forget all that Sharon Tamm has told them about her home in Daventry, about her father's mother who lives with the family and stirs up so much trouble, about her overweight sister Diane and her brother Leslie. The world of Sharon Tamm's family has entered theirs. They can see, even now, the grandmother in her special armchair in the kitchen, her face snagged with a sourness that has to do with her wastrel husband, long since dead. They can see the saucepans boiling over on the stove because Mrs Tamm can never catch them in time, and Leslie's motor-cycling gear on the kitchen table, and Diane's bulk. Mr Tamm shouts perpetually, at Leslie to take his motor-cycling clothes away, at Diane for being so fat, at his wife, at Sharon, making her jump. 'You are stupid to an extent,' is the statement he has coined specially for his wife and repeats for her benefit several times every evening. He speaks slowly when he makes this statement, giving the words air, floating them through tired exasperation. His noisy manner leaves him when he dispatches these words, for otherwise—when he tells his wife she is ugly or a bitch—he shouts, and bangs anything he can lay his hand on, a saucepan lid, a tin of mushy peas, a spoon. The only person he doesn't shout at is his mother, for whom he has an exaggerated regard, even, according to Sharon, loves. Every evening he takes her down to the Tapper's Arms, returning at closing time to the house that Sharon has so minutely described: rooms separated by walls through which all quarrels can be heard, cigarette burns on the edge of the bath, a picture of a black girl on the landing, a stair-carpet touched with Leslie's motor-cycling grease and worn away in places. To Henrietta's sitting-room—flowery in summer because the French windows bring the garden in, cheerful with a wood fire when it's cold—these images have been repeatedly conveyed, for Sharon Tamm derived considerable relief from talking.

'Well, she told me and I've told you. Please can we just put it all aside?'

She rises as she speaks and hurries to the kitchen. She opens the oven and places the pineapple pudding on the bottom shelf. She bastes the turkey breast and the potatoes and the parsnips. She washes some broccoli and puts it ready on the draining-board. He has not said, as she hoped he would, that Sharon Tamm is really a bit pathetic. Ka-Ki sniffs about the kitchen, excited by the smell that has come from the oven. She trots behind Henrietta, back to the garden.

'She told you too, didn't she, Roy? You knew all this?'

She didn't mean to say that. While washing the broccoli she planned to mention MacMelanie, to change the subject firmly and with deliberation. But the nervousness that Sharon Tamm inspired in her when she said that Roy couldn't hurt people has suddenly returned, and she feels muzzy due to the sherry, not entirely in control of herself.

'Yes, she told me,' he says. 'Well, actually, it isn't quite like that.'

He has begun to sweat again, little beads breaking on his forehead and his chin. He pulls the dotted handkerchief from his pocket and wipes at his face. In a slow, unwilling voice he tells her what some intuition already insists is the unbelievable truth: it is not just that the girl has a silly crush on him but that a relationship of some kind exists between them. Listening, she feels physically sick. She feels she is asleep, trying to wake herself out of a nightmare because the sickness is heaving through her stomach. The face of the girl is vivid, a whitehead in the crease of her chin, the rims of her eyes pink. The girl is an insult to her, with her dirty feet and broken fingernails.

'Let's not mention it ever again,' she hears herself urging repetitiously. 'MacMelanie,' she begins, but does not continue. He is saying something, his voice stumbling, larded with embarrassment. She can't hear him properly.

There has never been an uneasiness about their loyalty to one another, about their love or their companionship. Roy is disappointed because, professionally, he hasn't got on, but that has nothing to do with the marriage. Roy doesn't understand ambition, he doesn't understand that advancement has to be pursued. She knows that but has never said it.

'I'm sorry, Henrietta,' he says, and she wants to laugh. She wants to stare at him in amazement as he sprawls there, sweating and fat. She wants to laugh into his face so that he can see how ridiculous it all is. How can it possibly be that he is telling her he loves an unattractive girl who is thirty years younger than him?

'I feel most awfully dejected,' he mutters, staring down at the paving stones where they sit. Her dog is obedient at his feet. High above them an aeroplane goes over.

Does he want to marry the girl? Will she lead him into the house in Daventry to meet her family, into the kitchen where the awful grandmother is? Will he shake hands with stupid Mrs Tamm, with Leslie and Diane? Will he go down to the Tapper's Arms with Mr Tamm?

'I can't believe this, Roy.'

'I'm sorry.'

'Do you adore her?'

He doesn't answer.

'Have you hated me all these years, Roy?'

'Of course not.'

They have made love, the girl and he. He tells Henrietta so, confessing awkwardly, mentioning the floor of his room in the department. He would have taken off the girl's granny glasses and put them on the fawn vinyl by the leg of his desk. He would have run his fingers through the lustreless hair.

'How could you do this, Roy?'

'It's a thing that happened. Nobody did anything.' Red-faced, shame-faced, he attempts to shrug, but the effort becomes lost in his sprawling flabbiness. He is as unattractive as the girl, she finds herself reflecting: a stranded jellyfish.

'It's ridiculous, Roy,' she shouts, at last losing control. 'It's madness all this.' They have had quarrels before, ordinary quarrels about ordinary matters. Mild insults were later taken back, apologised for, the heat of the moment blamed.

'Why should it be ridiculous,' he questions now, 'that someone should love me? Why should it be?'

'She's a child, you're a man of fifty-two. How could there possibly be a normal relationship between you? What have you in common?'

'We fell in love, Henrietta. Love has nothing to do with having things in common or normal relationships. Hesselmann in fact points out—'

'For God's sake, Roy, this is not a time for Hesselmann.'

'He does suggest that love abnormalises—'

'So you're going to become a middle-aged hippy, are you, Roy? You're going to put on robes and dance and meditate in a field with the Orange People? The Orange People were phony, you said. You said that, Roy.'

'You know as well as I do that Sharon has nothing to do with the Orange People any more.'

'You'll love her grandmother. Not to mention Mr Tamm.'

'Sharon needs to be protected from her family. As a matter of fact, she doesn't want ever to go back to that house. You're being snide, you know.'

'I'm actually suffering from shock.'

'There are things we must work out.'

'Oh, for heaven's sake, Roy, have your menopausal fling with the girl. Take her off to a hotel in Margate or Benidorm.'

She pours herself more sherry, her hands shaking, a harsh fieriness darkening her face, reflecting the fury in her voice. She imagines the pair of them in the places she mentions, people looking at them, he getting to know the girl's intimate habits. He would become familiar with the contents of her handbag, the way she puts on and takes off her clothes, the way she wakes up. Nineteen years ago, on their honeymoon in La Grève, Roy spoke of this aspect of a close relationship. Henrietta's own particular way of doing things and her possessions—her lipstick, her powder compact, her dark glasses, the leather suitcase with her pre-marriage initials on it, the buttoning of her skirts and dresses—were daily becoming as familiar to him as they had been for so long to her. Her childhood existed for him because of what, in passing, she told him of it.

'D'you remember La Grève?' she asks, her voice calm again. 'The woman who called you Professor, those walks in the snow?'

Impatiently he looks away. La Grève is irrelevant, all of it far too long ago. Again he mentions Hesselmann. Not understanding, she says:

'At least *I* shall not forget La Grève.'

'I've tried to get over her. I've tried not seeing her. None of it works.'

'She said you would not have told me. What did you intend, Roy?'

'I don't know.'

'She said it wasn't fair, did she?'

'Yes, she did.' He pauses. 'She's very fond of you, you know.'

In the oven the breast of turkey would be shrivelling, the pineapple pudding of which he was so boyishly fond would be a burnt mess. She says, and feels ashamed of admitting it: 'I've always had affection for her too, in spite of what I say.'

'I need to talk to her now. I need to tell her we've cleared the air.'

He stands up and drinks what remains of his drink. Tears ooze from beneath his spectacles as he looks down at Henrietta, staring at her. He says nothing else except, yet again, that he is sorry. He shuffles and blows his nose as he speaks. Then he turns and goes away, and a few minutes later she hears the bang of the hall-door, as she heard it after Sharon Tamm had left the house also.

*

Henrietta shops in a greengrocer's that in the Italian small-town manner has no name, just *Fiori e Frutta* above the door. The shy woman who serves there, who has come to know her, adds up the cost of *fagiolini*, pears and spinach on a piece of paper.

'*Mille quattro cento.*' Henrietta counts out the money and gathers up her purchases.

'*Buon giorno, grazie,*' the woman murmurs, and Henrietta wishes her good-day and passes out into the street.

The fat barber sleeps in his customers' chair, his white overall as spotless as a surgeon's before an operation. In the window his wife knits, glancing up now and again at the women who come and go in the Malgri Moda. It is Tuesday the

Jollycaffè is closed. The men who usually sit outside it are nowhere to be seen.

Henrietta buys a slice of beef, enough for one. In the minimarket she buys eggs and a packet of *zuppa di verdura*, and *biscotti strudel 'cocktail di frutta*,' which have become her favourites. She climbs up through the town, to the *appartamento* in the Piazza Santa Lucia. She is dressed less formally than she thought suitable for middle age in England. She wears a denim skirt, blue canvas shoes, a blue shirt which she bought before the weekend from Signora Leici. Her Italian improves a little every day, due mainly to the lessons she has with the girl in the *Informazioni.* They are both determined that by the winter she will know enough to teach English to the youngest children in the orphanage. Sister Maria has said she would welcome that.

It is May. On the verges of the meadows and the wheat fields that stretch below the town pale roses are in bloom. Laburnum blossoms in the vineyards, wires for the vines stretching between the narrow trunks of the trees. It is the season of broom and clover, of poppies, and geraniums forgotten in the grass. Sleepy vipers emerge from crevices, no longer kept down by the animals that once grazed these hillsides. Because of them Henrietta has bought rubber boots for walking in the woods or up Monte Totona.

She is happy because she is alone. She is happy in the small *appartamento* lent to her by friends of her sister, who use it infrequently. She loves the town's steep, cool streets, its quietness, the grey stone of its buildings, quarried from the hill it is built upon. She is happy because the nightmare is distant now, a picture she can illuminate in her mind and calmly survey. She sees her husband sprawling on the chair in the garden, the girl in her granny glasses, and her own weeping face in the bathroom looking-glass. Time shrinks the order of events: she packs her clothes into three suitcases; she is in her sister's house in Hemel Hempstead. That was the worst of all, the passing of the days in Hemel Hempstead, the sympathy of her sister, her generous, patient brother-in-law, their children imagining she was ill. When she thinks of herself now she feels a child herself, not the Henrietta of the suburban sitting-room and the tray of drinks, with chiffon tidily in her hair. Her father makes a swing for her because she has begged so, ropes tied to the bough of an apple tree. Her mother once was cross because she climbed that tree. She cries and her sister comforts her, a sunny afternoon when she got tar on her dress. She skates on an icy pond, a birthday treat before her birthday tea when she was nine. 'I can't stay here,' she said in Hemel Hempstead, and then there was the stroke of good fortune, people she did not even know who had an *appartamento* in a Tuscan hill town.

In the *cantina* of the Contucci family the wine matures in oaken barrels of immense diameter, the iron hoops that bind them stylishly painted red. She has been shown the *cantina* and the palace of the Contucci. She has looked across the slopes of terracotta roof-tiles to Monticchiello and Pienza. She has drunk the water of the nearby spa and has sat in the sun outside the café by the bank, whiling away a morning with an Italian dictionary. *Frusta* means whip, and it's also the word for the bread she has with *fontina* for lunch.

Her husband pays money into her bank account and she accepts it because she must. There are some investments her father left her: between the two sources there is enough to live on. But one day, when her Italian is good enough, she will reject the money her husband pays her. It is degrading to look for support from someone she no longer respects. And one day, too, she will revert to her maiden name, for why should she carry with her the name of a man who shrugged her off?

In the cool of the *appartamento* she lunches alone. With her *frusta* and *fontina* she eats peppery radishes and drinks *acqua minerale.* Wine in the daytime makes her sleepy, and she is determined this afternoon to learn another thirty words and to do two exercises for the girl in the *Informazioni. Le Chiavi del Regno* by A. J. Cronin is open beside her, but for a moment she does not read it. A week ago, on the telephone to England, she described the four new villas of Signor Falconi to prospective tenants, Signora Falconi having asked her if she would. The Falconis had shown her the villas they had built near their *fattoria* in the hills, and she assured someone in Gloucester that any one of them would perfectly suit her requirements, which were sun and tranquillity and room enough for six.

Guilt once consumed her, Henrietta considers. She continued to be a secretary in the department for six years after her marriage but had given it up because she'd found it awkward, having to work not just for her husband but for his rivals and his enemies. He'd been pleased when she'd done so, and although she'd always intended to find a secretarial post outside the university she never had. She'd felt guilty about that, because she was contributing so little, a childless housewife.

'I want to stay here.' She says it aloud, pouring herself more *acqua minerale*, not eating for a moment. *'Voglio stare qui.'* She has known the worst of last winter's weather; she has watched spring coming; heat will not defeat her. How has she not guessed, through all those years of what seemed like a contented marriage, that solitude suits her better? It only seemed contented, she knows that now: she had talked herself into an artificial contentment, she had allowed herself to become a woman dulled by the monotony of a foolish man, his sprawling bigness and his sense of failure. It is bliss of a kind not to hear his laughter turned on for a television joke, not to look daily at his flamboyant ties and unpolished shoes. *Quella mattina il diario si aprí alla data Ottobre 1917:* how astonished he would be if he could see her now, childishly delighting in *The Keys of the*

Kingdom in Italian.

It was her fault, she'd always believed, that they could not have children—yet something informs her now that it was probably more her husband's, that she'd been wrong to feel inadequate. As a vacuum-cleaner sucks in whatever it touches, he had drawn her into a world that was not her own; she had existed on territory where it was natural to be blind—where it was natural, too, to feel she must dutifully console a husband because he was not a success professionally. 'Born with a sense of duty,' her father once said, when she was ten or so. 'A good thing, Henrietta.' She is not so sure: guilt and duty seem now to belong together, different names for a single quality.

Later that day she walks to the Church of San Biagio, among the meadows below the walls of the town. Boys are playing football in the shade, girls lie on the grass. She goes over her vocabulary in her mind, passing by the church. She walks on white, dusty roads, between rows of slender pines. *Solivago* is the word she has been trying to find—wandering alone. *Piantare* means to plant; *piantamento* is planting, *piantagione* plantation. Determinedly she taxes her atrophied memory: *sulla via di casa* and *in modo da; un manovale* and *la briciola.*

In the August of that year, when the heat is at its height, Signora Falconi approaches Henrietta in the *macelleria.* She speaks in Italian, for Henrietta's Italian is better now than Signora Falconi's rudimentary English. There is something, Signora Falconi reveals—a request that has not to do with reassuring a would-be tenant on the telephone. There is some other proposition that Signor Falconi and his wife would like to put to her.

'*Verrò,*' Henrietta agrees. '*Verrò martedí coll'autobus.*'

The Falconis offer her coffee and a little *grappa.* Their four villas, clustered around their *fattoria,* are full of English tenants now. Every fortnight these tenants change, so dirty laundry must be gathered for the *lavanderia*, fresh sheets put on the beds, the villa cleaned. And the newcomers, when they arrive, must be shown where everything is, told about the windows and the shutters, warned about the mosquitoes and requested not to use too much water. They must have many other details explained to them, which the Falconis, up to now, have not quite succeeded in doing. There is a loggia in one of the villas that would be Henrietta's, a single room with a balcony and a bathroom, an outside staircase. And the Falconis would pay just a little for the cleaning and the changing of the sheets, the many details explained. The Falconis are apologetic, fearing that Henrietta may consider the work too humble. They are anxious she should know that women to clean and change sheets are not easy to come by since they find employment in the hotels of the nearby spa, and that there is more than enough for Signor Falconi herself to do at the *fattoria*.

It is not the work Henrietta has imagined when anticipating her future, but her future in her *appartamento* is uncertain, for she cannot live for ever on strangers' charity and one day the strangers will return.

'*Va bene*,' she says to the Falconis. '*Lo faccio*.'

She moves from the Piazza San Lucia. *La governante* Signora Falconi calls her, and the tenants of the villas become her temporary friends. Some take her out to Il Marzucco, the hotel of the town. Others drive her to the sulphur baths or to the abbey at Monte Oliveto, where doves flutter through the cloisters, as white as the dusty roads she loves to walk on. On either side of the pink brick archway are the masterpieces of Luca della Robbia and sometimes the doves alight on them. This abbey on the hill of Oliveto is the most beautiful place she has ever visited: she owes a debt to the girl with the granny glasses.

In the evening she sits on her balcony, drinking a glass of *vino nobile,* hearing the English voices, and the voices of the Italians in and around the *fattoria.* But by October the English voices have dwindled and the only customers of the *fattoria* are the Italians who come traditionally for lunch on Sundays. Henrietta cleans the villas then. She scours the saucepans and puts away the cutlery and the bed linen. The Falconis seem concerned that she should be on her own so much and invite her to their meals occasionally, but she explains that her discovery of solitude has made her happy. Sometimes she watches them making soap and candles, learning how that is done.

*

The girl, walking up and down the sitting-room that once was Henrietta's, is more matter-of-fact and assured than Henrietta remembers her, though her complexion has not improved. Her clothes—a black jersey and a black leather skirt—are of a better quality. There is a dusting of dandruff on the jersey, her long hair has been cut.

'It's the way things worked out,' she says, which is something she has said repeatedly before, during the time they have had to spend together.

Henrietta does not reply, as she has not on the previous occasions. Upstairs, in blue-and-brown-striped pyjamas, purchased by herself three years ago, the man of whom each has had a share rests. He is out of danger, recovering in an orderly way.

'As Roy himself said,' the girl repeats also, 'we live in a world of mistakes.'

Yet they belong together, he and the girl, with their academic brightness and Hesselmann to talk about. The dog is no longer in the house. Ka-Ki has eaten a plastic bag, attracted by slivers of meat adhering to it, and has died. Henrietta blames herself.

No matter how upset she'd felt it had been cruel to walk out and leave that dog.

'I gave Roy up to you,' she says, 'since that was what you and he wanted.'

'Roy is ill.'

'He is ill, but at the same time he is well again. This house is yours and his now. You have changed things. You have let the place get dirty, the windows don't seem ever to have been opened. I gave the house up to you also. I'm not asking you to give it back.'

'Like I say, Henrietta, it was unfortunate about the dog. I'm sorry about that.'

'I chose to leave the dog behind, with everything else.'

'Look, Henrietta—'

'Roy will be able to work again, just as before: we've been quite assured about that. He is to lose some weight, he is to take care of his diet. He is to exercise himself properly, something he never bothered with. It was you, not me, they gave those instructions to.'

'They didn't seem to get the picture, Henrietta. Like I say, we broke up, I wasn't even living here. I've explained that to you, Henrietta. I haven't been here for the past five months, I'm down in London now.'

'Don't you feel you should get Roy on his feet again, since you had last use of him, as it were?'

'That way you're talking is unpleasant, Henrietta. You're getting at me, you're getting at poor Roy. Like you're jealous or something. There was love between us, there really was. Deep love. You know, Henrietta? You understand?'

'Roy explained it to me about the love, that evening.'

'But then it went. It just extinguished itself, like maybe there *was* something in the age-difference bit. I don't know. Perhaps we'll never know, Henrietta.'

'Perhaps not indeed.'

'We were happy for a long time, Roy and me. As happy as any two people could be.'

'I'm sure you were.'

'I'm sorry. I didn't mean to say that. Look, Henrietta, I'm with someone else now. It's different what I've got now. It's going to work out.'

A damp coldness, like the fog that hangs about the garden, touches Henrietta's flesh, insinuating itself beneath her clothes, icy on her stomach and her back. The girl had been at the hospital, called there because Roy had asked for her. She did not say then that she was with someone else.

'May I just, you know, say goodbye to Roy? May I be with him for just five minutes, Henrietta?'

She does not reply. The coldness has spread to her arms and legs. It oozes over her breasts; it reaches for her feet. In blurred vision she sees the steep cool streets of the town, the laburnums and the blaze of clover in the landscape she ran away to.

'I know it's terrible for you, Henrietta.'

Sharon Tamm leaves the room to have her last five minutes. The blur in Henrietta's vision is nothing now. She wonders if they have buried her dog somewhere.

'Goodbye, Henrietta. He's tons better, you know.'

She hears the hall-door close as she heard it on the afternoon when the girl came to talk to her, and later when Roy left the house. It's odd, she reflects, that because there has been a marriage and because she bears his name, she should be less free than the girl. Yet is not the life she discovered for herself much the same as finding someone else? Perhaps not.

'I'm sorry,' he says, when she brings him a tray. 'Oh God, I'm sorry about all this mess.'

He cries and is unable to cease. The tears fall on to the egg she has poached for him and into his cup of Bovril. 'Sorry,' he says. 'Oh God, I'm sorry.'

Cocktails at Doney's

'You've forgotten me,' were the first words Mrs Faraday spoke to him in the Albergo San Lorenzo. She was a tall, black-haired woman, wearing a rust-red suede coat cut in an Italian style. She smiled. She had white, even teeth, and the shade of her lipstick appeared subtly to match the colour of her coat. Her accent was American, her voice soft, with a trace of huskiness. She was thirty-five, perhaps thirty-seven, certainly not older. 'We met a long time ago,' she said, smiling a little more. 'I don't know why I never forget a face.'

She was married to a man who owned a paper mill near some town in America he'd never heard of. She was a beautiful woman, but he could remember neither her nor her husband. Her name meant nothing to him and when she prompted him with the information about her husband's business he could not remember any better. Her eyes were brown, dominating her classic features.

'Of course,' he lied politely.

She laughed, clearly guessing it was a lie. 'Well, anyway,' she said, 'hullo to you.'

It was after dinner, almost ten o'clock. They had a drink in the bar since it seemed the natural thing to do. She had to do with fashion; she was in Florence for the Pitti Donna; she always came in February.

'It's nice to see you again. The people at these trade shows can be tacky.'

'Don't you go to the museums as well? The churches?'

'Of course.'

When he asked if her husband accompanied her on her excursions to Florence she explained that the museums, the churches, and the Pitti Donna would tire her husband immensely. He was not a man for Europe, preferring local race-tracks.

'And your wife? Is she here with you?'

'I'm actually not married.'

He wished he had not met Mrs Faraday. He didn't care for being approached in this manner, and her condemnation of the people at the trade exhibitions she spoke of seemed out of place since they were, after all, the people of her business world. And that she was married to a man who preferred race-tracks to culture was hardly of interest to a stranger. Before their conversation ended he was certain they had not ever met before.

'I have to say good-night,' he said, rising when she finished her drink. 'I tend to get up early.'

'Why, so do I!'

'Good-night, Mrs Faraday.'

In his bedroom he sat on the edge of his bed, thinking about nothing in particular. Then he undressed and brushed his teeth. He examined his face in the slightly tarnished looking-glass above the wash-basin. He was fifty-seven, but according to this reflection older. His face would seem younger if he put on a bit of weight; chubbiness could be made to cover a multitude of sins. But he didn't want that; he liked being thought of as beyond things.

He turned the looking-glass light out and got into bed. He read *Our Mutual Friend* and then lay for a moment in the darkness. He thought of Daphne and of Lucy—dark-haired, tiny Lucy who had said at first it didn't matter, Daphne with her pale-blue, trusting eyes. He had blamed Daphne, not himself, and then had taken that back and asked to be forgiven; they were both of them to blame for the awful mistake of a marriage that should never have taken place, although later he had said that neither of them was, for how could they have guessed they were not suited in that way? It was with Lucy he had begun to know the truth; poor Lucy had suffered more.

He slept, and dreamed he was in Padua with a friend of another time, walking in the Botanical Gardens and explaining to his friend that the tourist guides he composed were short-lived in their usefulness because each reflected a city ephemerally caught. 'You're ashamed of your tourist guides,' his friend of that time interrupted, Jeremy it was. 'Why *are* the impotent so full of shame, my dear? Why *is* it?' Then Rosie was in the dream and Jeremy was laughing, playfully, saying he'd been most amusingly led up the garden path. 'He led me up it too, my God,' Rosie cried out furiously. 'All he could do was weep.'

*

Linger over the Giambologna birds in the Bargello, and the marble reliefs of Mino da Fiesole. But that's enough for one day; you must return tomorrow.

He liked to lay down the law. He liked to take chances with the facts, and wait for letters of contradiction. *At the height of the season there are twelve times as many strangers as natives in this dusty, littered city. Cascades of graffiti welcome them—the male sexual organ stylised to a Florentine simplicity, belligerent swastikas, hammers and sickles in the streets of gentle Fra Angelico . . .*

At lunchtime on the day after he had met her Mrs Faraday was in Doney's with some other Americans. Seeing her in that smart setting, he was surprised that she stayed in the Albergo San Lorenzo rather than the Savoy or the Excelsior. The San Lorenzo's grandeur all belonged to the past: the old hotel was threadbare now, its curtains creased, its telephones unresponsive. Not many Americans liked it.

'Hi!' she called across the restaurant, and smiled and waved a menu.

He nodded at her, not wishing to seem stand-offish. The people she was with were talking about the merchandise they had been inspecting at the Pitti Donna. Wisps of their conversation drifted from their table, references to profit margins and catching the imagination.

He ordered tagliatelle and the chef's salad, and then looked through the *Nazione*. The body of the missing schoolgirl, Gabriella, had been found in a park in Florence. Youths who'd been terrorising the neighbourhood of Santa Croce had been identified and arrested. Two German girls, hitchhiking in the south, had been made drunk and raped in a village shed. The *Nazione* suggested that Gabriella—a quiet girl—had by chance been a witness to drug-trafficking in the park.

'I envy you your job,' Mrs Faraday said, pausing at his table as he was finishing his tagliatelle. Her companions had gone on ahead of her. She smiled, as at an old friend, and then sat down. 'I guess I want to lose those two.'

He offered her a glass of wine. She shook her head. 'I'd love another cappucino.'

The coffee was ordered. He folded the newspaper and placed it on the empty chair beside him. Mrs Faraday, as though she intended to stay a while, had hung her red suede coat over the back of the chair.

'I envy you your job,' she said again. 'I'd love to travel all over.'

She was wearing pearls at her throat, above a black dress. Rings clustered her fingers, earrings made a jangling sound. Her nails were shaped and painted, her face as meticulously made up as it had been the night before.

'Did you mind,' she asked when the waiter had brought their coffee, 'my wondering if you were married?'

He said he hadn't minded.

'Marriage is no great shakes.'

She lit a cigarette. She had only ever been married to the man who owned the paper mill. She had had one child, a daughter who had died after a week. She had not been able to have other children.

'I'm sorry,' he said.

She looked at him closely, cigarette smoke curling between them. The tip of her tongue picked a shred of tobacco from the corner of her mouth. She said again that marriage was no great shakes. She added, as if to lend greater weight to this:

'I lay awake last night thinking I'd like this city to devour me.'

He did not comment, not knowing what she meant. But quite without wishing to he couldn't help thinking of this beautiful woman lying awake in her bedroom in the Albergo San Lorenzo. He imagined her staring into the darkness, the glow of her cigarette, the sound of her inhaling. She was looking for an affair, he supposed, and hoped she realised he wasn't the man for that.

'I wouldn't mind living the balance of my life here. I like it better every year.'

'Yes, it's a remarkable city.'

'There's a place called the Palazzo Ricasoli where you can hire apartments. I'd settle there.'

'I see.'

'I could tell you a secret about the Palazzo Ricasoli.'

'Mrs Faraday—'

'I spent a naughty week there once.'

He drank some coffee in order to avoid speaking. He sighed without making a sound.

(133)

'With a guy I met at the Pitti Donna. A countryman of yours. He came from somewhere called Horsham.'

'I've never been to Horsham.'

'Oh, my God, I'm embarrassing you!'

'No, not at all.'

'Gosh, I'm sorry! I really am! Please say it's all right.'

'I assure you, Mrs Faraday, I'm not easily shocked.'

'I'm an awful shady lady embarrassing a nice Englishman! Please say you forgive me.'

'There is absolutely nothing to forgive.'

'It was a flop, if you want to know.' She paused. 'Say, what do you plan to write in your guidebook about Florence?'

'Banalities mostly.'

'Oh, come *on*!'

He shrugged.

'I'll tell you a nicer kind of secret. You have the cleverest face I've seen in years!'

Still he did not respond. She stubbed her cigarette out and immediately lit another. She took a map out of her handbag and unfolded it. She said:

'Can you show me where Santo Spirito is?'

He pointed out the church and directed her to it, warning her against the motorists' signs which pursued a roundabout one-way route.

'You're very kind.' She smiled at him, lavishly exposing her dazzling, even teeth as if offering a reward for his help. 'You're a kind person,' she said. 'I can tell.'

*

He walked around the perimeter of the vast Cascine Park, past the fun-fair and the zoo and the race-track. It was pleasant in the February sunshine, the first green of spring colouring the twiggy hedges, birches delicate by the river. Lovers sprawled on the seats or in motor-cars, children carried balloons. Stalls sold meat and nuts, and Coca-Cola and 7-Up. Runners in training-suits jogged along the bicycle track. *Ho fame* a fat young man had scrawled on a piece of cardboard propped up in front of him, and slept while he waited for charity.

Rosie, when she'd been his friend, had said he wrote about Italian cities so that he could always be a stranger. Well, it was true, he thought in the Cascine Park, and in order to rid himself of a contemplation of his failed relationship with Rosie he allowed the beauty of Mrs Faraday to become vivid in his mind. Her beauty would have delighted him if her lipstick-stained cigarettes and her silly, repetitious chattering didn't endlessly disfigure it. Her husband was a good man, she had explained, but a good man was not always what a woman wanted. And it had come to seem all of a piece that her daughter had lived for only a week, and all of a piece also that no other children had been born, since her marriage was not worthy of children. It was the Annunciations in Santo Spirito she wanted to see, she had explained, because she loved Annunciations.

'Would it be wrong of me to invite you to dinner?' She rose from a sofa in the hall of the Albergo San Lorenzo as soon as she saw him, making no effort to disguise the fact that she'd been waiting for him. 'I'd really appreciate it if you'd accept.'

He wanted to reply that he would prefer to be left alone. He wanted to state firmly, once and for all, that he had never met her in the past, that she had no claims on him.

'You choose somewhere,' she commanded, with the arrogance of the beautiful.

In the restaurant she ate pasta without ceasing to talk, explaining to him that her boutique had been bought for her by her husband to keep her occupied and happy. It hadn't worked, she said, implying that although her fashion shop had kept her busy it hadn't brought her contentment. Her face, drained of all expression, was lovelier than he had so far seen it, so sad and fragile that it seemed not to belong to the voice that rattled on.

He looked away. The restaurant was decorated with modern paintings and was not completely full. A squat, elderly man sat on his own, conversing occasionally with waiters. A German couple spoke in whispers. Two men and a woman, talking rapidly in Italian, deplored the death of the schoolgirl, Gabriella.

'It must have been extraordinary for the Virgin Mary,' Mrs Faraday was saying. 'One moment she's reading a book and the next there's a figure with wings swooping in on her.' That only made sense, she suggested, when you thought of it as the Virgin's dream. The angel was not really there, the Virgin herself was not really reading in such plush surroundings. 'Later I guess she dreamed another angel came,' Mrs Faraday continued, 'to warn her of her death.'

He didn't listen. The waiter brought them grilled salmon and salad. Mrs Faraday lit a cigarette. She said:

'The guy I shacked up with in the Palazzo Ricasoli was no better than a gigolo. I guess I don't know why I did that.'

He did not reply. She stubbed her cigarette out, appearing at last to notice that food had been placed in front of her. She asked him about the painters of the Florentine Renaissance, and the city's aristocrats and patrons. She asked him why Savonarola had been burnt and he said Savonarola had made people feel afraid. She was silent for a moment, then leaned forward and put a hand on his arm.

'Tell me more about yourself. Please.'

Her voice, eagerly insistent, irritated him more than before. He told her superficial things, about the other Italian cities for which he'd written guidebooks, about the hill towns of Tuscany, and the Cinque Terre. Because of his reticence she said when he ceased to speak:

'I don't entirely make you out.' She added that he was nicer to talk to than anyone she could think of. She might be drunk; it was impossible to say.

'My husband's never heard of the Medicis nor any stuff like this. He's never even heard of Masaccio, you appreciate that?'

'Yes, you've made it clear the kind of man your husband is.'

'I've ruined it, haven't I, telling you about the Palazzo Ricasoli?'

'Ruined what, Mrs Faraday?'

'Oh, I don't know.'

They sat for some time longer, finishing the wine and having coffee. Once she reached across the table and put her hand on one of his. She repeated what she had said before, that he was kind.

'It's late,' he said.

'I know, honey, I know. And you get up early.'

He paid the bill, although she protested that it was she who had invited him. She would insist on their having dinner together again so that she might have her turn. She took his arm on the street.

'Will you come with me to Maiano one day?'

'Maiano?'

'It isn't far. They say it's lovely to walk at Maiano.'

'I'm really rather occupied, you know.'

'Oh, God, I'm bothering you! I'm being a nuisance! Forget Maiano. I'm sorry.'

'I'm just trying to say, Mrs Faraday, that I don't think I can be much use to you.'

He was aware, to his embarrassment, that she was holding his hand. Her arm was entwined with his and the palms of their hands had somehow come together. Her fingers, playing with his now, kept time with her flattery.

'You've got the politest voice I ever heard! Say you'll meet

(137)

me just once again? Just once? Cocktails tomorrow? Please.'

'Look, Mrs Faraday—'

'Say Doney's at six. I'll promise to say nothing if you like. We'll listen to the music.'

Her palm was cool. A finger made a circular motion on one of his. Rosie had said he limped through life. In the end Jeremy had been sorry for him. Both of them were right; others had said worse. He was a crippled object of pity.

'Well, all right.'

She thanked him in the Albergo San Lorenzo for listening to her, and for the dinner and the wine. 'Every year I hope to meet someone nice in Florence,' she said on the landing outside her bedroom, seeming to mean it. 'This is the first time it has happened.'

She leaned forward and kissed him on the cheek, then closed her door. In his looking-glass he examined the faint smear of lipstick and didn't wipe it off. He woke in the night and lay there thinking about her, wondering if her lipstick was still on his cheek.

*

Waiting in Doney's, he ordered a glass of chilled Orvieto wine. Someone on a tape, not Judy Garland, sang *Over the Rainbow*; later there was lightly played Strauss and some rhythms of the thirties. By seven o'clock Mrs Farady had not arrived. He left at a quarter to eight.

*

The next day he wandered through the cloisters of Santa Maria Novella, thinking again about the beauty of Mrs Faraday. He had received no message from her, no note to explain or apologise for her absence in Doney's. Had she simply forgotten? Or had someone better materialised? Some younger man she again hadn't been able to resist, some guy who didn't know any more about Masaccio than her good husband did? She was a woman who was always falling in love, which was what she called it, confusing love with sensuality. Was she, he wondered, what people referred to as a nymphomaniac? Was that what made her unhappy?

He imagined her with some man she'd picked up. He imagined her, satisfied because of the man's attentions, tramping the halls of a gift market, noting which shade of green was to be the new season's excitement. She would be different after her love-making, preoccupied with her business, no time for silliness and Annunciations. Yet it still was odd that she hadn't left a message for him. She had not for a moment seemed as rude as that, or incapable of making up an excuse.

He left the cloisters and walked slowly across the piazza of Santa Maria Novella. In spite of what she'd said and the compliments she'd paid, had she guessed that he hadn't listened properly to her, that he'd been fascinated by her appearance but not by her? Or had she simply guessed the truth about him?

That evening she was not in the bar of the hotel. He looked in at Doney's, thinking he might have misunderstood about the day. He waited for a while, and then ate alone in the restaurant with the modern paintings.

*

'We pack the clothes, *signore*. Is the carabinieri which can promote the enquiries for *la signora. Mi dispiace, signore.*'

He nodded at the heavily moustached receptionist and made his way to the bar. If she was with some lover she would have surfaced again by now: it was hard to believe that she would so messily leave a hotel bill unpaid, especially since sooner or later she would have to return for her clothes. When she had so dramatically spoken of wishing Florence to devour her she surely hadn't meant something like this? He went back to the receptionist.

'Did Mrs Faraday have her passport?'

'*Sí, signore. La signora* have the passport.'

He couldn't sleep that night. Her smile and her brown, languorous eyes invaded the blur he attempted to induce. She crossed and re-crossed her legs. She lifted another glass. Her ringed fingers stubbed another cigarette. Her earrings lightly jangled.

In the morning he asked again at the reception desk. The hotel bill wasn't important, a different receptionist generously allowed. If someone had to leave Italy in a hurry, because maybe there was sickness, even a deathbed, then a hotel bill might be overlooked for just a little while.

'*La signora* will post to us a cheque from the United States. This the carabinieri say.'

'Yes, I should imagine so.'

He looked up in the telephone directory the flats she had mentioned. The Palazzo Ricasoli was in Via Mantellate. He walked to it, up Borgo San Lorenzo and Via San Gallo. '*No*,' a porter in a glass kiosk said and directed him to the office. '*No*,' a pretty girl in the office said, shaking her head. She turned and asked another girl. '*No*,' this girl repeated.

He walked back through the city, to the American Consulate on the Lungarno Amerigo. He sat in the office of a tall, lean man called Humber, who listened with a detached air and then telephoned the police. After nearly twenty minutes he replaced the receiver. He was dressed entirely in brown, suit, shirt, tie, shoes, handkerchief. He was evenly tanned, another shade of the colour. He drawled when he spoke; he had an old-world manner.

'They suggest she's gone somewhere,' he said. 'On some kind of jaunt.' He paused in order to allow a flicker of amusement to develop in his lean features. 'They think maybe she ran up her hotel bill and skipped it.'

'She's a respectable proprietor of a fashion shop.'

'The carabinieri say the respectable are always surprising them.'

'Can you try to find out if she went back to the States? According to the hotel people, that was another theory of the carabinieri.'

Mr Humber shrugged. 'Since you have told your tale I must try, of course, sir. Would six-thirty be an agreeable hour for you to return?'

He sat outside in the Piazza della Repubblica, eating tortellini and listening to the conversations. A deranged man had gone berserk in a school in Rome, taking children as hostages and killing a janitor; the mayor of Rome had intervened and the madman had given himself up. It was a terrible thing to have happened, the Italians were saying, as bad as the murder of Gabriella.

He paid for his tortellini and went away. He climbed up to the Belvedere, filling in time. Once he thought he saw her, but it was someone else in the same kind of red coat.

'She's not back home,' Mr Humber said with his old-world lack of concern. 'You've started something, sir. Faraday's flying out.'

*

In a room in a police station he explained that Mrs Faraday had simply been a fellow guest at the Albergo San Lorenzo. They had had dinner one evening, and Mrs Faraday had not appeared to be dispirited. She knew other people who had come from America, for the same trade exhibitions. He had seen her with them in a restaurant.

'These people, sir, return already to the United States. They answer the American police at this time.'

He was five hours in the room at the police station and the next day he was summoned there again and asked the same questions. On his way out on this occasion he noticed a man who he thought might be her husband, a big blond-haired man, too worried even to glance at him. He was certain he had never met him, or even seen him before, as he'd been certain he'd never met Mrs Faraday before she'd come up to him in the hotel.

The police did not again seek to question him. His passport, which they had held for fifty-six hours, was returned to him. By the end of that week the newspaper references to a missing American woman ceased. He did not see Mr Faraday again.

'The Italian view,' said Mr Humber almost a month later, 'is that she went off on a sexual excursion and found it so much to her liking that she stayed where she was.'

'I thought the Italian view was that she skipped the hotel. Or that someone had fallen ill.'

'They revised their thinking somewhat. In the light of various matters.'

'What matters?'

'From what you said, Mrs Faraday was a gallivanting lady. Our Italian friends find some significance in that.' Mr Humber silently drummed the surface of his desk. 'You don't agree, sir?'

He shook his head. 'There was more to Mrs Faraday than that,' he said.

'Well, of course there was. The carabinieri are educated men, but they don't go in for subtleties, you know.'

'She's not a vulgar woman. From what I said to the police they may imagine she was. Of course she's in a vulgar business. They may have jumped too easily to conclusions.'

Mr Humber said he did not understand. 'Vulgar?' he repeated.

'Like me, she deals in surface dross.'

'You're into fashion yourself, sir?'

'No, I'm not. I write tourist guides.'

'Well, that's most interesting.'

Mr Humber flicked at the surface of his desk with a forefinger. It was clear that he wished his visitor would go. He turned a sheet of paper over.

'I remind sightseers that pictures like Pietro Perugino's *Agony in the Garden* are worth a second glance. I send them to the Boboli Gardens. That kind of thing.'

Mr Humber's bland face twitched with simulated interest. Tourists were a nuisance to him. They lost their passports, they locked their ignition keys into their hired cars, they were stolen from and made a fuss. The city lived off them, but resented them as well. These thoughts were for a moment openly reflected in Mr Humber's pale brown eyes and then were gone. Flicking at his desk again, he said:

'I'm puzzled about one detail in all this. May I ask you, please?'

'Yes, of course.'

'Were you, you know, ah, seeing Mrs Faraday?'

'Was I having an affair, you mean? No, I wasn't.'

'She was a beautiful woman. By all accounts, by yours, I mean, sir, she'd been most friendly.'

'Yes, she was friendly.'

She was naive for an American, and she was careless. She wasn't fearful of strangers and foolishly she let her riches show. Vulnerability was an enticement.

'I did not mean to pry, sir,' Mr Humber apologised. 'It's simply that Mr Faraday's detectives arrived a while ago and the more they can be told the better.'

(143)

'They haven't approached me.'

'No doubt they conclude you cannot help them. Mr Faraday himself has returned to the States: a ransom note would be more likely made to him there.'

'So Mr Faraday doesn't believe his wife went off on a sexual excursion?'

'No one can ignore the facts, sir. There is indiscriminate kidnapping in Italy.'

'Italians would have known her husband owned a paper mill?'

'I guess it's surprising what can be ferreted out.' Mr Humber examined the neat tips of his fingers. He re-arranged tranquillity in his face. No matter how the facts he spoke of changed there was not going to be panic in the American Consulate. 'There has been no demand, sir, but we have to bear in mind that kidnap attempts do often nowadays go wrong. In Italy as elsewhere.'

'Does Mr Faraday think it has gone wrong?'

'Faraday is naturally confused. And, of course, troubled.'

'Of course.' He nodded to emphasise his agreement. Her husband was the kind who would be troubled and confused, even though unhappiness had developed in the marriage. Clearly she'd given up on the marriage; more than anything, it was desperation that made her forthright. Without it, she might have been a different woman—and in that case, of course, there would not have been this passing relationship between them: her tiresomeness had cultivated that. 'Tell me more about yourself,' her voice echoed huskily, hungry for friendship. He had told her nothing—nothing of the shattered, destroyed relationships, and the regret and shame; nothing of the pathetic hope in hired rooms, or the anguish turning into bitterness. She had been given beauty, and he a lameness that people laughed at when they knew. Would her tiresomeness have dropped from her at once, like the shedding of a garment she had thought to be attractive, if he'd told her in the restaurant with the modern paintings? Would she, too, have angrily said he'd led her up the garden path?

'There is our own investigation also,' Mr Humber said, 'besides that of Faraday's detectives. Faraday, I assure you, has spared no expense; the carabinieri file is by no means closed. With such a concentration we'll find what there is to find, sir.'

'I'm sure you'll do your best, Mr Humber.'

'Yes, *sir.*'

He rose and Mr Humber rose also, holding out a brown, lean hand. He was glad they had met, Mr Humber said, even in such unhappy circumstances. Diplomacy was like oil in Mr Humber. It eased his movements and his words; his detachment floated in it, perfectly in place.

'Goodbye, Mr Humber.'

Ignoring the lift, he walked down the stairs of the Consulate. He knew that she was dead. He imagined her lying naked in a wood, her even teeth ugly in a rictus, her white flesh as lifeless as the virgin modesty of the schoolgirl in the park. She hadn't been like a nymphomaniac, or even a sophisticated woman, when she'd kissed his cheek good-night. Like a schoolgirl herself, she'd still been blind to the icy coldness that answered her naivety. Inept and academic, words he had written about the city which had claimed her slipped through his mind. *In the church of Santa Croce you walk on tombs, searching for Giotto's* Life of St Francis. *In Savonarola's own piazza the grey stone features do not forgive the tumbling hair of pretty police girls or the tourists' easy ways.* Injustice and harsh ambition had made her city what it was, the violence of greed for centuries had been its bloodstream; beneath its tinsel skin there was an iron heart. *The Florentines, like true provincials, put work and money first. In the Piazza Signoria the pigeons breakfast off the excrement of the*

(145)

hackney horses: in Florence nothing is wasted.

He left the American Consulate and slowly walked along the quay. The sun was hot, the traffic noisy. He crossed the street and looked down into the green water of the Arno, wondering if the dark shroud of Mrs Faraday's life had floated away through a night. In the galleries of the Uffizi he would move from Annunciation to Annunciation, Simone Martini's, Baldovinetti's, Lorenzo di Credi's, and all the others. He would catch a glimpse of her red coat in Santa Trinità, but the face would again be someone else's. She would call out from a gelateria, but the voice would be an echo in his memory.

He turned away from the river and at the same slow pace walked into the heart of the city. He sat outside a café in the Piazza della Repubblica, imagining her thoughts as she had lain in bed on that last night, smoking her cigarettes in the darkness. She had arrived at the happiest moment of love, when nothing was yet destroyed, when anticipation was a richness in itself. She'd thought about their walk in Maiano, how she'd bring the subject up again, how this time he'd say he'd be delighted. She'd thought about their being together in an apartment in the Palazzo Ricasoli, how this time it would be different. Already she had made up her mind: she would not ever return to the town where her husband owned a paper mill. 'I have never loved anyone like this,' she whispered in the darkness.

In his hotel bedroom he shaved and had a bath and put on a suit that had just been pressed. In a way that had become a ceremony for him since the evening he had first waited for her there, he went at six o'clock to Doney's. He watched the Americans drinking cocktails, knowing it was safe to be there because she would not suddenly arrive. He listened to the music she'd said she liked, and mourned her as a lover might.

Bodily Secrets

At fifty-nine, she was on her own, the widow of the O'Neill who had inherited the town's coal business, who had started, as an enterprise of his own, the toy factory. Her children had flown the nest, her parents and her parents-in-law were no longer alive. Her husband had been in his lifetime a smallish though heavily built man, with wide shoulders and an unrelenting, cropped head, like a battering wedge. His cautious eyes had been set well apart beneath woolly eyebrows; small veins had reddened his nose. He had died at the age of sixty-three, falling down in the big, airy hall of Arcangelo House and afterwards not regaining any real awareness of who he was or what had happened. He had built Arcangelo House after he and his wife had stayed in an Italian hotel of that name when they visited Rome on the occasion of Holy Year.

A beauty once, she was a handsome woman still, tall and imposing in her middle age, with a well-covered look that reflected her liking for sweet things. Her grey hair was shaded towards its original brown, and discreetly burnished; she bought clothes extravagantly. She made up her face with precision, taking her time over it; and attended similarly to her fingernails and, in season, her toenails. She had borne four children in all, two of her three daughters being married now, one in Dublin, the other in Trim; the third was a nurse in Philadelphia. Her son, married also, ran the coal business but was more interested in developing a thousand acres of turf bog he had bought and which he saw as the beginning of an enterprise which he believed would in time outstrip his father's and his grandfather's already established empire. He had inherited their entrepreneur's spirit, and since he'd first been aware of the role laid down for him he had seen himself as their rival. He was married to Thelma, daughter of a Portarlington publican, a girl whom Mrs O'Neill did not care for, considering her common. Particularly she did not care for the thought that one day Thelma would take her own place in Arcangelo House.

From the garden and the upstairs windows the house offered, over fields, a view of the town that was interrupted only by the toy factory. When the wind blew from the south it carried sounds rendered faint over the distance: the cries of children, a car being started somewhere, the saws in the timber works, the grind of a heavy lorry on Daly's Hill. And no matter where the wind came from there was always the bell at the convent, and the bell of Our Lady in Glory, and the Protestant bell on Sundays. At night the street lights and the lights of houses were spread out prettily—the town seen at its best, as Mrs O'Neill often reflected. But increasingly in the vacuum that Arcangelo House had become she reflected also that she felt like a pebble in a drum, and said as much to her bridge companions. They urged her to sell it and build a bungalow, but privately she felt that a bungalow was not her style.

When her husband had died Mrs O'Neill had been fifty-six, and although they had regularly disagreed in their thirty-seven years of marriage they had more often been affectionate companions. They had shared two interests in particular: golf and their children. Together they had attended the occasional race-meeting; and while her husband had not played bridge, she in turn had not inclined to join him in the bar of the Commercial Hotel, where he liked to spend an evening or two a week. Every summer they went to Lahinch or Bundoran for the

golf, and for several years after Holy Year they had returned to
Rome, to the hotel which had given their house its character
and its name. Often, on a night which wasn't a bridge night,
Mrs O'Neill wondered about the future and whether she
should indeed sell Arcangelo House. When the television
came to an end she sat alone in the big open drawing-room,
feeling just a little lonely and vaguely wishing that there was
another interest in her life besides bridge and golf and her
grown-up family. Time had dulled the loss that widowhood
had brought, but in no way had it filled the vacuum that was
somehow more apparent as time progressed. Once she'd been
the centre of things in Arcangelo House, looking after
everyone, in charge of other people's lives. 'Ah, come on now,'
she'd said a thousand times to the husband who'd died on her.
'You're as big a baby as any of them.' In her days as a beauty she
had more or less designed the house herself, standing over
MacGuire the architect and endeavouring to picture for him a
cool, well-organised hotel in Rome. It still pleased her that she
had succeeded so well, not that Arcangelo House was to
everyone's taste, she was well aware of that: it was too different,
too modern, in a way too grand. But old Canon Kenny, the
most educated man for miles about, said he would wager
money that the house was the most interesting to be found
outside Dublin. It had been featured in *Social and Personal* and
MacGuire, who was inordinately proud of it, had once asked if
a German architect, on a motoring holiday, might come and
see it. How could she just leave it all? The garden, once little
better than waste-land, had gorgeously matured. The portico,
with its clean white arches, was rich with different clematis
from June to August. The patio was warm enough to have
breakfast on in March. Yet the accomplishing of what she'd
wanted in the house and in the garden belonged to the time
when she'd been in charge, and was a reminder that nothing

now was changing or taking shape due to her efforts.

Occasionaly, pursuing such lines of thought, she wondered if she would marry again. She couldn't help herself; she had no desire to remarry, yet widows did so, it was something that quite often occurred. At the golf club there was Sweetman, a few years younger than herself, a bachelor all his life, pleasantly sociable but bleary when he had drink taken, and according to Dolores Fitzfynne a tightwad. There was O'Keefe, who was her own age, but it was hard to think of O'Keefe without thinking also of the Mrs O'Keefe there had been, a drear of a woman who had played neither golf nor bridge, who hadn't even had children: O'Keefe had been infected by her dreariness or else had infected her in the first place. There was no one else, except perhaps Agnew, with his long, thin face and his hands, which were long also, gesturing in the air, and his faintly high-pitched voice. He was younger than the others, younger than she was herself by seven or eight years, yet she often thought of him in this connection. She thought about him in a different way on the morning her son, Cathal, decreed that the toy factory would have to go. For seventeen years Agnew had been its manager.

In a blue and yellow paisley dressing-gown which she'd had all her married life she sat on the edge of her bed, listening to her son on the telephone saying that the people at the toy factory could easily be absorbed elsewhere, that for a long time now he had systematically been running the business down. The toy factory had been profitable only in the immediate post-war years, unable ultimately to sustain the competition which had so ominously built up: long before his death her husband had threatened that it would sooner or later have to close. It was a tiny concern, the loss would not be great.

'All they're making now are the fox-terriers,' Cathal said on the telephone, referring to wooden dogs on wheels.

'The building?' she said. 'Best to have it down, wouldn't it?'

'I could bale garden peat there. I'm going into that, you know.'

She did not say anything. She did not trust this dark-faced son she'd given birth to. Ceasing to be a toy factory, the building would be expanded when it became the location for one of his enterprises. There might be noise, even a smell of chemicals. You simply couldn't guess what would come along in order that more money might be made. And why should it matter since only a lone woman lived near by?

'We'll have to see,' she said.

'Ah, of course, of course. No hurry at all.'

She did not ask about Agnew. She could not see him being absorbed into the turf business or the coal business, and in any case Cathal didn't like him. Cathal would have him out on the street while you'd wink.

Cathal had his father's wedge of a head, his forehead and wide-apart, narrow eyes. He was the first of their children to be born, the one who had received most attention because the others were girls. Heir to so much, he had been claimed by a thrusting entrepreneur's world from infancy. The girls, except for Siobhan in Philadelphia, had been more mundanely claimed by men.

She wouldn't have minded any of the others being in Arcangelo House, but Thelma had a greedy way of looking at her, as if she couldn't wait to get into the place. Mrs O'Neill dearly wished that her son hadn't married this girl, but he had and that was that. She sighed as she replaced the receiver, seeing Thelma's slightly puffy face, her nose too small for the rest of it. She sat for a moment longer, endeavouring to release her imagination of that face and in the end succeeding. Then she dressed herself and went down to the toy factory. Agnew was in the inner office, standing by the window, his back to her as she entered.

'Mr Agnew.'

'Ah, Mrs O'Neill. Come in, come in, Mrs O'Neill.' He moved so swiftly in turning to greet her that she was reminded of the assured way he danced the quickstep. He came every December to the Golf Club Dance even though he was not a club member and had once confided to her that he had never played the game. 'Croquet,' he'd confided also. 'I used to be quite snappy at croquet.' He had his own expressions, a way of putting things that sometimes sounded odd. Typical that he should mention an old-fashioned game like croquet.

'I hope you're not busy, Mr Agnew. I'm not disturbing you, am I?'

'Heavens above, why would you be? Won't you take a chair, Mrs O'Neill? A cup of tea now?'

There was always this formality. He offered it and seemed shyly to demand it. Her husband had always used his surname, and so did Cathal; at the Golf Club Dance she'd heard other men call him by his initials, B.J. She couldn't in a million years imagine him addressing her as Norah.

'No, I won't have tea, thank you.'

'A taste of sherry at all? I have a nice sweet little sherry—'

'No, thanks. Really, Mr Agnew.'

He smiled, gently closing a glass-fronted cabinet he had opened in expectation of her accepting his hospitality. He was wearing a brown suit chalked with a pinstripe, and a brown silk tie. He said:

'Well, it seems we have come to the end of the road.'

'I know. I'm awfully sorry.'

'Mr O'Neill saw it coming years ago.'

'Yes, I'm afraid he did.'

He smiled again; his voice was unperturbed. 'The first day I came up to Arcangelo House I was terrified out of my wits. D'you remember, Mrs O'Neill? Your husband had an advertisement for the job in the *Irish Times*.'

'It seems an age ago.'

'Doesn't it, though? An age.'

His long face had acquired a meditative expression. He drew a packet of cigarettes from a pocket of his jacket and opened it slowly, folding back the silver paper. He advanced a single cigarette by knocking the packet on the surface of his desk. He leaned towards her, offering it. His wrists were slim and tanned: she had never noticed his wrists before.

'Thank you, Mr Agnew.'

He leaned across the desk again, holding the flame of a cigarette-lighter to the tip of her cigarette. It gleamed with the dull patina of gold, as slender as a coin.

'No, I don't entirely know what I'll do.' He lit his own cigarette and then held it, dangling, in his long fingers.

'Cathal should have something for you. It was my husband's intention, you know, that everyone at the toy factory should be offered something.'

She wanted to make that clear; she wanted to record this unequivocal statement in the inner office so that later on, if necessary, she could quote herself to Cathal. She inhaled some smoke and released it luxuriously through her nostrils. She was fond of the occasional cigarette, although she never smoked when she was on her own.

'I'm not so sure I'd entirely fit in, Mrs O'Neill. I don't know anything about selling turf.'

She mentioned coal, which after all was the fuel that had made the O'Neills wealthy. There was still a thriving coal business, the biggest in the county.

He shook his head. His hair, once reddish, was almost completely grey now. 'I don't think,' he said, 'I'd be at home in coal.'

'Well, I only thought I'd mention it.'

'It's more than kind, Mrs O'Neill.'

'My husband wouldn't have wanted anyone not looked after.'

'Oh, indeed I know it.'

She stared at the lipstick mark on her cigarette and then raised the cigarette to her mouth again. It was awkward because she didn't want to walk out of the factory smoking a cigarette, yet it was too soon to crush it out on the ashtray in front of her.

'If there's any way the family can help, you'll say, Mr Agnew?'

'I suppose I'll go to Dublin.'

The remark was not accompanied by one of his glancing smiles; he gave no sign whatsoever that he'd touched upon a fascinating topic. No one knew why he spent weekends occasionally in Dublin, and a certain curiosity had gathered round the mystery of these visits. There was some secret which he kept, which he had not even confided to her husband in his lifetime. He came back melancholy was all her husband had ever reported, and once or twice with bloodshot eyes, as if he had spent the time drinking.

'Though I'd rather not end up in Dublin,' he added now. 'To tell you the full truth, Mrs O'Neill, it's not a city I entirely care for.'

She bent the remains of her cigarette in half, extinguishing it on the ashtray. She stood up, thinking it odd that he'd said Dublin wasn't somewhere he cared for since he visited it so regularly.

'The toy factory was a favourite of my husband's. It saddened him to see it decline.'

'It had its heyday.'

'Yes, it had its day.'

She went, walking with him from the office, through a shed full of unassembled terriers on wheels. The white cut-out bodies with a brown spot around the tail, the brown heads, the little platforms that carried the wheels, the wheels themselves: all these dislocated parts lay about in stacks, seeming unwanted. No one was working in the shed.

He walked with her through other deserted areas, out on to the gravel forecourt that stretched in a semi-circle around the front of the small factory. A man loaded wired cartons on to a lorry. They were still meeting orders in England, Agnew told her. The paint shop was as active as ever, three girls on full time.

He held his hand out, his long, narrow features illuminated by another smile. His palm was cool, his grip gentle. He asked her not to worry about him. He assured her he'd be all right.

*

There were gusts of laughter in the club-house. Dessie Fitzfynne had told a Kerry joke, concerning eight Kerry gardaí and a cow. Dolores Fitzfynne, who'd just gone round in 82 and wanted to talk about that instead, requested that he shouldn't tell another. Sweetman was talking about horses, arranging something about going to the Curragh. Sweetman loved getting parties together to go racing or to Lansdowne Road, or for a weekend down in Kelly's at Rosslare. Paunchy and rubicund, Flanagan kept saying it was his turn and what did anyone want?

'I heard the factory's winding up,' the solicitor, Butler-Regan, remarked in his rowdy voice and she nodded, suddenly feeling dismal. She had forgotten about the toy factory while she'd been on the golf-course, going round in 91, taking three to get out of the rough at the eighth. She'd been playing with Dessie Fitzfynne, opposing Dolores and Flanagan. They'd been beaten, of course.

It was silly to feel dismal just because the facts of commerce dictated the closure of an unprofitable concern. As both Cathal and Agnew had intimated, the end had been a matter of anticipation for years. Only sentiment had prevented such a decision in the lifetime of her husband.

'Ah well, there you are,' Butler-Regan said noisily. ''Tis better let it go, Norah.'

Flanagan handed her another gin and French even though she hadn't asked for one. Overhearing the reference to the toy factory, he said:

'I hear Agnew's wondering what to do with himself.'

'The bold Agnew!' Butler-Regan laughed. He, too, was paunchy and rubicund. He added, laughing again, shouting through this laughter: 'Oh, Master Agnew'll fall on his feet, I'd say.'

They all liked Agnew even though he was so different. He was an easy companion for half an hour or so if you happened to run into him in the bar of the Commercial Hotel; he was always willing to drop into conversation with you on the street. He had digs with the Misses Malone in a house called St Kevin's, where he was regularly to be seen tending the front garden, behind silver-painted railings set in a low concrete wall. He also walked the Misses Malone's dog, Judy, about the town and on Sundays he attended the Protestant church unless he happened to be in Dublin.

'We'd all miss Agnew,' Flanagan said. 'That wild Protestant man.' He laughed, making much the same explosive sound that the solicitor did. Did any of them realise, she wondered, that Agnew's quickstep put them all to shame every December?

'Oh, wild is right,' Butler-Regan agreed. 'Wasn't he in the city again a week ago?'

The two men laughed in unison, the burst of noise causing Rita Flanagan to glance sharply across the bar to ascertain if her husband was already drunk. In dog's-tooth skirt and soft fawn golfing-jacket, Mrs O'Neill wondered what any of them would think if they knew that, quite involuntarily as she stood there, she had again begun to speculate on the possibility of not remaining for ever the widow she presently was. She sipped her gin and French, not taking part in a conversation about Sweetman's outing to the Curragh. In the same involuntary manner she found herself following a thread of thought that led her back to her wedding day. The O'Neills had insisted on paying for the reception, since her own family were not well-to-do. Old Canon Kenny—neither old nor a canon then—had conducted the service, assisted by a curate called Prendergast, who had later left the priesthood. They had gone to Bray for their honeymoon and on their first night in the International Hotel she had been jittery. She hadn't known how it should be, whether she should simply take her clothes off or wait for him to say something, whether or not there was going to be preliminary kissing. She'd gone as red as anything after they'd come up from the restaurant. 'I think that waiter knew,' she'd whispered on the stairs, not noticing there was a maid just behind them. He'd been jittery too, and in the end it was she who inaugurated the kissing and in fact had taken his tie off. What on earth would it be like being in a bedroom in Bray with Agnew? There was fat on her shoulders now, which hadn't been there before, and naturally her thighs and her hips were no longer the same. Her body had been forgotten in that particular way for many years before her husband's death, almost since the birth of Siobhan. They had come to occupy separate bedrooms in Arcangelo House, having reached the decision that Cathal and the three girls were enough. At first, when it was safe to do so, she had visited the other bedroom, but the habit had dwindled and then ceased. Would it be a form of unfaithfulness to resume it in different circumstances now?

It wasn't easy to guess how such things stood at fifty-nine.

O'Keefe, the widower of the woman who'd been a drear, approached her with the usual sorrowful look in his eyes, as if he still mourned the wife who had played neither bridge nor golf. The eyes themselves, lurking in their despondent wateriness behind spectacles, had pinkish rims and were the only feature you noticed in O'Keefe's flat face, except possibly his teeth, which moved uncomfortably in his jaw when he ate. He was eating now, chewing crisps from a transparent Tayto bag. His hair was like smooth lead; his bony limbs jutted from his clothes. There was no doubt whatsoever that O'Keefe, the manager of a butter business, was looking for a housekeeper in the form of a second wife. There was always a nudge or two in the clubhouse when he approached Mrs O'Neill for a chat.

'Ah, didn't I have a terrible round? Did you see me in front of you, Norah? Wasn't I shocking?'

She denied that. She hadn't noticed his misfortunes, she said, which indeed she hadn't. She might have added that the butter manager couldn't be shocking if he tried for the rest of his life.

'I've been meaning to ask you,' he said. 'Would you be interested in a bunch of sweet-peas from the garden, Norah?'

She drank more gin and French. She had plenty of sweet-peas at Arcangelo House, she replied, though it was very good of him to offer her more.

'Or the asparagus fern? D'you grow that stuff?'

'I grow asparagus all right. Only I eat it before the fern comes.'

'Ah well, why wouldn't you, Norah?'

Sweetman, at the bar, was sweating like an animal. No woman in her senses would want to marry Sweetman. His trouble with perspiration ironically denied his name, and the caginess Dolores Fitzfynne claimed for him would hardly have been easy to live with. He had a tendency towards forgetfulness when his round came up in the club-house and, according to Dolores, the parties he organised for race-meetings or Lansdowne Road were done so to his own pecuniary advantage. 'Too mingy with himself to look sideways at a woman,' Dolores had said, and probably she was right. He was a surveyor with the county council; and if he gave you a lift in his car he had a way of mentioning the high price of petrol.

She watched Sweetman while O'Keefe continued in his tedious manner, offering her marigold plants. It had surprised her when Agnew had said he'd never in his life played golf. She'd thought afterwards that he would probably have been good. He had the look of someone who had been athletic in his time. His dancing suggested ball sense, she didn't know why.

'To tell you the honest truth, I don't much care for marigolds.'

'The wife loved them. Give Mrs O'Keefe a box of marigolds and she'd be pricking them out till Kingdom come.'

He wagged his head; she nodded hers. She allowed a silence to develop in the hope that he'd go away. He said eventually:

'D'you ever watch that thing they have, *Dynasty* is it called?'

'I watched it the odd time.'

'Will you tell me this, Norah: where do they get the stories?'

'I suppose they invent them.'

'Isn't America the shocking place though?'

'I have a daughter there.'

'Ah, sure, of course you have.'

At the bar Butler-Regan looked as though he might sing. Very occasionally he did, striking the bar rhythmically with his fist, trying to make people join in. The club secretary, Dr Walsh, had had to speak to him, explaining that it wasn't usual to sing in a golf club, even adding that he didn't think it quite the thing for a solicitor to sing anywhere. But Butler-Regan had done so again, and had again to be warned. It was said that his wife, who like the late Mrs O'Keefe played neither bridge nor golf, had a terrible time with him.

'Does your girl ever remark on the *Dynasty* thing to you?' O'Keefe was enquiring. 'I mean, if it might be accurate?'

'Siobhan has never mentioned *Dynasty*.'

'Well, isn't that extraordinary?'

Ten minutes later the drinking in the club-house broke up and Mrs O'Neill drove back to Arcangelo House. She made scrambled egg and watched a film about drug-running on the television. The police of several nations pursued a foursome of gangsters and finally ran the ringleader to earth in Los Angeles. She dozed off, and when she woke up a priest with a Cork accent was talking about the feast of Corpus Christi. She listened to him until he'd finished and then turned the television off.

In her bedroom she did something she had not done for ten years at least: before she slipped into her nightdress she paused in front of the long looking-glass of her wardrobe and surveyed her naked body. It was most certainly no longer her best feature, she said to herself, remembering it when she was a child, standing up in the bath to be dried. She remembered being naked at last in the bedroom of the International Hotel in Bray, and the awkward voluptuousness that had followed. The bearing of four children, her fondness for sweet things, the insidious nips of gin in the club-house—in combination they had taken a toll, making clothes as necessary as all that meticulous care with make-up and hair. The first time she'd been pregnant, with Cathal, she had looked at herself in this same looking-glass, assuring herself that the enormous swelling would simply go away, as indeed it had. But nothing would go away now. Flesh hung loosely, marked with pink imprints of straps or elastic. If she slimmed herself to the bone there would be scrawny, empty skin, loops and pockets, hollows as ugly as the bulges. She drew her nightdress over her head and a pattern of pink roses in tight little bunches hid what she preferred not to see, transforming her again into a handsome woman.

*

Agnew had sensitive skin, yet could not resist the quality of finely woven tweed. He chose the sober colours, the greys and browns and inconspicuous greens. He bought his Donegal tweed in Kevin and Howlin's in Dublin and had the suits made up by a tailor in Rathmines. Because of his sensitive skin he had the trousers lined.

Agnew had never worn these suits to his office in the toy factory, for they did not seem to him to be sufficiently matter-of-fact for business. He wore them at weekends, when he went to church and on Sunday afternoons when he drove out to Rathfarran and walked around the cliffs, ending up in Lynch's Bar down by the strand, where by arrangement he took his Sunday supper. He wore them also on the weekends when he went to Dublin.

He would miss the cliffs and the strand, he reflected at breakfast one morning, a few weeks after his visit from Mrs O'Neill. He would miss the toy factory too, of course, and the people he had come to know in a passing kind of way, without intimacy or closeness but yet agreeably. In the snug, overcrowded dining-room of the terraced house called St Kevin's he broke a piece of toast in half and poured himself more tea. He had been fortunate in St Kevin's, fortunate because he was the only lodger and because the Misses Malone had never sought to share a meal with him, fortunate that the house was clean and the cooking averagely good. He'd been fortunate that his interest had never flagged in the job at the toy factory. He would take away with him a sample of every single wooden toy that had been manufactured during his time there: the duck with the quivering bill, the kangaroos, the giraffes, the little red steam engines, the donkeys and carts, the bricks, the elephants, the fox-terriers on wheels, and all the others. He was proud of these toys and of his part in their production. They were finer in every possible way—more ingeniously designed, constructed with greater craftsmanship, more fondly finished—than the torrent of shoddiness that had flooded them out of existence.

'I'll miss you too,' he said aloud in the overcrowded dining-room, staring down at the spaniel, Judy, who was wagging her tail in the hope of receiving a rind of bacon. She would eat rinds only if they were so brittle that they broke between her teeth. This morning, Agnew knew, what he had left would not satisfy her: the bacon had not been overdone. He lit a cigarette, folded the *Irish Times*, which earlier he had been reading, and left the dining-room, pursued by the dog. 'I'm off now, Miss Malone,' he called out in the hall, and one of the sisters called back to him from the kitchen. Judy, as she always did, followed him through the town to the toy factory, turning back when he reached the forecourt.

A woman called Mrs Whelan, who came to the factory three mornings a week to attend to whatever typing there was and to keep the books up to date, was to finish at the end of the week. She was there this morning, a prim, trim presence in navy-blue, conscientiously tapping out the last of the invoices. The final delivery was due to be dispatched that afternoon, for Cathal O'Neill had already laid down the peremptory instruction that further orders must not be accepted.

'Good morning, Mrs Whelan.'

'Good morning, sir.'

Interrupted for the briefest of moments, she went on typing.

She would be extremely useful to someone else, Agnew reflected, if she managed to find a position that suited her. 'I think I'm going to start cleaning the inner office,' he said, passing into it reluctantly, for it was not a task he anticipated with any pleasure. What on earth was he going to do with himself? Fifty-one was far too young simply to retire, even if he could afford to. It was all very well saying he couldn't see himself in the fuel business, either coal or turf, but what alternative was there going to be? In the failing toy factory he had had a position, he had been of some small importance, and he had often wondered if he himself—and the predicament he must find himself in when the factory closed—hadn't been an element in his late employer's sentiment. Had Mr O'Neill lived, the toy factory might have struggled on until a convenient moment was reached, when its manager might gracefully retire. Still, a father's sentiment rarely passed to a son, nor could it be expected to.

He took his jacket off and hung it up. As he did so the telephone rang and the widow of his late and sentimental employer invited him to what she described as a very small party on Friday evening. It would be in his honour, he said to himself after he had politely accepted. It was the kind of thing people did; there might even be a presentation, in the conventional way, of cutlery or Waterford glass or a clock.

*

'Now, this is bloody ridiculous!' Cathal glared at his mother, squinting in his extreme rage.

She remembered that squint in his pram. She remembered how his face would turn scarlet before exploding like a volcano, how he would beat his fists against her when she tried to lift him up. His father had had a bad temper also, though over the years she had learnt to ignore it.

'It isn't ridiculous at all, Cathal.'

'You are fifty-nine years of age.'

'I'm only too well aware of that.'

'Agnew's our employee, for God's sake!' He said something else and then broke off, his shout becoming an incomprehensible stutter. He began again, calming down and collecting himself. 'My God, when I think of Agnew!'

'I invited Basil Agnew—'

'Basil? *Basil?*'

'You knew his name was Basil. B. J. Agnew. It's on all the letters.'

'In no way did I know the man's name was Basil. I didn't know what his bloody name was.'

'Don't be violent, Cathal.'

'Aw, for God's sake now!' He turned away from her. He crossed the Italianate drawing-room and stood with his back to her, morosely looking out of the window.

'I invited Basil Agnew to a little evening I had and he stayed on afterwards to help me clear up a bit. The Flanagans were there, and the Fitzfynnes and a few others. It was all quite above board, Cathal. Father Doherty was there, quite happy with the arrangement.'

'You were seen out at Rathfarran with Agnew. You were in Lynch's with him.'

'That was later on, the following Sunday week it was. And of course we were in Lynch's. We had two glasses of whiskey each in Lynch's, and then we had our supper there.'

'Will you for God's sake examine what you're doing? You hardly know Agnew.'

'I've known him for seventeen years.'

Cathal mentioned his father, who, God rest him, would be disgusted if he knew, and probably he did know. He could not understand, Cathal repeated for the third time in this tempestuous conversation, how any sane woman could behave like this.

'Well, I have behaved like this, Cathal. I have been asked a question by Basil Agnew and I have answered in the affirmative. I wanted to tell you before I spoke a word to Father Doherty.'

'Agnew's a Protestant.'

'We'll be married by Father Doherty. Basil isn't the least particular about matters like that.'

'I bet he isn't. The bloody man—'

'I must ask you, Cathal, not to keep referring to Basil Agnew as a bloody man. I do not refer to Thelma as a bloody woman. When you informed me in this very room that you intended to marry her I held my peace.'

'The man's after your money and that's all there's to it.'

'You're being unpleasant, Cathal.'

He almost spat. As a child, he had had a most disagreeable habit of spitting. His eyes savaged her as he continued violently to upbraid her and to insult the man she had agreed to marry. He left eventually, barging his way out of the drawing-room, shouting back at her from the hall before he barged his way out of the house.

That evening her two married daughters, Eileen in Dublin and Rose in Trim, telephoned her. They were more diplomatic than Cathal, as they had always been. They beseeched her not to be hasty; both offered to come and talk it all over with her. She had written to them, she said; she was sorry Cathal had taken it upon himself to get in touch also, since she had particularly asked him not to. 'It's all in my letter,' she assured her daughters in turn. 'Everything about how I feel and how I've thought it carefully over.' The two men they'd married themselves were, after all, no great shakes. If you were honest you had to say that, one of them little better than a commercial traveller, the other reputed to be the worst veterinary surgeon in Trim. Yet she hadn't made much of a fuss when Eileen first brought her mousy little Liam to Arcangelo House, nor over Rose's Eddie, a younger version of Dessie Fitzfynne, with the same stories about Kerrymen and the same dull bonhomie. 'It'll work out grand,' she said to her daughters in turn. 'Was I ever a fool in anything I did?'

The following morning Thelma came round and in her crude way said how flabbergasted she was. She sat there with her vacant expression and repeated three times that you could have knocked her down with a feather when Cathal had walked in the door and informed her that his mother was intending to marry Agnew. 'I couldn't close my mouth,' Thelma said. 'I was stirring custard in the kitchen and declare to God didn't the damn stuff burn on me. "She's after getting engaged to Agnew," he said, and if you'd given me a thousand pounds I couldn't go on with the stirring.'

Thelma's rigmarole continued, how Cathal had stormed about the kitchen, how he'd shouted at the children and knocked a pot of blackcurrant jam on to the floor with his elbow, how she'd had to sit down to recover herself. Then she lowered her voice as if there were other people in her mother-in-law's drawing-room. 'Isn't there a lot of talk, though, about what Agnew gets up to when he goes off to Dublin for the two days? Is it women he goes after?' While she spoke, Thelma nodded vehemently, answering her own question. She'd heard it for certain, she continued in the same subdued voice, that Agnew had women of a certain description up in Dublin.

'That's tittle-tattle, Thelma.'

'Ah sure, I'd say it was, all right. Still and all, Mrs O'Neill.'

'What Mr Agnew does with his own time is hardly the business of anyone except himself.'

'Ah sure, of course 'tisn't. It's only Cathal and myself was wondering.'

The moon that was Thelma's face, its saucer eyes and jammy red mouth, the nose that resembled putty, was suddenly closer than Mrs O'Neill found agreeable. It was a way that Thelma had when she was endeavouring to be sincere.

'I had an uncle married late. Sure, the poor man ended demented.'

You are the stupidest creature God ever put breath into, Mrs O'Neill reflected, drawing herself back from her daughter-in-law's advancing features. She did not comment on Thelma's uncle any more than she had commented on the burning of the custard or the loss of the pot of blackcurrant jam.

'You know what I mean, Mrs O'Neill?' The subdued tones became a whisper. 'A horse-trainer's widow in Portarlington that went after the poor old devil's few pence.'

'Well, I'm most certainly not after Mr Agnew's few pence.'

'Ah no, I'm not saying that at all. I'd never say a thing like that, Mrs O'Neill, what you'd be after or what he'd be after. Sure, where'd I find the right to make statements the like of that?'

Thelma eventually went away. She would have been sent by Cathal, who would also have written to Siobhan. But Siobhan had always possessed a mind of her own and in due course a letter arrived from Philadelphia. *I'm delighted altogether at the news. I kind of hoped you'd do something like this.*

*

It had never, in the past, occurred to Agnew to get married. Nor would he have suggested it to his late employer's wife if he hadn't become aware that she wished him to. Marriage, she had clearly decided, would be the rescuing of both of them: she from her solitariness in Arcangelo House, he from the awkwardness of being unemployed. She had said she would like him to oversee the demolition of the toy factory and the creation of an apple orchard in its place. This enterprise was her own and had nothing to do with Cathal.

The women she played bridge with still addressed him friendlily when he met them on the street or in a shop. Her golfing companions—especially Flanagan and Fitzfynne—had even been enthusiastic. Butler-Regan had slapped him on the shoulders in the bar of the Commercial Hotel and said he was glad it hadn't been O'Keefe she'd gone for. Only O'Keefe had looked grumpy, not replying to Agnew's greeting when they met in Lawlor's one morning, both of them buying cigarettes. Dolores Fitzfynne telephoned him at the toy factory and said she was delighted. It was a good idea to plant an apple orchard on the site of the factory—Cox's and Beauty of Bath, Russets and Bramleys and Worcesters. In the fullness of time the orchard would become her own particular interest, as the toys had been her husband's and the turf-bogs were her son's. It was a pity the family were almost all opposed to the match, but naturally such a reaction was to be expected.

*

She was aware of eyes upon them when they danced together in the club-house bedecked with Christmas decorations. What did these people really think? Did all of them share, while appearing not to, the family's disapproval? Did fat Butler-Regan and fat Flanagan think she was ridiculous, at fifty-nine years of age, to be allowing a man to marry her for her money? Did Dolores Fitzfynne think so? Mrs Whelan, who had been his secretary for so long at the toy factory, always attended the Golf Club Annual Dance with her husband; the Misses Malone, his landladies for the same period of time in the terraced house called St Kevin's, came to help with the catering. Did these three women consider her beneath contempt because she'd trapped a slightly younger, attractive man as a companion for her advancing years?

'I've always liked the way you dance the quickstep,' she whispered.

'Always?'

'Yes, always.'

The confession felt disgraceful. Cathal and Thelma, dancing only yards away, would talk all night about it if they knew. With O'Keefe, she wouldn't have had to be unfaithful in that way.

'You're not entirely devoid of rhythm yourself.'

'I've always loved dancing actually.'

O'Keefe would have asked for more, and for less. Some hint of man's pride would have caused him scrupulously to avoid touching a penny of her money, nor would he have wanted to go planting apple trees under her direction. But O'Keefe would have entered her bedroom and staked his claim there, and she could not have borne that.

'We'll be married this time next week,' he said. 'Do you realise that?'

'Unless you decide to take to the hills.'

'No, I'll not do that, Norah.'

The Artie Furlong Band, new to the club-house this year and already reckoned to be a success, played an old tune she loved, *Smoke Gets in Your Eyes*. His step changed easily, he scarcely touched her as he guided her through the other dancers. Sweetman was appalling to dance with because of his perspiration troubles, Dessie Fitzfynne's knees were always driving themselves into you, Butler-Regan held you far too tight. She'd go on playing bridge and golf after they were married, no reason not to. He'd said he intended to continue exercising the Misses Malone's spaniel.

'You're sure about this?' he whispered, bending his long face closer to hers, smiling a little. 'You're absolutely sure, Norah?'

She remembered thinking how she couldn't imagine him ever calling her Norah, and how strange his own Christian name had felt when first she'd used it. She would never know him, she was aware of that; nor could he ever fully know her. There would never be the passion of love between them; all that must be done without.

'I'm sure all right.'

The music ceased. They went to get a drink and were joined immediately by the Fitzfynnes and Rita Flanagan. Thelma came up and said one of the children had spots all over his stomach. Cathal kept his distance.

'We're drinking to the happy couple,' Dessie Fitzfynne shouted, raising his glass. Thelma scuttled away, as if frightened to be seen anywhere near such a toast.

'Cheers to the both of you,' Rita Flanagan shrilled, and in another part of the decorated club-house Butler-Regan began to sing.

She smiled at the glasses that were raised towards them. 'That's very kind of you,' he said quietly. 'We're touched.'

She would have liked to add something, to have sorted out falsity from the truth. He was indeed marrying her for her money. But he, in return, was giving her a role that money could not purchase. Within a week the family would no longer possess her. Cathal's far-apart eyes would no longer dismiss her as a remnant of the dead.

'We're going to have an orchard, you know, where the toy factory is now.'

They looked a bit surprised, at first not quite grasping her meaning and then wondering why she should mention an orchard just then.

'Our wedding present to one another,' he explained. 'Norah's trees and I shall tend them.'

The band struck up again, drowning the raucous singing of Butler-Regan. Cathal at last approached his mother and asked her to dance, as every year he did on this Christmas occasion. But he did not at last say that he hoped it would work out all right, Agnew and herself in Arcangelo House. She had paid some price, Cathal believed, apart from the financial one. But Cathal, really, was not right and for him, too, she would have liked to sort out falsity from the truth.

*

'Well, that is that,' he said, turning off the television on a Sunday night, after he had returned from Dublin. He lurched a little as he moved towards her, holding out his packet of cigarettes. He had said, before their marriage, that he often became intoxicated in the course of these weekends. He met his friends and they went from place to place, all of them men who enjoyed the company of men. Sometimes, left alone, or unlucky in the new companions he had met, he wandered the quaysides of the city, thinking about the sailors of the ships. On the strand at Rathfarran his face had been averted when he told her this, and when he finished she had not spoken. Dessie Fitzfynne and Sweetman liked men's company also, she had thought, and so had her husband in his lifetime. But that, of course, was not the same.

'I don't think I'll go back there.' He swayed, like Flanagan did in drink. 'God knows, I don't want to.'

He always said that. He always offered her a cigarette after turning off the Sunday television. A moment later he made the renunciatory statement.

'It doesn't matter.' She tried to smile, imagining him in the public houses he had told her about, his dignified presence mocked by a man who was once particularly his friend, a waiter who no longer liked him.

'I dread for your sake that someone will find out one of these days. I hadn't thought of that when we married.'

'I knew what I was doing. You told me the truth, and you're honourable for that.'

When he'd told her she had not confessed a truth as well: that clothes and make-up disguised a loss she found it hard to bear. She was haunted by herself, by the beauty that had been there in a hotel in Bray. Lingering in the club-house on these Sunday nights, she drank more gin and French than usual, knowing he would be tipsy, too, when he returned. Once they'd fallen asleep in their chairs, and she'd woken up at twenty past three and crept away to bed. He'd seemed like a child, one arm hanging down, fingers resting on the carpet. On the strand at Rathfarran he'd told her he never wanted to go to sleep on these Sunday nights because he hated waking up so. In his bedroom at St Kevin's, the door locked against indiscreet entrance by one or other of the Misses Malone, he had sat with the whiskey bottle he'd bought for the purpose in Dublin. She'd listened while he'd told her that; concerning herself, there'd been no need to say what she might have said because, being the man he was, he guessed.

They passed together through the hall of Arcangelo House and mounted the stairs to their separate bedrooms. They paused before they parted, offering in their tipsiness a vague, unstated reassurance. Tomorrow none of this would be mentioned; their common ground would not be traversed on a mundane Monday morning. For a moment on the landing outside their bedrooms they spoke of the orchard that would replace the toy factory, and the trees they would watch growing up.

Virgins

Like a wasp, Laura says to herself, as she invariably does in the cathedral of Siena, with its violent argument of stripes. An uneasy place, her husband had been remarking only the other night, informing some other tourists in the Palazzo Ravizza.

In several languages, guides draw attention to the pulpit and Pastorino's *Last Supper*. Wilting Americans rest on chairs, Germans work their cameras. An old Italian woman lights a candle, children chatter and are silenced. With dark glasses dangling from her fingers, Laura makes her way through the cathedral crowds, having quickly verified that Francesco Piccolomini became Pius III. She knew she'd been right; her husband had said it was Pius II. Her husband is often wrong, about all sorts of things.

'Laura? Is it Laura?'

She stares at the round face, all freckles from the August heat. Hair, once coppery red, Laura guesses, is peppered now with grey; a dress is less elegantly striped than the architecture, in lettuce-green and blue. Laura smiles, but shakes her head. She passes her glance down the tired dress, to legs on which mosquitoes have feasted, to sandals whose shade of blue once matched the blue of the cotton above. She smiles again, knowing she knows this woman of fifty or so.

'You haven't changed a bit!' the woman says, and immediately Laura remembers because the voice is as it has always been. Polite to say she hasn't changed a bit; politely she lies herself.

'Nor you, now that I look, Margaretta.'

But her tone is nervous, and her confidence melts as they stand among the tourists and the angry stripes. How odd to meet here, she says, knowing it is not odd at all, since everyone's a tourist nowadays. She wishes they had not met like this; why could not Margaretta just have seen her and let her pass by?

'It's lovely to see you,' Margaretta says.

They continue to look at one another, and simultaneously, in their different moods, their distant friendship possesses them. Two marriages and their children are irrelevant.

*

The Heaslips' house was in a straggling grassy square, dusty in summer. A brass plate announced the profession of Dr Heaslip; the oak-grained hall-door was heavy and impressive, with brass that matched in weight and tone the nameplate. Near by, the Bank of Ireland was ivy-covered, less gaunt because of it than the Heaslips' grey stone façade. Other houses, each detached from its neighbour, were of grey stone also, or colour-washed in pink or cream or white. In the approximate centre of an extensive area of shorn grass, green railings protected an empty pedestal, which Queen Victoria in her day had dominated. A cinema—the De Luxe Picture House, as antique as its title—occupied a corner created by the edge of the square and the town's main street. Hogan's Hotel filled the corner opposite.

One day in June, during the second world war, a day when the brass plate shimmered in warm sunshine, a day Laura for all her life did not forget, Mrs Heaslip said in the drawing-room of the house:

'Laura, this is Margaretta.'

Laura held out her hand, as she had been taught, but Margaretta giggled, finding it amusing that two small girls should be so formal.

'Margaretta! Really, what will Laura think? Now, do at once apologise.'

'We're all like that in Ireland,' Margaretta pronounced instead. 'Bog-trotters, y'know.'

'Indeed we're not,' protested Mrs Heaslip, a thin, tall woman in a flowery dress. With some panache she wore as well a straw hat with a faded purple ribbon on it. The skin of her face, and of her arms and legs, was deeply brown, as if she spent the greater part of her time outside. 'Indeed, indeed, we're not,' she repeated, most emphatically. 'And do not say "y'know", Margaretta.'

They were nine, the girls, in 1941. Laura had been sent from England because of the war, called in Ireland 'the emergency': there was more nourishment to be had in Ireland, and a feeling of safety in an Irish provincial town. Years before Laura had been born, her mother, living in Ireland then, had been at a boarding-school in Bray with Mrs Heaslip. 'I think you'll like it in Ireland,' her mother had promised. 'If I didn't have this wretched job I'd come with you like a shot.' They lived in Buckinghamshire, in a village called Anstey Rye. In December 1939, when the war had scarcely begun, Laura's father had been killed, the Spitfire he'd been piloting shot down over the sea. Her mother worked in the Anstey Rye clothes shop, where she was responsible for the accounts, for correspondence with wholesalers and for considerable formalities connected with clothing coupons. It was all very different from Ireland.

'That's what's called a monkey puzzle, y'know,' Margaretta said in the garden, and Laura quietly replied that she knew a monkey puzzle when she saw one.

Unlike Mrs Heaslip, Margaretta wasn't thin. Nor was she

brown. She was pretty in a sleepy, careless kind of way: her eyes were sleepily blue, her cheeks carelessly dimpled, her red jumble of hair the most beautiful Laura had ever seen. Margaretta would be astonishing when she grew up—what, Laura imagined, looking at her on that first afternoon, Helen of Troy must have been like. She felt jealous of the promise that seemed to be in every movement of Margaretta's body, in every footstep that she took as she led the way through the garden and the house.

'I am to show you everything,' Margaretta said. 'Would you be enormously bored to see the town?'

'No, no, of course not. Thank you, Margaretta.'

'It isn't much, I'll tell you that.'

The girls walked slowly through the wide main street, Margaretta drawing attention to the shops. All of them were cluttered, Laura noticed, except one, connected with a bakery, which seemed to sell, not bread, but only flour and sugar. They passed Phelan's Café, Jas. Ryan's drapery, Shannon's Medical Hall, Clancy's grocery, which Margaretta said was a public house as well as a grocer's, the Home and Colonial, a hardware shop and a shoe shop, other public houses. They paused by a window full of exercise-books and bottles of Stephens' ink, which Margaretta said was her favourite shop of all. The window was strewn with packets of nibs and pencils, packets of rubber bands, rulers, pencil-sharpeners, and Waterman fountain pens in different marbled colours. There was an advertisement for Mellifont Books, and some of the books themselves, with garish paper covers: *Angela and the Pixies* in the Children's Series, *Murder from Beyond* in Crime and Detection. The shop, Margaretta said, was called Tracy's, although the name over the door was T. MacCarthy. She liked it because it smelt so pleasantly of paper. Clancy's smelt of whiskey and sawdust, the butcher's of offal.

'How're you, Margaretta?' Mr Hearne greeted her from his doorway, a heavy man in a blood-stained apron.

'Laura's come from England,' Margaretta said by way of reply.

'How're you, Laura?' Mr Hearne said.

In the weeks and months that followed, Laura came to know Mr Hearne well, for she and Margaretta did all the shopping for the household. 'Meat and women,' the butcher had a way of saying, 'won't take squeezing.' He used to ask riddles, of which he did not know the answers. His wife, Mrs Heaslip said, was frequently pregnant.

The sweetshops of the town became familiar to Laura also, Murphy's, O'Connor's, Eldon's, Morrissey's, Mrs Finney's. Different brands of ice-cream were sold: H. B., Lucan, Melville, and Eldon's own make, cheaper and yellower than the others. Murphy's sold fruit as well as confectionery, and was the smartest of the sweetshops. Margaretta said it smelt the nicest, a mixture of vanilla and grapes. They all sold scarlet money-balls, in which, if you were lucky, you got your money back, a brand-new ha'penny wrapped in a piece of paper. They all sold boxes of Urney chocolates, and liquorice pipes and strips, and Lemon's Nut-Milk Toffees and Rainbow Toffees. In their windows, boxes of Willwood's Dolly Mixtures were laid out, and slabs of Mickey Mouse Toffee, and jelly babies. Best value of all was the yellow lemonade powder, which Margaretta and Laura never waited to make lemonade with but ate on the street.

That first summer in Ireland was full of such novelty, but most fascinating of all was the Heaslip family itself. Dr Heaslip related solemn jokes in an unhurried voice and his equally unhurried smile came to your rescue when you were flustered and didn't know whether it was a joke or not. Mrs Heaslip read in the garden—books that had their covers protected with brown paper, borrowed from the library the nuns ran. Margaretta's two younger brothers, six and five, were looked after by Francie, a cross-eyed girl of nineteen who came every day to the house. Eileen and Katie between them did the cooking and cleaning, Katie for ever up and down the basement stairs, answering the hall-door to Dr Heaslip's patients. Eileen was quite old—Margaretta said sixty, but Mrs Heaslip, overhearing that, altered the estimation to forty-five—and made brown bread that Laura thought delicious. Katie was keeping company with Wiry Daly from the hardware's. Margaretta said she'd seen them kissing.

Dr Heaslip's motor-car, unlike the others in the town, which for the most part were laid up because of the emergency, was driven every day out of the garage at the back by a man called Mattie Devlin. He parked it in front of the house so that Dr Heaslip could hasten to it and journey out into the country to attend a child-birth or to do his best when there'd been an accident on a farm. 'Ah, well, we'll do our best' was a much-employed expression of his, issued in a tone of voice that did not hold out much hope of success though in fact, as Laura learnt, he often saved a life. 'She's out there ready, Doctor,' Mattie Devlin every morning shouted up through the house at breakfast-time. He then began his day's work in the garden, where, to Mrs Heaslip's displeasure, he refused to grow peas, broad beans or spinach, claiming that the soil was unsuitable for them. He grew instead a great number of turnips, both swedes and white, potatoes, and a form of kale which nobody in the family liked. He was a man in a striped brown suit who wore both belt and braces and tucked the ends of his trousers into his socks when he worked in the garden. He never took off either his jacket or his hat.

Sometimes when Dr Heaslip was summoned on a call that involved a journey in his car he would invite the girls to accompany him, but he was insistent that they should make themselves as inconspicuous as possible on the back seat in case their presence should be regarded as a misuse of his petrol allowance. When they arrived at whatever house it was that required his skill he relaxed this severity and permitted them to emerge. 'Go and look at the chickens and cows,' he'd urge. 'Show Laura what a chicken is, Margaretta.' If the day was fine and the farmhouse not too far from the town, they'd ask if they might walk home. Later he would pass them on the road and would blow his horn, slowing down to give them a lift if they wanted one. But they usually walked on and no one particularly minded when they were late for whatever meal it was. Their plates of meat and vegetables would be taken from the oven and they'd eat at the kitchen table, gravy dried away to nothing, mashed potatoes brown. Or tea, at teatime, would have gone black almost, keeping hot on the range.

Headstrong and impetuous, Dr Heaslip described his daughter as 'not like yourself, Laura. You're the wise virgin of the two.' He repeated this comparison often, asking Mrs Heaslip and sometimes Katie or Eileen, even Mattie Devlin, if they agreed. Margaretta ignored it, Laura politely smiled. Nothing much upset the Heaslip household and nothing hurried it. Mrs Heaslip's only complaints were the manner in which her daughter spoke and Mattie Devlin's ways with vegetables.

'*The Rains Came*,' Margaretta said. 'All about India, y'know.'

They went to it, as they did to all the films at the De Luxe Picture House, which hadn't yet acquired Western Electric Sound, so that the voices were sometimes difficult to hear. Dr Heaslip and Mrs Heaslip attended the De Luxe almost as regularly as Margaretta and Laura, who went three times a week, every time there was a change of programme. At breakfast the next day the girls reported on what they'd seen;

Dr and Mrs Heaslip then made up their minds. *Mr Deeds Goes to Town* had for years been Mrs Heaslip's favourite and *The House of Rothschild* her husband's. Margaretta thought *The House of Rothschild* the most enormously boring picture she'd ever seen in her life, worse even than *The Hunchback of Notre Dame*. For her, and for Laura, the highlights of that first summer were *Fast and Loose*, *Test Pilot*, *His Butler's Sister* and *Naughty Marietta*; and best of all, they easily agreed, was *The Rains Came*. On Saturdays there was a serial called *Flaming Frontiers*, and there were travelogues and the news, and shorts with Charlie Chase or Leon Errol. 'Don't you love the *smell* of the De Luxe?' Margaretta used to say after they'd dwelt at length on a performance by Franchot Tone or Deanna Durbin, exhausting the subject and yet unwilling to leave it. 'Hot celluloid, I think it is, and cigarette butts.'

The war ended in May 1945 and Laura brought back to England these memories of the family and the town, of the school she had attended with Margaretta, of the people and the shops. Margaretta wrote from time to time, a huge sprawling hand, words grotesquely misspelt: Mrs Hearne had called her latest baby Liam Pius, after the Pope; *Random Harvest* was on at the De Luxe, *The Way to the Stars* was coming.

Laura wrote neatly, with nothing to say because Margaretta couldn't be expected to be interested in all the talk about building things up again and descriptions of utility clothes. Margaretta had become her best friend and she Margaretta's. They had decided it the night before she'd returned. They'd shared Margaretta's bed, talking in whispers from ten o'clock until the Donald Duck clock said it was twenty past two. 'We'd better go to sleep, y'know,' Margaretta had said, but Laura had wanted to continue talking, to make the time go slowly. After Margaretta put the light out she lay in the darkness thinking she'd never had a friend like Margaretta before, someone who found the same things as boring as you did, someone you didn't have to be careful with. A wash of moonlight for a moment lightened the gloom, catching the untidy mass of Margaretta's hair on the pillow. She was breathing heavily, already asleep, smiling a little as if from some amusing dream. Then a cloud slipped over the moon again and the room abruptly darkened.

It was that night that Laura afterwards remembered most. 'You can't find friends in a town the like of this,' Margaretta had said. 'Well, I mean you can, y'know. Only it's different.' And she mentioned the girls she knew in the town, whom Laura knew also. None of them would have been fascinated, as they were, by the way Mrs Eldon of the sweetshop made her lips seem larger with the outline of her lipstick. None of them would have wondered how it was that Mr Hearne always had the same amount of stubble on his face. 'One day's growth,' Dr Heaslip had said when they'd asked him. How could a man, every day, have one day's stubble? 'They want to be nuns and things,' Margaretta said. These girls went to the De Luxe also, but they didn't take much interest in the performances, nor in the trade-marks of the films, the roaring lion, the searchlights, the statue with the torch, the snow-capped mountain, the radio aerial with electricity escaping from it. The girls of the town didn't go in for finding things funny. Sometimes Laura and Margaretta found a remark a shopkeeper had made so funny that they had to lean against some other shopkeeper's window, laughing so much it gave them a stitch. Sometimes the very sight of people made them laugh. Entranced, Margaretta listened when Laura had told her how her Uncle Gilbert had taken her on to his bony knee on her sixth birthday and softly spanked her for no reason whatsoever. Afterwards he'd given her a sweet and said it was their secret. 'Keep well away from that fellow,' Margaretta had sharply advised, and both of them had giggled, not quite knowing what they were giggling at. It was something Laura had never told anyone else.

It is so drab, Laura wrote. *As you would say, enormously drab. Everyone said at first, you know, that the war would be over by Christmas. I remember people saying Hitler was a knut and didn't know what he was doing. But now everything's so drab after Ireland that you'd think he had won the thing. I haven't had an egg for months.*

And so, for nourishment only, since safety wasn't in question any more, Laura's mother sent her to stay again with the Heaslips. Mrs Heaslip had pressed for this, had pressed that Laura's mother should accompany her.

'They can't spare her,' Laura explained when she arrived, reiterating what her mother had written. 'She'd really have loved to come.' The drab austerity was as confining as the war there had been.

For Laura, that summer had the pleasure of familiarity revisited in place of the novelty there had been when she'd first arrived in the town. Mrs Hearne might possibly be pregnant again, Mrs Eldon's lipstick still generously recreated her lips, *Murder from Beyond*, with curling, yellowed edges, was still in the window among the nibs and rubber bands.

Margaretta had acquired a bicycle during the year, and the saddle of Mrs Heaslip's Humber was lowered for Laura. For mile after mile of flat, undramatic landscape they talked, as they cycled, of the past performances at the De Luxe Picture House: Claudette Colbert in *Boom Town*, William Powell and Myrna Loy in *The Shadow of the Thin Man*, Ray Milland in *The Doctor Takes a Wife*. They turned off the tarred roads that were so easy to go fast on and explored countryside that was hilly and more interesting. Eileen made them sandwiches, which they carried in Margaretta's saddle-bag, and they were given money for lemonade. They usually ate the sandwiches in a field, leaving their bicycles by the roadside and chattering for ages in the sunshine. Once they took all their clothes off and bathed in a stream, shrieking because it was so cold. But what they liked best of all was to call in at some cottage and ask for a drink of water. They would be invited into the kitchen and two cups of water would be fetched from a bucket or a pump. On one occasion a very old woman insisted on giving them tea, with boiled eggs and bread, although they kept telling her they'd just eaten a lot of sandwiches. She showed them photographs of her son, who was in Chicago, and made them promise they would call at her cottage again. But even if all they received was the water they asked for there was always the excitement, afterwards, of talking about whoever had given it to them. Scrutinising people, remembering every word that was spoken and every detail of a kitchen: all that became a kind of game. If they were far enough away from the town they called themselves by names that were not their own. 'Annabella Morrissey,' Margaretta replied when asked, and Laura gave the name of girl she knew in England, Isabel Batchelor-Tate. They were Dublin girls, Margaretta once added, on holiday in Hogan's Hotel. Her father was a hay merchant and Laura's a taster of teas. 'I shouldn't tell people stuff like that,' Dr Heaslip reprimanded them one lunchtime. 'I'm quite well known, you know.' He went on humming after he'd spoken and they were unable to hide their fiery red faces, made to feel foolish because he had not been cross. Afterwards Mrs Heaslip looked at them amusedly, and suggested they should visit the de Courcys if they were bored.

'Oh, but we're not, Mrs Heaslip,' Laura protested vehemently. 'Not in the very least.'

'Take her to the de Courcys, Margaretta. I don't know what we've been thinking of not to introduce Laura to the de Courcys before this.'

'But, God, they're miles away.'

'Do not say "God", Margaretta. There is an invalid in that house. Of course a visit must be made. Eileen will make you salad sandwiches.'

They went the next morning. They cycled for nine miles and then they turned into an avenue with a gate-lodge from which a man carefully eyed them, from their sandals and white socks to their straw hats. He stood in the doorway, seeming to be listening to their conversation about Wiry Daly's courtship of Katie. He was wearing a Guard's uniform, the coarse navy-blue tunic open at the neck, a cigarette in the middle of his mouth. He had grey hair and a grey, mournful face. When Margaretta said hullo he wagged his head but did not speak. They began to giggle when they'd cycled on a bit.

The avenue was long, its surface badly broken, but pleasantly cool because the trees that lined it kept out the sun. Laura considered it romantic, like the avenue in *Rebecca*. But Margaretta said that was only wishful thinking: there hadn't been an avenue in *Rebecca* encased with trees and foliage. An argument began, which continued until the pink-washed house appeared, with white hydrangeas on either side of it, and tall windows, and an open hall-door. The bicycles crunched over gravel that made cycling difficult. The girls dismounted and walked the last bit.

'I'm Margaretta Heaslip,' Margaretta informed a maid who was winding a clock in the hall. 'We've been sent to see the de Courcys.'

The maid stared, appearing to be alarmed. She continued to wind the clock, which was on a table at the bottom of the stairs, and then she closed the glass of its face and put the key on a brass hook in an alcove; the time was half-past eleven.

Tapestries hung by the staircase, curving with it as it ascended. Rugs were scattered on the darkly stained boards of the floor, as threadbare as the stair carpet and the tapestries, which were so faded that whatever scenes they depicted had been lost. There was a smell in the hall, as Margaretta said afterwards, of flowers and bacon.

'Will you tell the de Courcys?' she suggested to the maid, since the maid appeared hesitant about how to proceed. 'Just say Margaretta Heaslip and a friend are here.'

'The de Courcys went up to Punchestown races, miss.'

'Is Ralph de Courcy here?'

'He is of course.'

'Will you tell him then?'

'He didn't go up to the races, miss, in case they'd strain him.'

'Will you tell him Margaretta Heaslip and a friend are here?'

The maid was as young as Katie, but not as pretty. She had protruding teeth and hair that was in disarray beneath her white cap. She hesitated again, and then visibly reached a decision.

'I'll tell him so, miss. Will ye sit in the drawing-room?'

She left them where they stood. One door they opened led to a panelled room, too small and businesslike for a drawing-room. Another, with blue blinds pulled down, had dining-chairs arranged around a long table, its other furniture shadowy in the gloom. The drawing-room itself had a fire, although the day was so exceedingly warm that the windows were open. There were vases of flowers on the mantelpiece and on tables and on a grand piano, and family portraits were close to one another on the walls. An old black-and-white dog was lying on the hearthrug and did not move when the girls entered. It was the most beautiful room, Laura considered, she had ever been in.

They sat cautiously on the edge of a sofa that was striped in two shades of faded pink. They spoke in whispers, discussing the maid: would she be keeping company with the uniformed man at the gate-lodge?

'Will ye wait a while?' the maid invited, appearing at the door.

Margaretta giggled and put her hand up to her mouth; Laura said they'd wait. 'I wonder what her name is,' she added when the maid had gone.

'Ludmilla, I'd say.'

The giggling began again, the dog snorted in his sleep. Through the open windows came the sound of pigeons.

'Well, this is an honour,' a voice said. 'How do you do?'

He was older than they were by maybe as much as three years. He was pale and dark-haired, his face hatched-shaped, his eyes brown. He was dressed in flannel trousers and a green tweed jacket.

'Margaretta Heaslip,' he continued, smiling extravagantly. 'I remember you when you were little.'

He spoke as if she still were, as if they were both not in the least grown up. His manner insisted that he himself belonged to the adult world, that he had long ago passed through theirs.

'My mother said to call,' Margaretta explained, disowning responsibility for their presence. 'To enquire how you were, and to introduce Laura.'

'How do you do, Laura?'

He held out a hand, which Laura received, allowing her own to be briefly clasped. His touch was cold. Like marble, she thought.

'Laura's English, y'know.'

'Well now, and whereabouts in England, Laura?'

'A village called Anstey Rye. In Buckinghamshire.'

'How attractive that sounds!'

'Dead as old mutton, Laura says. The war, y'know.'

'Ah, yes. The horrible war. But at least the Allies won. You're pleased, Laura?'

He had a precise way of speaking, his Irish accent drawling

out his sentences, a smile rarely absent from his face. Set in hollows, his dark eyes were fixed on Laura's, insistent that his interest in all she had to say was genuine.

'Well yes, I am pleased.'

'I used to listen to Lord Haw-Haw. He's most amusing.'

The maid returned with a tray of tea-cups, a tea-pot and biscuits on a plate.

'Thank you, Mary.'

As he spoke, Margaretta put her hand up to her face. But already he had noticed.

'What's the joke?' he politely enquired.

The maid left the room, and because she knew that she, too, would begin to giggle if she did not speak Laura said:

'Margaretta thought her name was Ludmilla.'

'Ludmilla?'

It wasn't funny any more, as it hadn't been when Dr Heaslip had not been cross. Politely, Ralph de Courcy handed them their cups of tea. He was right: they were children and he was not.

'Have a Marietta biscuit?'

They each took one. They felt silly and ashamed. Margaretta said:

'Are you feeling better these days?'

'I never feel ill at all.' He turned to Laura. 'My heart was weakened when I stupidly caught rheumatic fever as a boy. I'm meant to go carefully in case I die.'

They wanted to gasp in wonder at this reference to death, but they did not do so. Margaretta said:

'Are you getting better all the time?'

'Indubitably. I'm reading Thomas Mann. *Buddenbrooks.* Do you like Thomas Mann?'

They had never heard of this German author. Vaguely, they shook their heads. They had not yet read, Laura admitted, the book called *Buddenbrooks*.

'Shall I show you about the garden when you've finished your Marietta biscuits?'

'Yes, please,' Laura said. 'If you don't think the strain—'

'Strain is just a word they use. Your father came here once or twice, Margaretta, when I was at death's door—called in to offer a second opinion. It wasn't as disagreeable as it sounds, you know, being at death's door. Though nicer, perhaps, to be a few footsteps further off.'

His conversation was extraordinary, Laura considered. In a way everything about him was extraordinary, not least his detached smile and his eyes. His eyes did not flit about. They were the steadiest eyes she had ever seen, especially when he spoke of death.

'Oh, yes,' he said, 'they make a frightful fuss. Do you play tennis? You could stay to lunch and then we might play tennis.'

'But surely—' Margaretta began.

'I may play a *little* tennis. If I agree, and promise, not to sit about afterwards without a sweater and a blazer, then I may play a little tennis. Or at least that's what I say.'

Suppose he dies? Laura thought. Suppose he falls down on the tennis court and is unable to get up again? Imagine having to tell about that! Imagine Dr Heaslip saying nothing, but thinking what fools they were and how much they were to blame!

He took them to the garden. He didn't appear to know the names of any plants or flowers, but with his pale, cold hands he pointed about. He led them through a glasshouse full of tomatoes and out the other end. He pointed again: peaches flourished on a brick-lined wall. '*A la* Dean Swift,' he said: they'd no idea what he was talking about.

He sat between them on a wooden seat. A lawn stretched all around, bounded by white hydrangeas in front of towering cedar trees. Another dog, a brown spaniel, ambled from some corner and sat with them. Margaretta said the garden was beautiful.

'Sergeant Barry does it. Did you see Sergeant Barry by the gate-lodge?'

They said they had.

'He resigned from the force because he couldn't learn the Irish. He feared they might demote him and he couldn't bear the thought of that. So he resigned as sergeant.'

In the drawing-room, when she'd brought the tea and biscuits, he'd told the maid that they would stay to lunch. They hadn't dared to say that there were salad sandwiches in Margaretta's saddle-bag.

'You must be starving,' he said now, 'after such a journey. Heaven knows what they've managed to scrape together. Shall we go and see?'

He led the way back to the house and to the dining-room. The blinds had been raised, and places laid at the table. He pulled at a bell in the wall and some minutes later the maid brought in three soup-plates on a tray.

'Crosse and Blackwell's,' he said. 'Leave it if you don't like kidneys.'

All through the meal he asked questions, about Buckinghamshire and Anstey Rye, and if bombs had fallen near by; about the De Luxe Picture House, which he had been to once. There was a larger town, nearer to the de Courcys' house than their own, which had a cinema called the Palace, with Western Electric Sound. He'd seen *Gone with the Wind* there, which he described as 'light'. He'd like to see some German films, which he'd read about, but he doubted that they'd ever come to the Palace or the De Luxe. He related the plot of one, to do with the crimes committed by a man who was not sane, and enthusiastically they both said it sounded interesting. Perhaps now that the war was over these German films might be on in England, Laura added, and he agreed that that might be so. Then, quite abruptly, when they had all three finished their sago and stewed gooseberries, he said he was feeling a little tired. His smile continued. He was supposed to rest after lunch, he explained. It would perhaps be asking for trouble not to, today.

They stood up. They thanked him and hoped he would be completely better soon. It was as though tennis had never been mentioned; it was as though he had never said that people made a fuss. He did not move from where he sat at the head of the long table, but said that he had enjoyed their visit, that they were good to come all this way to bore themselves with the company of an invalid. Would they come again? he almost meekly asked.

'Yes, of course,' Laura replied, her assurance only moments ahead of Margaretta's.

'Please be careful,' Margaretta said. 'Please take a good rest.'

They rode in silence down the avenue, past the gate-lodge, where Sergeant Barry was reading a newspaper in his garden. He looked up from it to scrutinise them, another cigarette in the middle of his mouth. Again he wagged his head at them but did not attempt to speak.

'God!' Margaretta said when they were out of earshot. 'God, did you ever!'

'I hope we didn't cause a strain.'

'God, I know! I thought of that.'

When they next saw Dr Heaslip they asked him. 'Oh no, no,' he said. 'Company probably does the poor fellow good.' But neither Laura nor Margaretta could think of Ralph de Courcy as a poor fellow. A fortnight later they rode over to the de Courcys' house again, and Sergeant Barry, apprehending them as they turned into the avenue, told them the de Courcys were all away in Dublin.

'When will they be back?' Margaretta asked.

'Ah, not for a while. Not till the end of the month.'

A week later Laura returned to England. This time among the images she carried with her were the vivid ones of the hours they had spent in the de Courcys' house and in their garden. The indistinct tapestries, the key of the clock hanging in the alcove in the hall, the black-and-white dog asleep on the hearthrug: such images came and went in her mind, giving way to the face of the maid, and the sergeant at the gate-lodge, and Ralph de Courcy in his flannels and green tweed jacket. She dreamed that she and Margaretta walked among the white hydrangeas and the cedar trees, that they sat again on the pink-striped sofa. In her dream the hands fell off the clock in the hall, which Dr Heaslip said sometimes happened, owing to strain.

Margaretta wrote to say that the de Courcys had returned from Dublin, so she'd heard, but on her own she naturally hadn't had the nerve to cycle over. The De Luxe had at last acquired Western Electric Sound and the difference was tremendous. Wiry Daly had been to the house to see about marrying Katie, and when Mrs Heaslip suggested that they should wait a little longer he'd gone red in the face and said he thought waiting wasn't a good idea. Mr Hearne was dealing in black-market sugar and tea, making more than he'd ever made out of meat. But soon, so people said, he'd be arrested.

*

The following summer, to her great disappointment, and to Margaretta's, Laura did not visit Ireland. The reason for this was that her mother, suffering a bout of pneumonia in the early part of the year, did not recover quickly. She struggled back to her desk in the cubbyhole behind the Anstey Rye clothes shop, but an exhaustion that the illness had left her with would not lift, and when Laura's summer holidays came Dr Pace advised that she should be responsible for all the housework and all the cooking, taking this burden at least from her mother. Had it not been for the post-war effort that was still required of everyone, he would have stipulated total rest for her mother, three months simply doing nothing. And he knew that ends had to be made to meet.

So Laura cooked her mother's meals and her own, and Hoovered the rooms of their cottage. She made her mother rest on Sundays, bringing her trays in bed. She was conscientious about taking the wet battery of the wireless to be recharged once a week, she weeded the garden and transplanted the lettuce plants. All the time she cherished the hope that at the end of the summer, even for a week, she might be permitted to visit Margaretta. Her mother was clearly regaining her strength. She stopped spending Sundays in bed and instead sat in the garden. By mid-August she began to do the cooking again.

Letters from Margaretta asked if there was any chance, but in Anstey Rye Ireland was not mentioned. Instead, Laura's mother spoke of their straitened circumstances this year: because of her pneumonia, she had not earned as much for those few months as she might have; ends had not yet begun to meet again. So Laura wrote to Margaretta, explaining.

Isn't it strange, Margaretta herself wrote, long after that summer had passed and Laura's mother had entirely recovered, *that there should have been two invalids, your mother and Ralph de Courcy?* Her handwriting was less wild than once it had been, her spelling much improved. *My father says he's only slowly mending.* And in a daydream Laura allowed herself to pretend that it was him she had looked after, carrying trays up the curving staircase, carrying cushions to a chair in the garden. She wondered if she'd ever see that house again, and Sergeant Barry at the gate-lodge. *Isn't Linda Darnell beautiful?* Margaretta wrote. *I'd love to look like that. Have you seen* Tortilla Flat?

In 1948 Laura went again to Ireland. Katie had married Wiry Daly and had had a baby. There was a new maid with Eileen in the kitchen, Mattie Devlin's daughter, Josie. The shopkeepers said Laura was getting prettier all the time, but Laura knew that it was Margaretta who was the beautiful one and always would be, her marvellous hair and her headstrong manner that Laura admired so. She'd been going to a boarding-school ever since Laura had last visited the Heaslips, the one in Bray where Mrs Heaslip and Laura's mother had met. 'You're better looking than Linda Darnell,' Laura said, meaning it.

They were too shy to cycle to the de Courcys' house. They didn't realise at first that such a shyness had developed in them, but when they talked about that warm day two summers ago they realised that they could not attempt to repeat it. Two children, with white socks and straw hats, had cycled up the avenue, chattering and giggling: it would be awkward now. But one evening, watching *Thunder Rock* at the De Luxe, they saw Ralph de Courcy two rows in front of them, with a blonde-haired girl. 'You're never Margaretta and Laura?' he said when the film had come to an end and they met him face to face in the aisle.

'Yes,' Laura said, aware that she reddened as she spoke. When she glanced at Margaretta she saw that she had reddened also.

'This is a sister of mine,' he introduced. 'Hazel.'

Margaretta said:

'I think I met you, Hazel, years ago when we were kids.'

'Yes, you did.'

'This is my friend Laura.'

'I've heard about the day you both came to see us, when we were all at Punchestown except Ralph.'

'You never came again,' he chided, through the smile that was always there. 'You said you would, you know.'

'Laura didn't stay with us last year.'

'You could have come on your own.'

Margaretta laughed, blushing again.

'That was really an appalling film,' he said. 'A waste of money.'

'Yes,' Laura agreed, although she did not think so. 'Yes, it was.'

The de Courcys had driven to town in a car powered by propane gas, a relic of the emergency. To Laura and Margaretta it looked like any other car except for an attachment at the back. Although the night was warm, Ralph put on a muffler and an overcoat before taking his place at the driver's wheel. Unlike her mother, Laura thought, he was not totally well again.

'Come and play tennis one day,' his sister invited. 'Come in the morning and stay to lunch.'

'Come on Friday,' he said.

*

'My husband is an antiquarian bookseller,' Laura says in the cathedral.

'Mine makes radio components.'

Margaretta had remained in the town, marrying Shulmann, who had set up his factory there in 1955. Shulmann was with her in Siena, resting now in their pensione. Their three children are grown up.

'I guessed you would have married,' Laura says.

'And I you.'

What does the antiquarian bookseller look like? Is Shulmann thin or fat? Laura remembers Margaretta's hair on the pillow, spread out in the moonlight, and Margaretta saying that the smell in the De Luxe Picture House was of hot celluloid and cigarette butts, and how they giggled because they'd considered Sergeant Barry comic. How different would their lives have been if the friendship had continued? Some instinct tells her as they stand there among the tourists that their friendship in its time went deeper than the marriages they have mentioned. She sees them on their bicycles, and the curiosity of Sergeant Barry passing from their sandals and their white socks to their beribboned straw hats. 'Ludmilla,' Margaretta says on the pink-striped sofa. Is friendship more fragile, Laura wonders, the more precious it is? And Margaretta reflects that in the thirty-eight years that have passed the friendship might have made a difference in all sorts of ways. They are tourists like the others now, strangers among strangers.

*

They rode over early on the Friday of the tennis party, but as they arrived at the de Courcys' house rain began to fall. Other people were there, friends of Hazel de Courcy who had also come to play tennis but who now stood about forlornly because the rain persisted. Then someone suggested whist and the occasion became a different one from the occasion the visitors had anticipated. The fire blazed in the drawing-room, there was tea and Marietta biscuits at eleven o'clock, and lunch at one, there was tea and cake, with bread and butter and scones, at four. Ralph de Courcy rested after lunch, but soon appeared again. He talked to Margaretta alone, questioning her about the boarding-school at Bray, about the buildings and the playing-fields and the food. He asked her if she was happy there.

'Oh, it's all right,' Margaretta replied, and she described the big assembly hall that was known as the ballroom because that was what it had been before the house became a school. A draughty conservatory served as the senior lounge; cold, gaunt dormitories contained rows of beds, each with its narrow pine cupboard and washstand. The two headmistresses were sisters, in tweed skirts and jumpers on which necklaces bounced. The food was inedible.

'Poor Margaretta,' he murmured.

She was about to say it wasn't as awful as it sounded but changed her mind because his sympathy was pleasant. He said he would think of her at the school, eating the inedible food, being polite to the headmistresses. She felt a shiver of warmth, in her head or her body, she wasn't sure which: a delicious sensation that made her want to close her eyes.

'It'll be lovely for me,' Ralph de Courcy said, 'being able to imagine you there, Margaretta.'

The rain ceased after tea but the tennis court was too sodden by now to permit play that day, and soon afterwards the party broke up. Hardly speaking at all—not once commenting as they might have on Hazel de Courcy's friends—the girls cycled back to the town, and when Dr Heaslip asked at supper how Ralph de Courcy had seemed neither at first replied. Then Margaretta said that he was quite recovered from his illness, even though he'd had his usual rest. Every day he was recovering a little more. Soon he would be just like anyone else, she said.

Laura cut her ham and salad into tiny shreds, not wanting to hear anything in the dining-room in case it impinged on what the day already meant to her. The sun had been warm during their ride back from the de Courcys' house; the damp fields and hedges had acquired a beauty as if in celebration of what had happened. 'Shall we write to one another?' he had suggested in the moments when they'd been alone. He had asked her about England, about Anstey Rye and her mother. He smiled more than ever while he spoke, making her feel complimented, as if smiling was natural in her presence.

'I didn't know till now,' Margaretta said a few days later, 'that I fell in love with him the first time we rode out there.'

They were walking together on a dull road, just beyond the town. Margaretta did not add that he'd asked her about her school, that he had been interested in all that ordinary detail so that he could picture her there that autumn. She refrained from this revelation because she knew that Laura was in love with him also. Laura had not said so but you could see, and it would hurt her horribly to know that he had asked—passionately almost—about the gaunt dormitories and the ballroom that had become an assembly hall.

'Well, of course,' Laura said, 'he's very nice.'

There was nothing else she could say. Bidding her goodbye, he had clasped her hand as though he never wanted to let it go. His deep, brown eyes had held hers in a way she knew she would never forget; she was certain he had almost kissed her. 'Are you good at secrets?' he had asked. 'Are you, Laura?' She had only nodded in reply, but she'd known that what he meant was that all this should be kept between themselves, and she intended to honour that.

'I simply think he's a marvellous person,' Margaretta said, possessively.

'Oh, yes, of course.'

Already it was September, and they did not speak of him again. Laura within a week returned to England and a few days after that Margaretta began another term at the boarding-school in Bray.

I see you so very clearly, he wrote. *I think of you and wonder about you. I'll never forget our being in the garden that day, I sometimes imagine I can still taste the tinned soup we had for lunch. Whatever can you have thought of me, going away to rest like that? Was it rude? Please write and tell me it wasn't rude and that you didn't mind. I rested, actually, with your face beside me on the cushion.*

He did not beg for love in vain, and in Bray and Buckinghamshire they exulted in their giving of it, though both felt saddened that in their own communications, one to another, they did not mention Ralph de Courcy or his letters. *I was glad when it rained because, actually, I don't play much tennis. Oh, heavens, how I should love to be walking with you beneath the beech trees! Did you think I was at death's door that first day—the day when I said to myself you were an angel sent to me? When we met in the De Luxe it was marvellous. Was it for you? Please write. I love your letters.*

In Bray and Buckinghamshire they loved his letters also. They snatched at them impatiently: from the letter table in the senior lounge, from the hallstand in Anstey Rye. They bore them away to read in private, to savour and learn by heart. They kept them hidden but close at hand, so that when the yearning came they could raise them to their lips. *Shall I come and see you in the holidays?* Margaretta wrote. *Or could you drive over in your father's gas contraption and maybe we'd go to the De Luxe? I can't wait till the holidays, to tell the truth. December the sixteenth.*

These suggestions provoked a swift response. Their friendship was a secret. If Margaretta came to the de Courcys' house would they be able to disguise it beneath the eye of the family? Of all absurd things, the family might mention strain, and a visit to the Picture House was out of the question. *Dear Margaretta, we must wait a little while yet. Please wait. Please let's just write our letters for the moment.*

But Margaretta, on the eighteenth of that December, was unable to prevent herself from cycling out of the town in the direction of the de Courcys' house. It was a cold morning, with frost heavy on the hedges and beautifully whitening the fields. All she wanted was a single glimpse of him.

I cannot tell you the confusion it caused, he wrote, weeks later, to Laura, *and how great the unhappiness has been for me. It was so sad because she looked bulky and ridiculous in the trousers she had put on for cycling. They thought she was a thief at least. Why on earth did she come?*

Sergeant Barry found her among the rhododendrons and led her, weeping, to the house. 'Goodness, Margaretta!' Hazel de Courcy exclaimed in the hall while Margaretta tried to pull herself together. She said she'd just been passing by.

She seemed a different person from the girl who'd first come here with you, but that was perhaps because you were with her then. No one knew what to say when she stood there in the hall. I turned away and went upstairs. What else could I do?

Margaretta rode miserably back to the house in the square. She wrote immediately, apologising, trying to explain, but her letter elicited no reply. She was unable to eat properly all the holidays, unable in any way to comfort herself. No letter arrived at the boarding-school in Bray. No letter, ever again, arrived for Margaretta from Ralph de Courcy.

Oafish, my sister said, and although it's hard I thought the same. Not beautiful in the least, her cheeks all red and ugly. I had never thought Margaretta was stupid before.

Laura was hurt by this description of her friend, and she wished she might have sent her a line of consolation. Poor Margaretta had ridden out that day with no companion to lend her courage, and to everyone in the de Courcys' house it must have been obvious that she was a lovesick girl. But by the summer she would have recovered, and Laura could gently tell her then that she and Ralph loved one another, because secrets could not remain secrets for ever.

But the summer, when it came, was not like that. In the

February of that year Laura had become upset because her letters from Ralph de Courcy had ceased. A month later she received a note from Margaretta. *I thought I'd better tell you. Ralph de Courcy died.*

That summer, Margaretta and Laura were sixteen; and Mr Hearne, who had survived his years as a black-marketeer, was once again an ordinary butcher. 'Women and meat won't take squeezing,' he said, eyeing the girls with lasciviousness now. At the De Luxe Picture House they saw *Blithe Spirit* and *Green for Danger.* Laura asked about Ralph de Courcy's grave.

'God knows where it is,' Margaretta replied. 'He could be buried under a road for all I care.'

'We liked him.'

'He was cheap.'

'He's dead, Margaretta.'

'I'm glad he's dead.'

Still Margaretta had not told her about her cycle ride on that bitter morning. She offered no explanation for this violent change of heart, so Laura asked her.

'Well, something happened if you must know.'

She related all of it, telling how she had begun to receive letters from Ralph de Courcy, how they had come, two and three a week sometimes, to the boarding-school at Bray.

'I didn't mean any harm, Laura. All I wanted was a glimpse of him. Of course I should have gone at night, but how could I? Nine miles there and nine miles back?'

Laura hardly heard. 'Letters?' she whispered in a silence that had gathered. 'Love letters, you mean?'

The conversation took place in Margaretta's bedroom. She unlocked a drawer in her dressing-table and produced the letters she spoke of, tied together with a piece of red string.

'You can read them,' she said. 'I don't mind.'

I rested, actually, with your face beside me on the cushion. In

Laura's own bedroom, among the love letters she had so sadly and so fondly brought with her to Ireland, were those words also. *I said to myself you were an angel sent to me.*

'What kind of love was it,' Margaretta cried, 'that could evaporate in a second? Just because I made a mistake?'

The letters were returned to the dressing-table drawer, the key turned in the lock, the key itself secreted beneath a frilled cloth. Laura, catching a reflection of herself in the dressing-table looking-glass, saw that she had turned as white as powder. She felt weak, and imagined that if she stood up she would faint.

'I don't know why I keep his old letters,' Margaretta said. 'I honestly don't know.'

That it had been Margaretta and not she who had been foolish was no consolation for Laura. That it was she, not Margaretta, to whom he had written for longer, until the day before his death, was none either. His protestations of passion seemed like mockery now.

'Except I suppose,' said Margaretta, 'that I went on loving him. I always will.'

And I, too, thought Laura. She would love him in spite of the ugly pain she felt, in spite of not understanding why he had behaved so. Had two girls' longing simply been more fun than one's? Had he been as cruel as that?

'I have a headache,' she said. 'I think I'll lie down for a little.'

*

The days that followed were as unbearable for Laura as the days that followed her foolishness had been for Margaretta. Dr Heaslip said twice that their guest was looking peaky; she did her best to smile. 'It's all right, really,' Margaretta reassured her, assuming that Laura's lowness was a kind of sympathy. 'It's over now. He's dead and gone.'

He was buried in a country churchyard a mile or so from the de Courcys' house: that much at least Laura had elicited from Margaretta. One early morning, as dawn was just beginning to glimmer, she let herself out of the tall wooden doors through which Matt Devlin every day drove Dr Heaslip's car, and cycled out into the countryside. Trees that were at first only shadows acquired foliage as dawn advanced, hedges and fields softened into colour, stone walls and gates offered again the detail that night had claimed. Around the churchyard, rooks were noisy, and on the grave of Ralph de Courcy there were fresh flowers that Laura knew were Margaretta's, conveyed there secretly also. She picked honeysuckle and laid it on the earth above his head. She knelt and spoke his name; she repeated what so often she had written in her letters. She couldn't help loving him in spite of still not understanding.

'You went, didn't you?' Margaretta accused. 'You went in the middle of the night?'

'In the early morning.'

'He loved me, y' know, before I was so stupid. It was me he wrote letters to.'

The summer crept by. They talked much less than they had talked before. Politeness began between them, and smiles that were not meant. They missed the past but did not say so, and then—on the night before Laura was to return to England— Margaretta said:

'I've hated you this summer.'

'There is no reason to hate me, Margaretta.'

'It has to do with him. I don't know what it is.'

'Well, I don't hate you, Margaretta, and I never could.'

'That's nice.'

'Don't be unhappy, Margaretta.'

Why could she not have shared the truth? Why could she not have said that in the game he'd played he'd wanted to know all about Anstey Rye also? She might have pointed out that when you scraped away the superficialities of her early-morning journey—the peaceful dawn, the rooks, the honeysuckle—it had been less honourable and less courageous than Margaretta's. In her wise virgin way, she had taken no chances in visiting only the dead.

'Margaretta . . .'

She hesitated, unable to go on. And Margaretta said:

'I'll never forgive you for going to his grave.'

'I only went to say goodbye.'

'It was me he wrote to.'

Again Laura tried to say that she, as much as Margaretta, had been shamed. Sharing their folly, would they have laughed in the end over Ralph de Courcy, she wondered, as they had laughed over so much else? Would they have talked for half the night in Margaretta's bedroom, exorcising that lingering pain?

'Margaretta,' Laura began, but still could not go on.

*

The De Luxe Picture House has gone. Mr Hearne is dead. So is Mrs Eldon, her lips trimmed down to size. But Tracy's still smells pleasantly of paper, and Murphy's of vanilla and grapes. Wiry Daly and Katie are grandparents now.

'But oh, it's not much changed, y'know.'

Dr Heaslip and his wife might or might not be dead also: this is not mentioned in Margaretta's news. Her voice is spiritless, and Laura has to think as each name is mentioned. Margaretta's features mourn the loss: a conversation, through desuetude, has lost its savour. It was harsh, so casually and so swiftly, to have considered her bland and fat, implying insensitivity. Laura should reach out and kiss her, but the gesture would be false.

Margaretta remembers the flowers that year after year she

has placed on the grave, and the bitterness she felt when she thought of Laura. She cycled in that same secret way to the churchyard, not caring if the de Courcys guessed that it was she who had picked the weeds from the mound that marked his presence. When she ceased to make the journey she had at first felt faithless, but the feeling had worn away with time.

For Laura there is the memory of the guilt that had remained for so long, the letters she had tried to compose, her disappointment in herself. *Dear Margaretta:* so many times she had begun her message, certain that there were words to soften her treachery and then discovering that there were not. In time she ceased also, weary of the useless effort.

Regret passes without words between them; they smile a shrugging smile. If vain Ralph de Courcy had chosen their girlish passion as a memorial to himself he might have chosen as well this rendezvous for their middle age, a waspish cathedral to reflect a waspish triumph. Yet his triumph seems hollow now, robbed by time of its drama and the heady confusions of an accidental cruelty. Death's hostage he had been, a ghost who'd offered them a sleight of hand because he hadn't the strength for love. They only smile again before they part.

Her Mother's Daughter

Her mother considered it ill-bred to eat sweets on the street, and worse to eat fruit or ice-cream. Her mother was tidy, and required tidiness in others. She peeled an apple in a particular way, keeping the peel in one long piece, as though it were important to do so. Her mother rarely smiled.

Her father, now dead, had been a lexicographer: a small, abstracted man who would not have noticed the eating of food on the street, not even slices of meat or peas from their pods. Most of the time he hadn't noticed Helena either. He died on her eighth birthday.

Her mother had always ruled the household. Tall and neat and greyly dressed, she had achieved her position of command without resort to anger or dictatorial speech; she did not say much, and what she did say she never found necessary to repeat. A look informed the miscreant, indicating a button undone, an unwashed hand. Helena, possessing neither brother nor sister, was the only miscreant.

The house where she and her mother lived was in a south-western suburb of London. Next door on one side there was a fat widow, Mrs Archingford, who dyed her hair a garish shade of red. On the other an elderly couple were for ever bickering in their garden. Helena's mother did not acknowledge the presence of Mrs Archingford, who arrived at the house next door when Helena was nine; but she had written a note to the elderly man to request him to keep his voice down, a plea that caused him to raise it even more.

Helena played mainly by herself. Beneath the heavy mahogany of the dining-room table she cut the hair of Samson while he slept, then closed her eyes while the table collapsed around her, its great ribbed legs and the polished surface from which all meals were eaten splintering into fragments. The multitude in the temple screamed, their robes wet with blood. Children died, women wept.

'What are you doing, Helena?' her mother questioned her. 'Why are you muttering?'

Helena told a lie, saying she'd been singing, because she felt ashamed: her mother would not easily understand if she mentioned Delilah. She played outside on a narrow concrete path that ran between the rockery and the wooden fence at the bottom of the garden, where no one could see her from the windows. 'Now, here's a book,' her mother said, finding her with snails arranged in a semi-circle. Helena washed her hands, re-tied the ribbon in the hair, and sat in the sitting-room to read *Teddy's Button*.

Few people visited the house, for Helena's mother did not go in for friends. But once a year Helena was put in a taxi-cab which drove her to her grandparents on her father's side, the only grandparents she knew about. They were a grinning couple who made a fuss of her, small like her father had been, always jumping up and down at the tea table, passing plates of buttered bread to her and telling her that tea tasted nicer with sugar in it, pressing meringues and cake on her. Helena's mother always put a bowl beside Helena's bed on the nights there'd been a visit to the grandparents.

Her mother was the first teacher Helena had. In the dining-room they would sit together at the table with reading-books and copy-books and history and geography books. When she began to go to school she found herself far in advance of other children of her age, who because of that regarded her with considerable suspicion. 'Our little genius,' Miss Random used to say, meaning it cheerfully but making Helena uncomfortable because she knew she wasn't clever in the least. 'I don't consider that woman can teach at all,' her mother said after Helena had been at the school for six weeks and hadn't learnt anything new. So the dining-room lessons began again, in conjunction with the efforts of Miss Random. 'Pathetic, we have to say': her mother invested this favourite opinion with an importance and a strength, condemning not just Miss Random but also the milkman who whistled while waiting on the doorstep, and Mrs Archingford's attempt at stylish hair. Her mother employed a series of charwomen but was maddened by their chatter and ended by doing the housework herself, even though she found anything like that exceedingly irksome. She far preferred to sit in the dark study, continuing the work that had been cut short by death. In the lifetime of Helena's father her mother had assisted in the study and Helena had imagined her parents endlessly finding words in books and dissecting them on paper. Before the death conversations at mealtimes usually had to do with words. 'Fluxion?' she remembered her father saying, and when she shrugged her mother tightened her lips, her glance lingering on the shrug long after its motion had ceased. 'A most interesting derivation,' her father had supplied, and then went on to speak about the Newtonian calculus. The words he liked to bring up at mealtimes had rare meanings, sometimes five or six, but these, though worthy of record, had often to be dismissed on what he called the journey to the centre of interest. 'Fluxion, Helena, is *the rate at which a flowing motion increases its magnitude*. The Latin *fluxionem*. Now *flux*, Helena, is different. The familiar expression, *to be in a state of flux*, we know of course. But there is interestingly a variation: in mathematical terms, a drawn line is the flux of a point. You understand that, Helena? You place a dot with your pencil in your exercise-book, but you change your mind and continue the dot so that it becomes a line. With *flux* remember our pleasant word, *flow*. Remember our Latin friend, *fluere*. A flowing out, a flowing in. With *fluxion*, we have the notion of measuring, of calculation.' Food became cold while he explained, but he did not notice. All that was her memory of him.

More interesting than Helena's own household were the households round about. The death that had taken place, the honouring of the unfinished work, her mother's seriousness, were far less fascinating than the gaudy hair and dresses of Mrs Archingford or the arguments of the elderly couple in the garden of the house next door. Sometimes a son visited this couple, an unkempt figure who intrigued Helena most of all. Now and again she noticed him in the neighbourhood, usually carrying a cage with a bird in it. On one occasion he sat in the garden next door with a cage on either side of him, and Helena watched from a window while he pointed out to his mother the features of the budgerigars these cages contained. His mother poured tea and his father read a newspaper or protested, in a voice loud enough to carry to Helena's window, that the conversation about budgerigars was inane. On another occasion Helena saw the unkempt son entering Mrs Archingford's house with a cage and later leaving empty-handed, having presumably made a successful sale. She would have liked to report these incidents to her mother, but when once she referred to the elderly couple's son her mother stared at her in astonishment.

When she was twelve, Helena brought a girl called Judy Smeeth back to tea. She had asked her mother if she might, since she had herself been to tea several times with Judy Smeeth, who was considered at school to be stupid. She was stout, with spectacles, and experienced difficulty in covering her large thighs with her gymslip. When teachers drew attention to this immodest display she laughed and said she did the best she could.

Helena's mother looked at Judy Smeeth blankly, and afterwards said she didn't think she'd ever met a more unattractive person.

'She's my friend at school,' Helena explained.

'Biscuit after biscuit. No wonder she's the size she is.'

'She invited me to her house five times.'

'You mean by that, do you, Helena, that when she comes here she must make up for all those visits by grabbing as much as she can, by filling herself with biscuits and Swiss roll? Is there not a more attractive girl you could have as a compaion?'

'No, there isn't.'

'That was said roughly, Helena.'

'She's my best friend.'

Helena's mother vaguely shook her head. She never talked about friends, any more than she talked about her mother or her father. Helena didn't know if she'd had brothers or sisters, and certainly that was not a question she could ask. 'Gosh, *your mother*!' Judy Smeeth said in her amazed way. 'Didn't half give me the jitters, your mother.'

Many months later, in answer to Helena's repeated pleas, Judy Smeeth was permitted to come to the house again. On this occasion they played with a tennis ball in the garden, throwing it to one another. Unfortunately, due to a clumsy delivery of Judy's, it crossed the fence into Mrs Archingford's garden. 'Hey!' Judy cried, having climbed on to a pear tree that grew beside the fence. 'Hey, lady, could we have the ball back?'

Her plump hams, clad only partially in navy-blue school-regulation knickers, were considerably exposed as she balanced herself between the pear tree and the fence. She shouted again, endeavouring to catch the attention of Mrs Archingford, who was reading a magazine beneath her verandah.

'Hey! Yoo-hoo, lady!'

Mrs Archingford looked up and was surprised to see the beaming face of Judy Smeeth, bespectacled and crowned with frizzy hair. Hearing the sound, she had expected the tidier and less extrovert presence of the girl next door. She rose and crossed her garden.

'It's only the ball, missus. We knocked the ball a bit hard.'

'Oh, I *see*,' said Mrs Archingford. 'D'you know, dearie, for a minute I thought your appearance had changed *most* peculiarly.'

'Eh?'

Mrs Archingford smiled at Judy Smeeth, and asked her what her name was. She picked the tennis ball out of her lupins.

'Judy the name is. Smeeth.'

'Mine's Mrs Archingford. Nice to meet you, Judy. Come to tea, have you?'

'That's right. Thanks for the ball.'

'Tell you what, why don't you and what's-her-name climb over that fence and have a glass of orangeade? Like orangeade, do you?'

'Yeah. Sure.'

'Tell you what, I've got a few Danish pastries. Almond and apple. Like Danish pastries, Judy?'

'Hey, Helena, the woman wants us to go over her place.'

'No,' Helena said.

'Why not?'

'Just no.'

'Sorry, missus. Cheerio then.'

Judy descended, having first thrown the ball to Helena.

'Hey, look,' she said when she was standing on the lawn,

'that woman was on about pastries. Why couldn't we?'

'Let's go into the house.'

Her mother would have observed the incident. She would have noticed the flesh of Judy's thighs and Judy's tongue sticking out of the corner of her mouth as she struggled to retain her balance. Two of a kind, she'd probably say when Judy had gone, she and vulgar Mrs Archingford. Her lips would tighten, her whole face would look like iron.

'I don't want that girl here again, Helena,' was what in fact she did say. 'She is far from suitable.'

Helena did not protest, nor attempt to argue. She had long since learnt that you could not win an argument with her mother because her mother refused to engage in arguments. 'Gor, she don't half frighten me,' Judy Smeeth remarked after that second visit to the house. Helena had realised a long time ago that she was frightened of her also.

'The completion of your father's work,' her mother announced one day, 'is taking a great deal longer than I had anticipated, even though he left such clear and copious notes. I am unworthy and ill-equipped, but it is a task that must be undertaken. So much begun, so much advanced. Someone must surely carry it to fruition.'

'Yes,' Helena said.

'I cannot manage you and the work together, child. I do not wish you to go away to school, I prefer to have you by me. But circumstances dictate. I have no choice.'

So Helena went to a boarding-school in Sussex, and it never at that time occurred to her to wonder how the fees at this expensive place were afforded, or indeed to wonder where any money at all came from. She returned at the end of that first term to find her mother more deeply involved in the unfinished work and also somewhat changed in her manner, as if affected by the lack of a companion. Sarcasm snapped more freely from her. Her voice had become like a whip. She hates me, Helena thought, because I am a nuisance.

The house had become even more reclusive than it had been, no friend from school could ever be invited there now. The wireless, which had occasionally been listened to, was silent. The telephone was used only to order food and house-hold goods from Barker's of Kensington. Letters rarely came.

Then one afternoon just after Easter, when Helena was fifteen, a visitor arrived. She heard the doorbell from her bedroom and went to answer it because her mother wouldn't bother to. It would be an onion-seller, she thought, or one of those people who pressed the *Encyclopaedia Britannica* on you.

'Hullo,' a middle-aged man said, smiling at her from a sandy face. His short hair was sandy also. He wore a greenish suit. 'Are you Helena?'

'Yes.'

'Then I'm your uncle. One of your mother's brothers. Did you know you had uncles and an aunt?'

She shook her head. He laughed.

'I was the one who made up the games we used to play. Different games for different parts of the garden. Aren't you going to let me in?'

'I'm sorry.'

He stepped into the hall, that awful fusty hall she hated so, its grim brown curtains looping in the archway at the bottom of the stairs, it grim hallstand, the four mezzotints of Australian landscape, the stained ceiling.

She led him into the sitting-room, which was awful also, cluttered with tawdry furniture her mother didn't notice had grown ugly with wear and time, the glass-fronted cabinets full of forgotten objects, the dreary books drearily filling bookcase after bookcase.

'I heard about your father's death, Helena. I'm sorry.'

'It's ages ago now. Seven years actually. He died on my birthday.'

'I only met your father once.' He paused. 'We've often wondered about you, you know.'

'Wondered?'

'The family have. We've known of course that your mother wouldn't be short, but even so.'

He smiled his easy smile at her. It was her mother who had supplied the money there had been, Helena intuitively realised. Something about the way he had mentioned the family and had said her mother wouldn't be short had given this clear impression. Not just obsessive in his scholarship, her father had been needy also.

'I thought I'd call,' he said. 'I've written of course, but even so I just thought I'd call one of these days.'

She left him and went to knock on the study door, as her mother liked her to do. There was no reply, and when she knocked a second time her mother called out in irritation.

'An uncle has come,' Helena said.

'Who?'

'Your brother.'

'Is here, you mean?' Her mother, wearing reading glasses on a chain, which she had recently taken to, had a finger marking the point on a page at which she had been interrupted. She was seated at the desk, papers and books all around her, the desk light turned on even though it was the middle of the afternoon.

'He's downstairs.'

Her mother said nothing, nor did she display further surprise, or emotion. She stared at Helena, her scrutiny suggesting that Helena was somehow to blame for the presence of this person, which in a sense Helena was, having opened the hall door to him and permitted his entrance. Her mother drew a piece of paper towards her, at the same time releasing her finger from the place it marked. She picked up a fountain pen and then opened a drawer and found an envelope.

'Give him this,' she said, and returned to her books.

Helena carried the missive to the sitting-room. The man had pulled back an edge of the grubby lace curtain and was gazing out into the empty street. He took the envelope from Helena and opened it.

'Well, there you are,' he said when he had read the message, and sighed. He left the note behind when he went. Her mother had simply ordered him to go away. *Please me by not returning to this house,* her mother had added, signing her full name.

*

In the dormitory called the Upper Nightingale Helena retailed the excesses of her mother. How the elderly couple in the house next door had been written to and requested to make less noise. How Mrs Archingford had been snubbed. How Judy Smeeth had been forbidden the house, how her mother's sandy-faced brother had been summarily dismissed. She told how her mother had never visited the grinning little grandparents, and how they had never come to the house. She described the house—the Australian mezzotints, the fustiness, the dim lights and curtained windows, the dirtiness that was beginning to gather. In their beds, each with a blue cover, other girls of Upper Nightingale listened with delight. None of them had a mother whose tongue was like a whip. None feared a mother's sarcasm. None dreaded going home.

When she closed her eyes after lights-out Helena saw her mother in the dark study, listing words and derivations, finding new words or words no longer used, all in loving memory. 'Oh God,' pleaded Helena in those moments given up to private prayer at the beginning and end of church. 'Oh God, please make her different.'

Her mother supplied her with money so that at the end of each term she could make her way from the school by train and then across London in a taxi-cab. It was not her mother's way to stand waiting at a railway station; nor, indeed, when Helena did arrive, to answer the doorbell until it had been rung twice or three times. It was not her way to embrace Helena, but instead to frown a little as if she had forgotten that her advent was due on a particular day. 'Ah, Helena,' she would say eventually.

These holiday periods were spent by Helena in reading, cleaning the kitchen, cooking, and walking about the avenues and crescents of the neighbourhood. When she painted the shelves in her bedroom, her mother objected to the smell of paint, causing Helena to lose her temper. In awkward, adolescent rage, unreasonably passionate, she shouted at her mother. The matter was petty, she was being made petty herself, yet she could not, as she stood there on the landing, bear for a second longer her mother's pretence that the smell of paint could not possibly be coming from within the house since no workman had been employed to paint anything. There was astonishment in her mother's face when Helena said she had been painting her shelves.

'I went out and bought paint,' she cried, red-faced and furious. 'Is there something sinful in that? I went into a shop and bought paint.'

'Of course there's nothing sinful, Helena.'

'Then why are you blaming me? What harm is there in painting the shelves in my bedroom? I'm seventeen. Surely I don't have to ask permission for every single action I take?'

'I merely wondered about the smell, child.'

'You didn't wonder. You knew about the smell.'

'I do not care for that, Helena.'

'Why do you hate me?'

'Now, Helena, please don't be tiresome. Naturally I do not hate you.'

'Everyone knows you hate me. Everyone at school, even Mrs Archingford.'

'Mrs Archingford? What on earth has Mrs Archingford to do with it?'

'She is a human being, that's all.'

'No one denies that Mrs Archingford is a human being.'

'You never think of her like that.'

'You are in a tiresome mood, Helena.'

Her mother turned and went away, descending the stairs to the study. Without a show of emotion, she closed the door behind her, quietly, as if there had not been an angry scene, or as if no importance could possibly attach to anything that had been said.

In her bedroom, that afternoon, Helena wept. She lay on her bed and pressed her face into her pillow, not caring how ugly she was making herself, for who was there to see? In waves of fury that came and calmed, and then came on again, she struck at her thighs with her fists until the repeated impact hurt and she guessed there would be black and blue marks. She wished she had reached out and struck her mother as she stood at the top of the stairs. She wished she had heard the snap of her mother's neck and had seen her body lifeless, empty of venom in the hall.

Twilight was gathering when she got up and washed her face in the bathroom. She held a sponge to each puffed-up eye in turn, and then immersed her whole face in a basin of cold water, holding it there for as long as she could. Her hair was bedraggled as a result, clinging to her damp face. She looked awful, she thought, her mouth pulled down with wretchedness, but she didn't care.

She walked along the crescents and the avenues, and down by the river, finding a common she'd only visited once before.

She wished she could simply go on walking through the evening, and never return to her mother's house. She wished that some young man in a motor-car would call out to her and ask her where she was going and say jump in. She would have, she knew she would have.

Instead she turned around and found her way back to the house, her footsteps dawdling and reluctant the closer she came to it. It was ten past nine by the clock in the sitting-room. Her mother, sitting by the electric fire, did not ask where she'd been.

'He will be forgotten,' she said instead, 'if I cannot complete his work.'

She spoke in a voice so matter-of-fact, so dry and spiritless that she might have been reciting a grocery list. Vaguely, Helena had listened when once she'd been told that the work consisted of the completion of a scholarly book, an investigation into how, over centuries, the meanings of words had altered. 'Difficult as it is,' her mother vowed, still without emotion, 'it shall not go unfinished.'

Helena nodded, for some reason feeling sorry she'd been so cross. There was a silence. Her mother stared without interest at the electric fire.

'When you were little,' Helena dared to begin.

'Little?'

'A child.'

'I didn't much care for being a child.'

'I just wondered if—'

'When you don't much care for something you prefer not to dwell upon it, Helena.'

The conversation ended, as abruptly as other attempts to elicit information always had. 'Of course I shall endeavour,' her mother said. 'I intend to continue to make an effort. He would consider it pusillanimous if I did not.'

Helena tried to imagine her as a child and then as an older girl but in neither of these efforts was she successful. The only photograph in the house was of her mother and her father on their wedding day, standing against an undefined background. Her father was smiling because, Helena had always guessed, the photographer had asked him to. But her mother had not heeded this request.

'I've cooked us moussaka,' Helena said the next day, wanting to make up for her outburst. 'A kind of shepherd's pie.'

'Good heavens, child, how very ambitious of you!'

Her mother left most of it on her plate and went away to find herself a slice of bread. Some time later they spoke again of cooking. Helena said:

'There's a course you can take.'

'A course, Helena?'

She explained, her mother carefully listened. Her mother said:

'But surely you can take a more interesting course? What would be at the end of this, for instance?'

'A job, if I am lucky.'

'You would cook in some kitchen, is that it? Other people's food? Food for mouths in a hotel—or a hospital or a school? Is that it?'

'Well, perhaps.'

'I can only call it pathetic, Helena, to cook food for people in an institution.'

'Cooking is something I like.'

'I do not understand that.'

Genuinely, Helena knew, her mother didn't. The meals they ate—which as a child she had assumed to be as all meals were—had never been prepared with interest. Meat and vegetables arrived from the food department of the Kensington store and had, with as scant attention as possible, found their way on to the mahogany surface of the dining-table.

'The course doesn't cost a lot.'

'Child, it doesn't matter what it costs. Your father would be disappointed is what matters.'

There was resentment in her mother's voice. There was astonished disbelief, as if Helena had confessed to a crime. 'I'm glad he's dead,' her mother said, 'so that he need not suffer to see his only child becoming a cook.'

'I'm sorry it's such a tragedy.'

'It makes no sense, child.'

Her mother turned away, leaving the sitting-room, where the brief conversation had taken place. Helena might have told the truth: that any course, in cooking, in typing and shorthand, in nursery management, in accountancy or gardening, would have fulfilled her need, which was to close the door of the house behind her and never to return.

*

She worked in the kitchens of Veitch and Company, paper manufacturers, helping to cook canteen food for two hundred employees. Braised steak, silverside, gammon, beef, roast potatoes or mashed, peas, carrots, Brussels sprouts, broad beans in season, trifle or Black Forest gâteau, stewed plums or custard tart: they were dishes and tastes which represented a world as distant as it could possibly be from her mother's and father's. 'Helena!' a voice shouted in the kitchens one day and there was Mrs Archingford on the telephone, talking about the police and how the name of Veitch and company had been discovered on a postcard in the dark study, where Helena's mother had been found also. It was Mrs Archingford who had noticed the curtains not drawn back in the sitting-room of her mother's house, who had worried and had finally spoken to a policeman on the beat. Starvation was given as the cause of death on the death certificate: still struggling with the work in the study, Helena's mother had not bothered to eat. Not having visited her for more than three years, Helena had tried not to think about her while that time passed.

'You'll forgive me, dear, if I fail to attend the funeral,' Mrs Archingford requested. 'She didn't care for the look of me and no bones about it. Would be a trifle hypocritical, should we say?'

Helena was the only person who did attend the funeral. While a clergyman who had never known her mother spoke his conventional farewell she kept thinking of the busy kitchens of Veitch and Company—all that mound of food, while her mother had absentmindedly starved.

She cleared the house, taking a week off from the kitchens. She gathered together her mother's clothes—and her father's, which still remained—and placed them ready in the hall, to be collected by a charitable organisation. She telephoned a firm which a girl in the kitchens had told her about, which purchased the contents of empty houses. She telephoned a house agents' and put the house on the market.

She found nothing, in her mother's bedroom or the study, that belonged to the past, before the time of the marriage. There were no personal letters of any kind, no photographs privately kept, no diaries. There was dust everywhere, some of her mother's clothes were unwashed; the gas cooker in the kitchen, the refrigerator and the kitchen cupboards, were all filthy. But the order which was absent elsewhere dominated the study. The papers and notebooks dealing with lexicographic matters were arranged tidily on the long rectangular table beneath the window, and on the desk itself were two stacks of lined foolscap, one covered with the tiny handwriting of Helena's father, the other with her mother's, larger and firmer. The pages were numbered: there were seven hundred and forty-six of them. *I do not know about a title for the work,* her mother had written in the draft of a letter she had clearly been intending to dispatch to a publisher. *My husband left no instruction, but some phrase may particularly strike you from what he has written himself, and a title thus emanate. The work is now complete, in the form my husband wished it.* Had her mother put aside all other form of life as the final pages were composed, pathetically clinging to the relationship her wealth had bought? Helena wondered if she had bothered to go to bed since she had not bothered with food. She might have died of exhaustion as well as of starvation. She might have lost track of day and night, afraid to leave the study in case the long task should by some awful mischance be lost when the end was so very close. She imagined her mother struggling with sleep, weak in her body, the clarity of her bold handwriting now the most important fragment of her existence. She imagined her blinking away a sudden dizziness, and then moving in the room, one hand still on the desk to balance her progress, another reaching out into the gloom. She imagined her dead, lying on the unclean carpet.

On the foolscap pages there were underlined words, printed in capital letters: *Nympholepsy. Disembogue. Graphotype. Imagist. Macle. Rambunctious.* The precision of alphabetical order, the endlessly repeated reflections of her mother's seriousness, the intensity of her devotion to the subject out of which she and the man she'd married had spun a life together: all that lingered in the study, alive in the conjoined handwriting on the foolscap pages and the notebooks. The explanations of the paragraphs were meaningless to Helena and the burden of reading them caused her head to ache. She didn't know what to do with all the paper and the writing that had been left so purposefully behind. She didn't know what to do about the letter to a publisher, probably the last effort her mother had made. She closed the study door on all of it.

She did not sleep in the house. Each evening she returned to her two-room flat near Shepherd's Bush, where she turned the television on immediately to drive the house out of her thoughts. She sat in front of the bustling little screen with a glass of whisky and water, hoping that it, too, would help to cloud the images of the day. She longed to be back in her noisy kitchens, surrounded by different kinds of food. Sometimes, when she'd had a second and a third glass of whisky, the catalogue of the food which had become her life reminded her in a wry way of the catalogue of words in the study, one so esoteric, one so down-to-earth. Toad-in-the-hole, cabinet pudding, plaice and chips, French onion soup, trifle, jelly surprise.

One morning she arrived at the house with a cardboard carton into which she packed the foolscap pages. She carried it upstairs and placed it in a corner of the bedroom that had been her parents', with a note to the effect that it should not be taken away by the firm she had employed to take everything else. The books in the study would go, of course. In her small flat she could not possibly store them, and since they were of no possible interest to her what was the point?

Mrs Archingford kept ringing the doorbell, to ask if she would like a cup of tea or if she could help with anything. Mrs Archingford was, not unnaturally after the years that had gone by, curious. She told Helena that at Number 10 the elderly couple's son had moved in, to look after them in their now extreme old age. Birds flew about the rooms, so Mrs Archingford reported; the son was odd in the extreme.

'I dare say you'll be relieved to turn your back on the house?' she probed. 'No place for a young person, I shouldn't wonder?'

'Well, I don't want to live here, certainly.'

'My dear, however could you?'

Mrs Archingford's tone implied a most distressful childhood. She wouldn't be surprised to hear, her tone suggested, that Helena had been beaten and locked in cupboards, just to teach her. 'Most severe, your mother was, I always thought.'

'It was her way.'

'Forgive a nosy neighbour, dear, but your mother didn't look happy. Her own worst enemy, as I said one time to the gas man. "Be brisk about it," she ordered him, really sharply, you know, when the poor fellow came to read the meter. Oh, years ago it must have been, but I often remember it. Imagine that said to a meter man, when all the time he has to go careful in case of errors! And of course if he had made an error she'd be the first—'

'Actually, my mother wouldn't have noticed.'

'Why don't you slip in for a Nescafé and a Danish, eh? Smells like a morgue this hall does—oh, there, what a clumsy I am! Now, take that as unsaid, dear!'

Helena replied that it was quite all right, as indeed it was. Mrs Archingford pressed her invitation.

'What about a warming cup, though? D'you know, I've never in all my days been inside this house? Not that I expected to, I mean why should I? But really it's interesting to see it.'

Mrs Archingford poked a finger into the dust on the hall-stand, and as she did so the doorbell rang. Women from the charitable organisation had come for the clothes, so Helena was saved from having to continue the conversation about Nescafé and Danish pastries. That morning, too, a man arrived to estimate the value of the house and its contents so that death duties might be calculated. Then a man who was to purchase the contents came. He looked them over and suggested a figure far below that of the death duties man, but he pointed out that he was offering a full removal service, that in some unexplained way Helena was saving a fortune. She didn't argue. In the afternoon Mrs Archingford rang the bell again to say the estate agents Helena had chosen were not the best ones, so the woman in the Express Dairy had told her when she'd happened to allude to the matter while buying smoked ham. But Helena replied that the choice had been made.

A few days later she watched the furniture being lifted away, the books and ornaments in tea-chests, the crockery and saucepans and cutlery, even the gas cooker and the refrigerator. When everything was gone she walked about the empty rooms. Why had she not asked the sandy-haired man who had come? Why had she not made tea for him and persuaded him to tell her anything at all? Through a blur of mistiness she saw her mother as a child, playing with her brother in the garden he had mentioned. Helena stood in the centre of the room that had been her mother's bedroom and it seemed to her then that there were other children in the garden also, and voices faintly echoing. Trees and shrubs defined themselves; a house had lawns in front of it. 'Come on!' the children good-naturedly cried, but her mother didn't want to. Her mother hated playing. She hated having to laugh and run about. She hated being exposed to a jolliness that made her feel afraid. She wanted peace, and the serious silence of her room, but they always came in search of her and they always found her. Laughing and shouting, they dragged her into their games, not understanding that she felt afraid. She stammered and her face went white, but still they did not notice. Nobody listened when she tried to explain, nobody bothered.

These shadows filled her mother's bedroom. Helena knew that the playing children were a figment without reality, yet some instinct informed her that such shadows had been her mother's ghosts, that their dreaded world had accompanied her even after she had hidden from them in a suburban house where the intolerable laughter was not allowed. Companions too ordinary to comprehend her mother's different nature had left her afraid of ordinariness, and fear was what she had passed on to an ordinary daughter. Helena knew she would never marry; as long as she lived she would be afraid to bring a child into the world, and reflecting on that now she could feel within her the bitterness that had been her mother's, and even the vengeful urge to destroy that had been hers also.

Curtains had been taken down, light-shades removed. Huge patches glared from ancient wallpaper where furniture had stood or pictures hung. The bare boards echoed with Helena's footsteps. She bolted what it was necessary to bolt and saw that all the windows were secure. She banged the hall-door behind her and for the last time walked through the avenues and crescents she knew so well, on her way to drop the keys through the estate agents' letter-box. The cardboard carton containing her father's work, and her mother's achievement in completing it, remained in a corner of an empty bedroom. When the house was sold and the particulars completed the estate agents would telephone her in the kitchens at Veitch and Company to point out that this carton had been overlooked. Busy with meat or custard tart, she'd say it didn't matter, and give the instruction that it should be thrown away.

Music

At thirty-three Justin Condon was a salesman of women's undergarments, regularly traversing five counties with his samples and his order book in a Ford Fiesta. He had obediently accepted this role, agreeing when his father had suggested it to him. His father in his day had been a commercial traveller also and every Friday Justin returned to the house his father had returned to, arriving at much the same hour and occupying a room he had in childhood shared with his three brothers. His mother and his father still lived in the house, in the Dublin suburb of Terenure, and were puzzled by their youngest son because he was so unlike their other children, both physically and in other ways. His dark-haired head was neat; remote, abstracted eyes made a spherical, ordinary face seem almost mysterious. At weekends Justin took long walks on his own, all the way from Terenure to the city, to St Stephen's Green, where he sat on a seat or strolled among the flowerbeds, to Herbert Park, where he lay in the sunshine on the grass: people had seen him and remarked upon it. He had never in his life been known to listen to the commentary on a hurling match or a Gaelic match, let alone attend such an event. When he was younger he had come back one Friday with a greyhound, an animal he had proceeded to rear as a pet, apparently not realising that such creatures had been placed in the world for the purpose of racing one another. 'Ah, poor Justin's the queer old flute,' his father had more than once privately owned in

McCauley's public house. His mother wished he'd get married.

Justin's reason for remaining in his parents' house had not been shared with them, although it was a simple one: he considered that any other dwelling would be of a temporary nature and not worth the nuisance of moving to because one day he would leave, not just the suburb of Terenure but Dublin, and Ireland, for ever. He would leave his samples in the Ford Fiesta; he would leave the Ford Fiesta in a lay-by. He was not truly a purveyor of garments in imitation silk, his destiny was not the eternal entering of drapers' shops. He would escape as others had escaped before him; James Joyce he thought of particularly in this respect, and Gauguin. He liked the photograph of James Joyce in the broad-brimmed black hat, with the black coat reaching to his ankles; Gauguin had been a businessman. When Joyce had left Ireland he'd had to borrow a pair of boots. Later he'd tried to sell tweed to the Italians.

Dwelling on such matters, Justin watched the light of a May morning from a bed in Co. Waterford. There wasn't much to see: streaks of brightness along the edges of the drawn curtains, the ceiling of the bedroom mistily illuminated through rosy fabric. A man called Fahy, travelling in fertilisers, had assured him that when he stayed in this house he occupied the bed of Mrs Keane, its widowed landlady. When Garda Foley, who lodged on a more permanent basis in the house, drank his eleven o'clock Bournville and stated his intention of retiring for the night, Fahy would rise from the kitchen table also, saying he'd had a long day. He would mount the stairs a few paces behind Garda Foley and in full view of the policeman would enter the bedroom known as the 'overnight room' because it was set aside by Mrs Keane for her casual trade among commercial travellers. Garda Foley, long since retired from the force, a lifelong bachelor, was a moral presence in Mrs Keane's house, a man who could be relied upon by Canon Tighe or Father Reedy, selflessly working behind the scenes for the Legion of Mary and organising the tug of war at the Nore Fête every Whit. Fahy said he gave him a quarter of an hour and then listened on the landing to the depth of his snoring. He smoked a final cigarette in the overnight bedroom, taking a good ten minutes over it, before listening again at the panels of Garda Foley's door. If the rhythm of sleep had not altered, he made his way to the bed of Mrs Keane.

Justin supposed it was true. With some precision, Fahy had described the body of the widow, a woman of fifteen stone and in her sixty-first year. The hair that was grey about her head sprouted blackly and abundantly, according to the traveller in fertilisers, on other areas of her. Buttocks and stomach were vast; Hail Marys were repeated after sinning.

In the overnight room Justin imagined without pleasure the scenes Fahy described. Fahy was a little runt of a Dublin man, married with five or six children, always sticking his elbow into you to make a point. Sometimes in his ramblings he mentioned Thomasina MacCarthy, the dentist, who was the only other lodger in Mrs Keane's house. She had a great notion of Justin, Fahy insisted, the implication being that Justin could easily arrive at the same arrangement with Thomasina MacCarthy as he himself had arrived at with Mrs Keane. No man was an island was a repeated observation of Fahy's.

Justin rose in order to break his train of thought, and crossed to the window. He drew back the curtains and stood in his pyjamas looking out at the line of houses across the street. No blind had yet been released, no curtain or shutter opened. A cat crept along the grey pavement, interested in the empty bottles outside each door. The houses themselves were colour-washed in pink or cream, in yellow, grey or blue, their hall-doors painted in some contrasting shade, or grained. The street was wide, with lamp-posts between every second house, and a single visible telegraph pole. Just visible also, where the street met another as it curved away to the left, was Hayes's shop, which traded in newspapers, tobacco and confectionery. The sight of it, with its hanging *Players Please* sign, reminded Justin that he was in need of a cigarette himself. He left the window and crossed to the bedside table.

Inhaling, he slipped out of his pyjamas and dressed himself in shirt and trousers, preparatory to making his way to Mrs Keane's bathroom. Still intent on keeping Fahy's reports and innuendoes at bay, he dwelt upon his earliest memory, which was the leg of a chair. That same chair was still in the house in Terenure and he often found himself looking at it, his eye travelling down one particular leg, to the rings cut into the timber, the varnish worn partially away. With three brothers and three sisters, he had grown up the baby of the family, surrounded by people who shouted more than he did, who were for ever arguing and snatching. At school the textbooks were inkstained and dirty, the blackboards so pitted you could hardly read the chalk marks on them, the desk-tops slashed with messages and initials. 'Come here and I'll show you,' Sha McNamara used to whisper; and forcibly he'd insist, no choice about it, on displaying the promise of his sexuality. Ikey Breen had been paid a threepenny piece by a woman under cover of darkness in the Stella Cinema. All Riordan's jokes had to do with excrement.

Justin shaved in Mrs Keane's bathroom, hurrying to finish before Garda Foley came rattling at the door. Long before he began to go to school he remembered his father driving away from the house in Terenure on a Monday morning. His father had taught him how to strike a match, and would let him hold it over the tobacco in his pipe while he sucked at the smoke, making a bubbling noise. His father used to take him on to his knee and ask him if he'd been a good boy, but Justin always had to turn his head away because of the whiff on his father's breath. The stench of stout, his mother said it was, bottle after bottle of stout that made the whole house stink like a brewery. He associated his father particularly with Sundays, with leading the family into mass, with saying he was starving on the walk home. Sunday dinner was different from ordinary dinner, always meat and a pudding. Afterwards his father had his bath, with the door of the bathroom open so that he could listen to whatever sporting commentary there was on the radio. Justin's sisters were forbidden to go upstairs at this time in case they'd catch a glimpse from the landing. His brothers roller-skated in the yard.

Justin washed the remains of the shaving foam from his face. It was on a Sunday that his Aunt Roche had first put a record on her gramophone: John Count McCormack singing *The Rose of Tralee*. After that he had begun to visit her sitting-room regularly, a room full of ferns in pots and framed embroideries. It was she and Father Finn who had given him faith in himself and in his musical aptitude, who hadn't laughed when he'd hinted that Mahler was his hero.

He dried his face and left the bathroom. Somewhere in the house he could hear the heavy tread of Garda Foley. The smell of frying rashers and the chatty voice of a radio disc-jockey drifted from the kitchen.

'Mr Condon!' called Thomasina MacCarthy. 'Mr Condon, Mrs Keane has the breakfast ready.'

*

In her tiny sitting-room she dusted the ornaments on the mantelpiece, the brass gondola, the tuskless elephants, the row of trinket containers, the framed photograph of Justin as a child, specially taken by Mr Boland the insurance man, whose hobby was photography. She was not really his aunt: when he was six he had stood by the railings of her front garden, staring at her while she cut the grass. 'What's your name?' she'd asked, and he'd said it was Justin Condon. 'Ah now, isn't that a great name?' She'd smiled at him, knowing he was shy. Her face had been damp with perspiration due to the exertion of pushing the lawnmower. He had watched her closely while she took her glasses off and wiped them on her apron.

She was a slight, frail woman of seventy-nine, with thin hands, and hair the colour of the ashes she now carried in a cardboard box from her sitting-room. She moved slowly, suffering a little from arthritis in one of her knees and in her arms. 'I think I have some Mi-Wadi,' she'd said that first day. 'D'you like Mi-Wadi lemonade, Justin?'

He had followed her into the house and in the kitchen she had poured an inch or two of Mi-Wadi into two glasses and filled them with water from the cold tap. She'd found some biscuits, raspberry wafers she'd bought for the weekend. He had three brothers and three sisters, he said; his father was in business and was never at home during the week. When he was older he told her about the Christian Brothers' school, the white-painted windows and the rowdy, concrete playground. He said that Brother Walsh had picked him out as someone who was useless.

The Sunday when she'd wound up the gramophone and put on the record of John Count McCormack was a special memory for her because she always thought of the occasion as marking the beginning of his interest in music. Later she had played him her selected arias from *La Traviata* and *Carmen* and *Il Trovatore*—on the same Sunday in September when he had posed for Mr Boland in the garden. He'd had to stand in front of the hydrangea bush but Mr Boland hadn't been happy with that so he'd had to sit on a chair on the front-door step. In the end the photograph had been taken against the rose trellis.

'Well, that's disgraceful!' Father Finn had said on another Sunday, when he heard how a Christian Brother had described the child as useless.

*

'That's a right bit of bacon,' Garda Foley complimented Mrs Keane. 'Isn't bacon in this country a greatly improved commodity?'

Neat as a napkin across the table from him, Thomasina MacCarthy smiled shyly at Justin, as if they shared some private opinion. Justin pretended not to notice. He bent his head over the bacon on his plate, over the slices of black pudding and the fried bread and the egg. Garda Foley would think Stravinsky was the name of a race-horse, and so would Mrs Keane. 'Ah, sure, I knew all right,' Thomasina MacCarthy would protest, lying because she couldn't help herself. Her two prominent front teeth were like an advertisement for her trade; her eyes were prominent also, her nose and chin slight. She wore clothes in pastel shades, pale blues and pinks and greens. Like himself, she returned every weekend to Dublin, to stay with her parents.

'It's a sign of the advance the country has made,' continued Garda Foley, 'the way the bacon is better these days.'

'The price of it would murder you,' Mrs Keane reminded him.

He nodded and continued to nod, dwelling on that. 'Well, isn't it another sign in that case,' he suggested eventually, 'the way the people would have the means for it?'

'Nearly a pound a pound. Sure, it's a holy disgrace.'

Mrs Keane's dining-room was heavy with furniture: rexine-covered chairs, a large ornate sideboard, a great mahogany dining-table, wax fruit on occasional tables, armchairs with antimacassars, pictures of forest scenes. Bottles of sauce stood on the sideboard, and empty decanters, and a pile of table-mats. Shells decorated the mantelpiece, and small cups and saucers, gifts from Tramore and Youghal.

'Well, it's the same way that's in it with everything.' The policeman's delivery of this statement was ponderous, the words punctuated by the munching of his jaws. He was a match for Mrs Keane in size, his rounded hill of a stomach tightly engaging the buttons of his waistcoat. A bulbous nose was set carelessly in a crimson countenance, short hair was as spiky as a hedgehog's.

'Wouldn't you say the prices is shocking?' Mrs Keane enquired of Thomasina MacCarthy, in a voice that insisted women knew best.

'Ah, they are of course.'

Garda Foley turned to Justin, a piece of egg, already dipped in mustard, on the end of his fork. 'Have they inflation beat? Fahy was here last week and said inflation was beat.'

Justin shook his head. He didn't know, he said. He'd heard somewhere that, far from being defeated, inflation was gaining ground.

'Has your father a word to say on it? I remember a thing about your father when he used to stay with us here. He had a keen sense of politics.'

'I don't think I heard him mention inflation.'

'Give him a message from me, will you? Tell him Garda Foley was asking for him.'

'I will of course.'

'Oh, Mr Condon, I meant to tell you: I saw you in Stephen's Green on Sunday.' Thomasina MacCarthy's two large teeth announced interest in him; the eyes blinked rapidly. Her pastel-green suit was trim on her trim form; he imagined her fingers, trim also, in a patient's mouth.

'I'm often in Stephen's Green.'

'I thought you lived in Terenure, Mr Condon.'

'I walk into the city.'

'God, I love walking.'

The fingers, in a hurry, would layer a gum with cotton-wool; sharply, they'd jab a hypodermic needle home. She'd talk to you when your mouth was full of implements; she'd tell you to have a wash-out with the pink stuff, and say she was nearly finished. Fahy said she had an eye on a bungalow out on the Cappoquin road. 'Wouldn't the two of you be snug in a bed there?' Fahy had said.

'I have a few friends coming in, Saturday fortnight. Would you care to join us, Mr Condon?'

He felt a tightening in the atmosphere. Both Garda Foley and Mrs Keane were aware of the implication of what had just been said. An attempt was being made to develop the casual acquaintanceship that existed between Justin and the dentist in Mrs Keane's house; the relationship was to be extended to Dublin. Fahy would be told; so would Canon Tighe and Father Reedy. 'Sure, if some girl like Thomasina MacCarthy doesn't do something about it that fellow'll be a bachelor at seventy': he could hear Mrs Keane saying that, or his father or his mother. Fahy would put it differently.

'Saturday fortnight?'

'About a quarter to eight. You know Clontarf? 21 Dunlow Road. Just a few friends and a bit of dancing.'

'I don't dance at all.'

'I'm not much at it myself.'

Garda Foley and Mrs Keane were pleased. They had enjoyed this flutter of excitement. They would think about the party at 21 Dunlow Road, and discuss it. They would be unpleasantly agog after it had taken place.

'21 Dunlow Road,' Thomasina MacCarthy repeated, writing it clearly on a piece of paper she'd found in her handbag.

'You might ask him that,' requested Garda Foley. 'Does he consider inflation beat? If there's one man in Ireland would know, it's your father.'

Justin nodded again, finishing the fried food on his plate. He promised to discuss the matter with his father and to obtain his father's opinion. He wouldn't turn up at 21 Dunlow Road, he said to himself. When he next spent a night at Mrs Keane's he'd say he'd lost the address.

*

When he was ten she had asked him if he'd like to learn how to play the piano and when he'd said yes she'd arranged for Father Finn to give him lessons in her sitting-room. She had paid for them and when she'd asked him not to tell his family he had eagerly agreed because apparently his family would have laughed at the idea of a boy playing a musical instrument. 'It's a great thing for him,' Father Finn later reported. 'And hasn't he a rare aptitude for it?' In the circumstances Father Finn wasn't averse to keeping the knowledge of the lessons from the Condons, and after a while he refused to accept any fee for the tuition. 'Well, that's one thing at any rate he's not useless at,' he remarked, later still.

God had arranged it, she often thought during those years that went by. God had arranged for the child to come by her gate that first afternoon, and for the music she played him on her gramophone to delight him. God had arranged a way for the three of them, Father Finn and herself and Justin. When the Condons had eventually discovered about the piano lessons they'd been bewildered but not cross, mainly because it was Father Finn who was giving them. And as well as the lessons every Wednesday Father Finn began to come round on Sunday afternoons and they all three listened to John Count McCormack or the operatic arias. It was a natural thing for the priest to do since everyone knew now of the musical aptitude of Justin Condon and how it needed to be fostered and encouraged.

*

The sun warmed his exposed chest; beside him his shirt was laid out on the grass; his eyes were closed. Faintly the sound of the river by which he lay penetrated his sleep.

He dreamed of the queen who had inspired the choral symphony he was attempting to write. In his dream she trailed wolfhounds on leather thongs through her garden and listened to the spirits of the otherworld. From among them one took visible form: a young girl rose from the mists and the flowers and warned the queen of her folly.

Two flies tormented Justin's plump chin. Their tickling silenced music that had the resonance of music composed by Mahler. He smacked at his face but already the flies had gone.

The symphony told of a journey from the royal palaces in the West to the territory of Cúchulainn in Ulster. The queen's great army, fattened with the soldiers of her allies, with the long line of camp followers, with druids and jesters, storytellers, soothsayers, military men and servitors, travelled into heroic battle, while the mystical hero awaited their arrival. Sometimes, on Saturdays, Justin hired a piano cubicle in a music shop and spent the morning there, advancing his composition. Shortly after the death of Father Finn the piano in his Aunt Roche's sitting-room had gone hopelessly out of tune and apparently couldn't be much improved.

Justin reached for his shirt. When he had buttoned it he neatly tightened the knot of his tie. Since breakfast-time in Mrs Keane's dining-room he had visited sixteen drapers in seven different towns. He had O'Leary's and Callaghan's to call on yet, and then that would be that for the day. He drove on and did the business he had to do. He spent the night in Dungarvan in a room above a fish-and-chip café. The smell of the frying wafted up and through his open window. From his bed he listened to people talking about the film they had been to, and to a drunk man who proclaimed that he intended to stand no nonsense from his wife. He fell asleep at half-past eleven and dreamed of the journey in his symphony, of the queen in her magnificence, and the chorus of otherworld spirits.

'Wait now till I get the brother,' said Mr McGurk, the joint proprietor of McGurk's Arcade, the following day. He left the shop and called up through the house. In a moment the older Mr McGurk appeared.

Justin's samples were laid out on the counter. Some were familiar to the McGurks and presented no problem when it came to deciding the size of the order. Others, lines that were new this spring, had to be considered with care.

'Would a woman of this area dress herself in that?' enquired the younger Mr McGurk, poking at a black garment trimmed flimsily with lace of the same colour.

'I don't know would she.'

'The gusset is strong,' Justin pointed out, since it said so on his sales sheet. 'A man-made fibre.'

'It isn't the gusset would sell that article,' replied the older Mr McGurk. 'What I'm thinking is, is it too ritzy for this area?'

'Will we call down Eileen?' suggested his brother.

'I'd say we would.'

Eileen, wife of the older Mr McGurk, was summoned from the house. She picked up the garment in question and meticulously examined it.

'Would you wear it?' her husband demanded.

'I would in a shade of peach. Does it come in a peach?'

Justin said it did, and in a shade of coffee.

'Order it in the peach,' advised Mrs McGurk. 'Black's not the tone for stuff the like of that.'

'Too ritzy,' agreed her husband. 'I'm just after saying it.'

'How's your father?' Mrs McGurk asked Justin.

'He's grand.'

'Has he still got the hilarious way with him?'

Justin replied that he supposed his father had. One after the other, the McGurk brothers said they'd never laughed at any traveller's jokes the way they'd laughed at Justin's father's. Justin could feel them thinking that he himself wasn't half the man his father was, that he didn't enter into the spirit of things, that all he seemed concerned with was writing down orders in his book. 'I'll tell you a thing about Thomasina MacCarthy,' Fahy had said. 'She has a notion of making a man of you. There's women like that around.'

He left the McGurks' shop and drove out to the estuary. He walked by the green, seaweedy water, wondering if Mahler would have composed a note if he'd been incarcerated in a bungalow on the Cappoquin road, listening every night to talk about cavity linings.

*

'Now, there never was,' she remembered Father Finn saying when Justin was thirteen, 'a great man of music that came out of Ireland.'

He made the pronouncement while eating a slice of buttered toast she had prepared for him. She had loved doing that, toasting the bread and spreading the butter on it, arranging blackcurrant jam in a glass dish. Blackcurrant was Father Finn's favourite, raspberry was Justin's.

'We had singers and harpists. We had all classes of instrumentalists. We have a proud tradition, but we never yet had a composer that could rank with the Germans. To this day,

Justin, we have to turn to Germany for musical composition.'

Pouring tea for both of them, she mentioned Italy and the priest agreed that the Italians had made a contribution. He told the story of Puccini's life. He referred to the burden of a musical gift and to the reward it brought in time. 'A precious freedom of the spirit. A most glorious thing.'

She had delighted in listening to him. She was never happier than on those Sunday afternoons when he and Justin sat together by her fire or on the Wednesdays when she made a cup of tea after the piano lesson. No admission of affection had ever been made by the priest or by herself; no admission could be. Until Justin arrived in her life there had been no way of creating a relationship that went beyond that of priest and parishioner.

'There's a little thing Justin composed for me,' Father Finn said one Sunday. 'A short little piece, but I'd say it displayed promise.'

*

'We had a complaint, Mr Condon,' Miss Murphy reported in Castlemartyr. 'We had this slip brought back to us after it fell into holes.'

Only Thomasina MacCarthy and Miss Murphy called him Mr Condon, Thomasina MacCarthy because any other mode of address might have sounded forward, Miss Murphy for reasons he had never been able to fathom.

'Would it be the way it was washed, Miss Murphy? Was it put into a machine?'

'Oh, it would have been washed all right, Mr Condon. Naturally you'd expect it to have been washed.'

'No, I mean in a machine though. Or maybe it got boiled in error. It's all tinged with blue, look. Some blue garment has run into it.'

'It would save an argument with the customer, Mr Condon, if you replaced it. It's good for business when something gets replaced.'

Justin made a note in his order book and said that Miss Murphy would have a replacement within a fortnight. He had a new line he wanted to show her, he added, and displayed for her the sample he had displayed for fifty-seven other drapers, including the McGurks, since he'd left Dublin. Miss Murphy picked it up gingerly.

'It comes in a peach, Miss Murphy, and a coffee. The gusset is guaranteed sturdy. Man-made fibre.'

'I never saw that type of cut before.'

'It's the fashion in Dublin.'

Miss Murphy shook her head. She folded the piece of clothing in a professional manner and Justin returned it to the suitcase in which he carried his samples. Miss Murphy ordered a supply of summer vests and made arrangements to replenish her stock of first-communion stockings. 'Is your father fit?' she asked as Justin closed his order book, and for the first time since he had known Miss Murphy it idly occurred to him that she and his father might have had the same relationship as Fahy claimed to have with Mrs Keane. Miss Murphy was elderly now, a woman with a face like an arrow, with spectacles on a chain. Once she might have been pretty; it was odd that she had never married.

'He's grand,' Justin said.

'Remember me to him, will you?'

Her tone was different from Garda Foley's when he mentioned Justin's father, different from the McGurks' and all the other drapers'. Had there always been a hint of bitterness in Miss Murphy's voice when she sent this message to his father? He looked up from the suitcase he was fastening and found her eyes upon him. They held his own until he felt embarrassed.

He had noticed before that there was a similarity between his father and Fahy. They were both small men, rotund, bald-headed, pink-skinned, given to banter. He snapped the clasps on his suitcase and Miss Murphy turned away to attend another customer.

*

She made a cake, the banana cake he liked. Usually she wrapped in tin-foil what remained of it after their Sunday tea and he took it away to eat during the week, on his travels. She enjoyed thinking of him eating the cake, sitting out in the sunshine as he liked to do, in some quiet place.

Slowly she chopped up two bananas. He had belonged to them as he never had to his parents. On Sunday afternoons and again on Wednesdays they had been a family. She left the kitchen and in her sitting-room she delicately placed the needle on the same worn record of John Count McCormack singing *The Rose of Tralee*. Soon she would die, as the old priest had, six months ago. She would fall down, or she would die in her sleep. And before any of it happened she might become muzzy in her thoughts, unable to explain to Justin Condon and properly to ask for his forgiveness. Father Finn had known also in the end, death banishing his illusions. 'We did a terrible thing,' the old priest had said, sending for her specially.

The record came to an end and she sat there for a moment longer, listening to the scratchy sound of the needle. She had once, long before the child had come into her life, tried to become Father Finn's housekeeper. 'Ah no, no,' he had murmured, gently rejecting her because it wouldn't have done.

*

'And how were things in West Waterford?' his father enquired.

'Has Joe Bolger retired from Merrick's?'

Glistening, as if he had just scrubbed his face with a nailbrush, Mr Condon held a glass of whiskey in his right hand. As well as his face, the backs of his hands glistened, as did his glasses, his even false teeth, the dome of his hairless head. Justin imagined him with Miss Murphy in her shop, telling a joke, driving out into the country with Miss Murphy when it was dark, the way Fahy said he'd had to with some woman in Claremorris before he got going with Mrs Keane.

'I didn't see Joe Bolger,' Justin said. 'I think maybe he's retired.'

'I always liked West Waterford.'

They were in the sitting-room. His father was standing in front of a coal fire that was too hot for the time of year. In the kitchen Justin's mother was frying their evening meal. Recently Mr Condon had taken to giving himself a glass of whiskey at a quarter to six in the evening instead of making his usual journey to McCauley's at the corner. When he'd eaten his food he returned to the sitting-room and occupied the chair nearest the television, pouring himself another glass of whiskey at a quarter past seven. Justin's mother said the whiskey was bad for him but he said it was doctor's orders. 'It's ready for you,' she shouted from the kitchen, reminding Justin of Thomasina MacCarthy calling out in Mrs Keane's that the breakfast was ready.

'I could eat an elephant,' said Mr Condon, swallowing the last of his whiskey.

Between them, his brothers and sisters had brought thirty-seven children into existence: Justin often thought of that. At Christmas they all crowded into the house, shouting and quarrelling and reminding Justin of what the house had been like in his childhood. On Saturdays there were visits from one or another of those families, and on Sundays also.

'There was a time I was below in Dungarvan,' Mr Condon recalled in the kitchen, 'the day Golden Miller won at Fairyhouse. Joe Bolger was footless behind the counter.'

Mrs Condon cut slices of loaf bread, and pushed the butter past her husband in Justin's direction. Mr Condon had never been known to pass anyone anything.

'God, you'd have died laughing.' As if to lend greater verisimilitude to this claim, Mr Condon laughed rumbustiously himself, exposing egg and bread partially chewed. 'He was handing out skeins of wool and not charging for it. He gave a gross of safety-pins to a farmer's wife by the name of Mrs Quinn. "Sure, aren't they always handy," he said, "in case you'd have something falling down?"'

Mrs Condon, who did not always care for her husband's humour, asked what the weather had been like down the country. Justin replied that it had been fine.

'There was another time,' Mr Condon went on, 'when the boys in the digs took poor Joe's clothes when he was asleep in bed. I didn't see it myself but didn't he have to descend the stairs with the sheets on him?'

'It rained on Wednesday,' Mrs Condon said. 'It didn't cease the whole day.'

'There wasn't a drop down the country.'

'Well, isn't that strange?'

'It's often that way.'

'They say it's settled in Dublin for the weekend.'

Mrs Condon was as thin as his Aunt Roche, with a worried look that Justin couldn't remember her ever having been without. She wore flowered overalls even when she went shopping, beneath her black coat.

'The wildest lads in West Waterford was in Joe Bolger's digs,' continued Mr Condon. 'There wasn't a trick they didn't have knowledge of.'

Justin, who had heard about these exploits in West Waterford before, nodded. Mrs Condon poured more tea.

'They went into the Bay Hotel one night when a pile of boxes
containing young chicks had just come off the bus. Your men
had them released in the hall before anyone could lift a hand.
They had them flying up and down the stairs and into the
dining-room, knocking down the sauce bottles. The next thing
is, didn't they have them fluttering about the bedrooms?'

'You told us, Ger,' Mrs Condon said.

'I did of course. Didn't I come back that Friday and go
through the whole thing? It could kill you stone dead to wake up
in your bedroom and find chickens squawking all over you.'

'It must have been unpleasant certainly.'

'Well, that's West Waterford for you. Are you still telling that
story, Justin?'

Justin nodded again. He wouldn't have known how to begin
telling such a story, and he had never attempted to. He thought
about the symphony, hearing the theme that the queen and her
consort in their palace bed had inspired. A slow movement,
lyrical in tone.

'Is that girl still stopping at Mrs Keane's?' his mother
enquired. 'The dentist.'

He'd once mentioned Thomasina MacCarthy in order to fill
a gap in some conversation; he wished he hadn't because his
mother had somehow sensed his apprehension and appeared
to have mistaken it for interest.

'Yes, she's still there.'

'Sounds a nice type of girl.'

Fortunately, Mr Condon had begun to laugh in anticipation
of some further antics on the part of the lodgers in Joe Bolger's
digs. When his laughter ceased he retailed them, as he had
many times done in the past. Obediently Justin and his mother
laughed in turn.

'There was a curate from Milecross,' Mr Condon said, 'a Father Dolan. Well, the lads in the digs had him tied in knots.'

'You told us about Father Dolan, Ger.'

'He was down at his tea and when he went upstairs there wasn't a stick of furniture left in the room. They had the bed and the wardrobe carried out, and the pictures off the walls. They took the wash-stand, and the Holy Mother off of the mantelpiece. The poor man thought he'd gone insane.'

The music was different now: brassy and wild as the journey across Ireland began. While it echoed, Justin saw for a moment his favourite picture of James Joyce, in the broad-brimmed hat and the long black coat. He wondered what Mahler had been like.

'Another time those eejits drew a sideboard across the entrance to the Gents, the day of Slip Hennessy's wedding. There wasn't a man in the place knew what to do with himself.' Mr Condon threw his head back and laughed, permitting his teeth to move about in his open mouth. When he'd finished, Mrs Condon said:

'Didn't you say the dentist was a Dublin girl?'

'I think she is.'

'It's nice she's at Mrs Keane's'

He did not reply. His father said again that you'd have died laughing, and his mother rose from the table. Justin began to gather up the dishes, resolving that tomorrow he would spend the morning in the piano cubicle of the music shop. Afterwards he'd walk out to Herbert Park and lie in the sun, with a new bit of music lingering the way it always did.

*

On Sunday afternoon he told her about his time in West Waterford and East Cork, about the McGurk brothers and all the other drapers he had visited. He mentioned Garda Foley and Mrs Keane and Miss Murphy. He spoke of Thomasina MacCarthy's party at 21 Dunlow Road but he didn't go into details and he didn't retail what had passed through his mind concerning any of these people. He'd spent four hours yesterday in the piano cubicle, he said, and he'd lain down in Herbert Park.

'It's nice to get the sun,' she said, offering him a piece of the banana cake.

'Sure, we don't get enough of it.'

She nodded and then, to his astonishment, she spoke of his simplicity. It was that, she said, that the priest and she should have pointed out to him; it was that that was notable.

He sipped his tea, wondering if she was rambling in her elderliness. She never had done so before, she'd always been as sharp as a needle.

'Simplicity?' he said. 'Are you feeling yourself?'

'Father Finn liked to come here on a Sunday. He liked it particularly and I liked it myself. With the piano lessons on a Wednesday it was the same.'

He frowned, then nodded. He'd watched the tennis-players in Herbert Park, he said, after it had become too chilly to go on lying on the grass. It would be a long time yet, he said, before the symphony was complete; there'd be years in the piano cubicle and years lying out in the sun, letting the music run through his head. It was no good being in a hurry; you knew instinctively the pace that suited you.

'You were like a child to us all those years, Justin.'

'Ah, sure, it was enjoyable all round.'

He reached for another slice of cake. His tea-cup was empty and he wondered why she didn't fill it. He looked at her closely and saw that she had begun to weep, something she had never done in his presence before.

'My father was telling us last night,' he said, 'about a time some lads let a crate of chickens loose in the Bay Hotel, Dungarvan.'

He spoke in desperation: he wanted to stop her talking about Father Finn and about his own simplicity, how he'd been a child to them all those years. Her voice had a peculiar note in it.

'It's gone now,' he said, 'the old Bay Hotel.'

He knew she had no interest in a hotel she'd never seen nor heard of before; why should she have? Yet he went on talking about it, about the barricading of the Gents at the time of Slip Hennessy's wedding, and the removal of the furniture from Father Dolan's bedroom while he was having his tea. He spoke hurriedly, his words tumbling and juddering. Urgently they rushed from him, preventing her from speaking. But when he paused for breath she said:

'We damaged you between us, Justin. We took advantage of your simplicity.'

'Ah no, no.'

Again he spoke swiftly, endeavouring to convey through his agitation that he did not want to hear; that once she had spoken, the words could not be undone. For a long time now he had known he could play the piano in a tidy, racy way, that possibly he possessed no greater gift. It was his longing to walk away from his Ford Fiesta, from his parents' house and from Ireland, that made him different from his father, not his modest musical aptitude. And yet his fantasy sprang from a lingering sliver of hope, from words that had once been spoken in his Aunt Roche's sitting-room. He had clutched at the straw they had offered him and it had kept him going. He had played his part, not knowing what it was, offering them a straw also: for the first time, he realised that.

'Father Finn couldn't die guilty,' she said. 'No more than I can. He asked me to tell you the truth before he went, Justin, and I have to do that. No harm or damage was ever intended.'

Justin put down his tea-cup and saucer on a round glass-topped table as familiar to him as any piece of furniture in his parents' house. She was right to have mentioned his simplicity: she might as easily have called him a fool. He felt ashamed of being in the room with her since she knew so much about his foolishness; she might even have guessed that he had seen himself in the broad-brimmed hat and the long black overcoat, or on an island with Gauguin's dark-skinned girls.

'I'd have deprived you of the piano and the gramophone if I'd sent you away.'

He stared at her. She should have sent him away all the same, she said, she should have sent him off to play with other children; and in time she should have urged him to embark on a friendship with a girl.

He stood up. 'That's a nice little piece you composed for me,' Father Finn had said, and he saw again the priest's face as he spoke those words, seeing it differently now. He saw his Aunt Roche's differently also, with anxiety twitching in it as the priest murmured his praise and his encouragement, both of them fearful for the safety of their Wednesday and Sunday afternoons.

'Don't go, Justin. Don't go.'

But there was no point in staying, any more than there was a point in saying he would end by marrying Thomasina MacCarthy. His Aunt Roche, who had seemed to understand so much, wouldn't understand that such things happened when you had nothing to keep you going. He had thought the world of her, just as he had of Father Finn, but she wouldn't understand if he said that in time he would acquire his father's bonhomie, even his popularity with the drapers of the provinces. A woman like Miss Murphy might enter his life, or a woman like Mrs Keane.

He did not look again at the frail presence in the room he had come to know so well. She cried out at him, only repeating that she'd had to tell the truth, that the truth was more important than anything. She caught at the sleeve of his jacket, begging him to forgive her for the past. He pushed her hand away, and swore at her before he went.

Two More Gallants

You will not, I believe, find either Lenehan or Corley still parading the streets of Dublin, but often in the early evening a man called Heffernan may be found raising a glass of Paddy in Toner's public house; and FitzPatrick, on his bicycle, every working day makes the journey across the city, from Ranelagh to the offices of McGibbon, Tait & FitzPatrick, solicitors and commissioners for oaths. It is on his doctor's advice that he employs this mode of transport. It is against the advice of *his* that Heffernan continues to indulge himself in Toner's. The two men no longer know one another. They do not meet and, in order to avoid a confrontation, each has been known to cross a street.

Thirty or so years ago, when I first knew Heffernan and FitzPatrick, the relationship was different. The pair were closely attached, Heffernan the mentor, FitzPatrick ready with a laugh. All three of us were students, but Heffernan, a Kilkenny man, was different in the sense that he had been a student for as long as anyone could remember. The College porters said they recalled his presence over fifteen years and, though given to exaggeration, they may well have been accurate in that: certainly Heffernan was well over thirty, a small ferrety man, swift to take offence.

FitzPatrick was bigger and more amiable. An easy smile perpetually creased the bland ham of his face, causing people to believe, quite incorrectly, that he was stupid. His mouse-coloured hair was kept short enough not to require a parting, his eyes reflected so profound a degree of laziness that people occasionally professed surprise to find them open. Heffernan favoured pin-striped suits, FitzPatrick a commodious blue blazer. They drank in Kehoe's in Anne Street.

'He is one of those chancers,' Heffernan said, 'we could do without.'

'Oh, a right old bollocks,' agreed FitzPatrick.'

' "Well, Mr Heffernan," ' he says, ' "I see you are still with us." '

'As though you might be dead.'

'If he had his way.'

In the snug of Kehoe's they spoke of Heffernan's *bête noire*, the aged Professor Flacks, a man from the North of Ireland.

' "I see you are still with us," ' Heffernan repeated. 'Did you ever hear the beat of that?'

'Sure, Flacks is senile.'

'The mots in the lecture giggle when he says it.'

'Oh, an ignorant bloody crowd.'

Heffernan became meditative. Slowly he lit a Sweet Afton. He was supported in his continuing studentship by the legacy left to him for that purpose by an uncle in Kilkenny, funds which would cease when he was a student no longer. He kept that tragedy at bay by regularly failing the Little-go examination, a test of proficiency in general studies to which all students were obliged to submit themselves.

'A fellow came up to me this morning,' he said now, 'a right eejit from Monasterevin. Was I looking for grinds in Little-go Logic? Five shillings an hour.'

FitzPatrick laughed. He lifted his glass of stout and drank from it, imposing on his upper lip a moustache of foam which was permitted to remain there.

'A minion of Flacks's,' Heffernan continued. 'A Flacks boy and no mistake, I said to myself.'

'You can tell them a mile off.'

' "I know your father," I said to him. "Doesn't he deliver milk?" Well, he went the colour of a sunset. "Avoid conversation with Flacks," I told him. "He drove a wife and two sisters insane." '

'Did your man say anything?'

'Nothing, only "Cripes".'

'Oh, Flacks is definitely peculiar,' FitzPatrick agreed.

In point of fact, at that time FitzPatrick had never met Professor Flacks. It was his laziness that caused him to converse in a manner which suggested he had, and it was his laziness also which prevented him from noticing the intensity of Heffernan's grievance. Heffernan hated Professor Flacks with a fervour, but in his vague and unquestioning way FitzPatrick assumed that the old professor was no more than a passing thorn in his friend's flesh, a nuisance that could be exorcised by means of complaint and abuse. Heffernan's pride did not at that time appear to play a part; and FitzPatrick, who knew his friend as well as anyone did, would not have designated him as a possessor of that quality to an unusual degree. The opposite was rather implied by the nature of his upkeep and his efforts not to succeed in the Little-go examination. But pride, since its presence might indeed be questioned by these facts, came to its own support: when the story is told in Dublin today it is never forgotten that it has roots in Professor Flacks's causing girls to giggle because he repeatedly made a joke at Heffernan's expense.

Employed by the University to instruct in certain aspects of literature, Professor Flacks concentrated his attention on the writings of James Joyce. Shakespeare, Tennyson, Shelley, Coleridge, Wilde, Swift, Dickens, Eliot, Trollope, and many another familiar name were all bundled away in favour of a Joycean scholarship that thirty or so years ago was second to none in Irish university life. Professor Flacks could tell you whom Joyce had described as a terrified YMCA man, and the date of the day on which he had written that his soul was full of decayed ambitions. He spoke knowledgeably of the stale smell of incense, like foul flowerwater; and of flushed eaves and stubble geese.

'Inane bloody show-off,' Heffernan said nastily in Kehoe's.

'You'll see him out, Heff.'

'A bogs like that would last for ever.'

Twelve months later, after he and Heffernan had parted company, FitzPatrick repeated all that to me. I didn't know either of them well, but was curious because a notable friendship had so abruptly come to an end. FitzPatrick, on his own, was inclined to talk to anyone.

We sat in College Park, watching the cricket while he endeavoured to remember the order of subsequent events. It was Heffernan who'd had the idea, as naturally it would be, since FitzPatrick still knew Professor Flacks only by repute and had not suffered the sarcasm which Heffernan found so offensive. But FitzPatrick played a vital part in the events which followed, because the elderly woman who played the main part of all was a general maid in FitzPatrick's digs.

'Has that one her slates on?' Heffernan enquired one night as they passed her by in the hall.

'Ah, she's only a bit quiet.'

'She has a docile expression all right.'

'She wouldn't damage a fly.'

Soon after that Heffernan took to calling in at FitzPatrick's digs in Donnybrook more often than he had in the past. Sometimes he was there when FitzPatrick arrived back in the evening, sitting in the kitchen while the elderly maid pricked sausages or cut up bread for the meal that would shortly be served. Mrs Redmond, the landlady, liked to lie down for a while at that time of day, so Heffernan and the maid had the kitchen to themselves. But finding him present on several occasions when she came downstairs, Mrs Redmond in passing mentioned the fact to her lodger. FitzPatrick, who didn't himself understand what Heffernan's interest in the general maid was, replied that his friend liked to await his return in the kitchen because it was warm. Being an easy-going woman, Mrs Redmond was appeased.

'There's no doubt in my mind at all,' Heffernan stated in Kehoe's after a few weeks of this behaviour. 'If old Flacks could hear it he'd have a tortoise's pup.'

FitzPatrick wagged his head, knowing that an explanation was in the air. Heffernan said: 'She's an interesting old lassie.'

He then told FitzPatrick a story which FitzPatrick had never heard before. It concerned a man called Corley who had persuaded a maid in a house in Baggot Street to do a small service for him. It concerned, as well, Corley's friend, Lenehan, who was something of a wit. At first FitzPatrick was confused by the story, imagining it to be about a couple of fellow-students whom he couldn't place.

'The pen of Jimmy Joyce,' Heffernan explained. 'That yarn is Flacks's favourite of the lot.

'Well, I'd say there wasn't much to it. Sure, a skivvy never would.'

'She was gone on Corley.'

'But would she steal for him?'

'You're no romantic, Fitz.'

FitzPatrick laughed, agreeable to accepting this opinion. Then, to his astonishment, Heffernan said: 'It's the same skivvy Mrs Redmond has above in your digs.'

FitzPatrick shook his head. He told Heffernan to go on with himself, but Heffernan insisted.

'She told me the full story herself one night I was waiting for you—maybe the first night I ever addressed a word to her. "Come into the kitchen outa the cold, Mr Heffernan," she says. D'you remember the occasion it was? Late after tea, and you didn't turn up at all. She fried me an egg.'

'But, holy Christ, man—'

'It was the same night you did well with the nurse from Dundrum.'

FitzPatrick guffawed. A great girl, he said. He repeated a few details, but Heffernan didn't seem interested.

'I was told the whole works in the kitchen, like Jimmy Joyce had it out of her when she was still in her teens. A little gold sovereign was what she fecked for your man.'

'But the poor old creature is as honest as the day's long.'

'Oh, she took it all right and she still thinks Corley was top of the bill.'

'But Corley never existed—'

'Of course he did. Wasn't he for ever entertaining that fine little tart with the witticisms of Master Lenehan?'

The next thing that happened, according to FitzPatrick, was that a bizarre meeting took place. Heffernan approached Professor Flacks with the information that the model for the ill-used girl in Joyce's story 'Two Gallants' had come to light in a house in Donnybrook. The Professor displayed considerable excitement, and on a night when Mrs Redmond was safely at the pictures he was met by Heffernan at the bus-stop and led to the kitchen.

He was a frail man in a tweed suit, not at all as FitzPatrick had imagined him. Mrs Redmond's servant, a woman of about the same age, was slightly deaf and moved slowly owing to rheumatism. Heffernan had bought half a pound of figroll biscuits which he arranged on a plate. The old woman poured tea.

Professor Flacks plied her with questions. He asked them gently, with courtesy and diplomacy, without any hint of the tetchiness described so often by Heffernan. It was a polite occasion in the kitchen, Heffernan handing round the figrolls, the maid appearing to delight in recalling a romance in her past.

'And later you told Mr Joyce about this?' prompted Professor Flacks.

'He used come to the house when I worked in North Frederick Street, sir. A dentist by the name of O'Riordan.'

'Mr Joyce came to get his teeth done?'

'He did, sir.'

'And you'd talk to him in the waiting-room, is that it?'

'I'd be lonesome, sir. I'd open the hall-door when the bell rang and then there'd be a wait for maybe an hour before it'd ring again, sir. I recollect Mr Joyce well, sir.'

'He was interested in your—ah—association with the fellow you mentioned, was he?'

'It was only just after happening, sir. I was turned out of the place in Baggot Street on account of the bit of trouble. I was upset at the time I knew Mr Joyce, sir.'

'That's most understandable.'

'I'd often tell a patient what had happened to me.'

'But you've no hard feelings today? You were badly used by the fellow, yet—'

'Ah, it's long ago now, sir.'

Heffernan and FitzPatrick saw the Professor on to a bus and, according to FitzPatrick, he was quivering with pleasure. He clambered into a seat, delightedly talking to himself, not noticing when they waved from the pavement. They entered a convenient public house and ordered pints of stout.

'Did you put her up to it?' FitzPatrick enquired.

'The thing about that one, she'd do anything for a scrap of

the ready. Didn't you ever notice that about her? She's a right old miser.'

It was that that Heffernan had recognised when first he'd paid a visit to Mrs Redmond's kitchen: the old maid was possessed of a meanness that had become obsessional with her. She spent no money whatsoever, and was clearly keen to add to what she had greedily accumulated. He had paid her a pound to repeat the story he had instructed her in.

'Didn't she say it well? Oh, top of the bill, I'd say she was.'

'You'd be sorry for old Flacks.'

'Oh, the devil take bloody Mr Flacks.'

Some months went by. Heffernan no longer visited the kitchen in Donnybrook, and he spoke hardly at all of Professor Flacks. In his lazy way FitzPatrick assumed that the falsehoods which had been perpetrated were the be-all and end-all of the affair, that Heffernan's pride—now clearly revealed to him— had somehow been satisfied. But then, one summer's afternoon while the two idled in Stephen's Green in the hope of picking up girls, Heffernan said: 'There's a thing on we might go to next Friday.'

'What's that?'

'Mr Flacks performing. The Society of the Friends of James Joyce.'

It was a public lecture, one of several that were to be delivered during a week devoted by the Society to the life and work of the author who was its *raison d'être*. The Society's members came from far afield: from the United States, Germany, Finland, Italy, Australia, France, England and Turkey. Learned academics mingled with less learned enthusiasts. Mr James Duffy's Chapelizod was visited, and Mr Power's Dublin Castle. Capel Street and Ely Place were investigated, visits were made to the renowned Martello Tower, to Howth and to Pim's. Betty Bellezza was mentioned, and Val from Skibbereen. The talk was all Joyce talk. For a lively week Joyce reigned in Dublin.

On the appointed evening FitzPatrick accompanied his friend to Professor Flacks's lecture, his premonitions suggesting that the occasion was certain to be tedious. He had no idea what Heffernan was up to, and wasn't prepared to devote energy to speculating. With a bit of luck, he hoped, he'd be able to have a sleep.

Before the main event a woman from the University of Washington spoke briefly about Joyce's use of misprints; a bearded German read a version of 'The Holy Office' that had only recently been discovered. Then the tweeded figure of Professor Flacks rose. He sipped at a tumbler of water, and spoke for almost an hour about the model for the servant girl in the story, 'Two Gallants'. His discovery of that same elderly servant, now employed in a house in Donnybrook, engendered in his audience a whisper of excitement that remained alive while he spoke, and exploded into applause when he finished. A light flush enlivened the paleness of his face as he sat down. It was, as Heffernan remarked to his dozy companion, the old man's finest hour.

It was then that FitzPatrick first became uneasy. The packed lecture-hall had accepted as fact all that had been stated, yet none of it was true. Notes had been taken, questions were now being asked. A voice just behind the two students exclaimed that this remarkable discovery was worth coming two thousand miles to hear about. Mental pictures of James Joyce in a dentist's waiting-room flashed about the hall. North Frederick Street would be visited tomorrow, if not tonight.

'I'd only like to ask,' Heffernan shouted above the hubbub, 'if I may, a simple little question.' He was on his feet. He had caught the attention of Professor Flacks, who was smiling benignly at him. 'I'd only like to enquire,' Heffernan continued, 'if that whole thing couldn't be a lot of baloney.'

'Baloney?' a foreign voice repeated.

'Baloney?' said Professor Flacks.

The buzz of interest hadn't died down. Nobody was much interested in the questions that were being asked except the people who were asking them. A woman near to FitzPatrick said it was extraordinarily moving that the ill-used servant girl, who had been so tellingly presented as an off-stage character by Joyce, should bear no grudge all these years later.

'What I mean, Professor Flacks,' said Heffernan, 'is I don't think James Joyce ever attended a dentist in North Frederick Street. What I'm suggesting to you, sir, is that the source of your information was only looking for a bit of limelight.'

FitzPatrick later described to me the expression that entered Professor Flacks's eyes. 'A lost kind of look,' he said, 'as though someone had poked the living daylights out of him.' The old man stared at Heffernan, frowning, not comprehending at first. His relationship with this student had been quite different since the night of the visit to Mrs Redmond's kitchen: it had been distinguished by a new friendliness, and what had seemed like mutual respect.

'Professor Flacks and myself', continued Heffernan, 'heard the old lady together. Only I formed the impression that she was making the entire matter up. I thought, sir, you'd formed that opinion also.'

'Oh, but surely now, Mr Heffernan, the woman wouldn't do that.'

'There was never a dentist by the name of O'Riordan that practised in North Frederick Street, sir. That's a fact that can easily be checked.'

Heffernan sat down. An uneasy silence gripped the lecture-hall. Eyes turned upon Professor Flacks. Weakly, with a hoarseness in his voice, he said: 'But why, Mr Heffernan, would she have made all that up? A woman of that class would hardly have read the story, she'd hardly have known—'

'It's an unfortunate thing, sir,' interrupted Heffernan, standing up again, 'but that old one would do anything for a single pound note. She's of a miserly nature. I think what has happened,' he went on, his tone changing as he addressed the assembly, 'is that a student the Professor failed in an examination took a chance to get his own back. Our friend Jas Joyce,' he added, 'would definitely have relished that.'

In misery Professor Flacks lifted the tumbler of water to his lips, his eyes cast down. You could sense him thinking, FitzPatrick reported, that he was a fool and he had been shown to be a fool. You could sense him thinking that he suddenly appeared to be unreliable, asinine and ridiculous. In front of the people who mattered to him most of all he had been exposed as a fraud he did not feel himself to be. Never again could he hold his head up among the Friends of James Joyce. Within twenty-four hours his students would know what had occurred.

An embarrassed shuffling broke out in the lecture-hall. People murmured and began to make their way into the aisles. FitzPatrick recalled the occasion in Mrs Redmond's kitchen, the two elderly puppets on the end of Heffernan's string, the figrolls and the tea. He recalled the maid's voice retailing the story that he, because he knew Heffernan so well, had doubted with each word that was uttered. He felt guilty that he hadn't sought the old man out and told him it wasn't true. He glanced through the throng in the lecture-hall at the lone figure in porridgy tweeds, and unhappily reflected that suicide had been known to follow such wretched disgrace. Outside the lecture-hall he told Heffernan to go to hell when a drink in Anne Street was suggested—a remark for which Heffernan never forgave him.

'I mean,' FitzPatrick said as we sat in College Park a long time later, 'how could anyone be as petty? When all the poor old fellow ever said to him was "I see you are still with us"?'

I made some kind of reply. Professor Flacks had died a natural death a year after the delivery of his lecture on 'Two Gallants'. Earlier in his life he had not, as Heffernan had claimed, driven a wife and two sisters mad: he'd been an only child, the obituary said in the *Irish Times*, and a bachelor. It was an awkward kind of obituary, for the gaffe he'd made had become quite famous and was still fresh in Dubliners' minds.

We went on talking about him, FitzPatrick and I, as we watched the cricket in College Park. We spoke of his playful sarcasm and how so vehemently it had affected Heffernan's pride. We marvelled over the love that had caused a girl in a story to steal, and over the miserliness that had persuaded an old woman to be party to a trick. FitzPatrick touched upon his own inordinate laziness, finding a place for that also in our cobweb of human frailty.

The Wedding in the Garden

Ever since Dervla was nine the people of the hotel had fascinated her. Its proprietor, Mr Congreve, wore clothes that had a clerical sombreness about them, though they were of a lighter hue than Father Mahony's stern black. Mr Congreve was a smiling man with a quiet face, apparently not in the least put out by reports in the town that his wife, in allying herself with a hotel proprietor, had married beneath her. Ladylike and elegant, she appeared not to regret her choice. Mrs Congreve favoured in her dresses a distinctive blend of greens and blues, her stylishness combining with the hotel proprietor's tranquil presence to lend the couple a quality that was unique in the town. Their children, two girls and an older boy, were imbued with this through the accident of their birth, and so were different from the town's other children in ways that might be termed superficial. 'Breeding,' Dervla's father used to say. 'The Congreves have great breeding in them.'

She herself, when she was nine, was fair-haired and bony, with a graze always healing on one knee or the other because she had a way of tripping on her shoe-laces. 'Ah, will you tie up those things!' her mother used to shout at her: her mother, big-faced and red, blinking through the steam that rose from a bucket of water. Her brothers and sisters had all left the house in Thomas MacDonagh Street by the time Dervla was nine; they'd left the town and the district, two of them in America even, one in London. Dervla was more than just the baby of the family: she was an afterthought, catching everyone unawares, born when her mother was forty-two. 'Chance had a hand in that one,' her father liked to pronounce, regarding her affectionately, as if pleased by this intervention of fate. When his brother from Leitrim visited the house in Thomas MacDonagh Street the statement was made often, being of family interest. 'If her mother didn't possess the strength of an ox,' Dervla's father liked to add, 'God knows how the end of it would have been.' And Dervla's Leitrim uncle, refreshing himself with a bottle of stout, would yet again wag his head in admiration and wonder at his sister-in-law's robust constitution. He was employed on the roads up in Leitrim and only came to the town on a Sunday, drawn to it by a hurling match. Dervla's father was employed by O'Mara the builder.

Even after she went to work in the Royal Hotel and came to know the family, her first image of them remained: the Congreves in their motor-car, an old Renault as she afterwards established, its canvas hood folded back, slowly making the journey to the Protestant church on a sunny Sunday morning. St Peter's Church was at one end of the town, the Royal Hotel at the other. It had, before its days as an hotel, apparently been owned by Mrs Congreve's family, and then people in the grocery business had bought it and had not lived there, people who had nothing to do with the town, who were not well known. After that Mr Congreve had made an offer with, so it was said, his wife's money.

The motor-car in the sunlight crept down Draper's Street, the bell of St Peter's Church still monotonously chiming. The boy—no older than Dervla herself—sat between his sisters in the back; Mr Congreve turned his head and said something to his wife. Daddy Phelan, outside Mrs Ryan's bar, saluted them in his wild way; Mrs Congreve waved back at him. The boy wore a grey flannel suit, the girls had fawn-coloured coats and tiny bows in their pigtails. The motor-car passed from view, and a moment later the bell ceased to chime.

*

Christopher couldn't remember the first time he'd been aware of her. All he knew was that she worked in the kitchen of the hotel, walking out from the town every day. Playing with Molly and Margery-Jane in the shrubberies of the garden, he had noticed now and again a solitary figure in a black coat, with a headscarf. He didn't know her name or what her face was like. 'Count to ten, Chris,' Margery-Jane would shrilly insist. 'You're not counting to ten!' Some game, rules now forgotten, some private family game they had invented themselves, stalking one another among the bamboos and the mahonias, Molly creeping on her hands and knees, not making a sound, Margery-Jane unable to control her excited breathing. The girl passed through the yard near by, a child as they were, but they paid her no attention.

A year or so later Mary, the elderly maid whose particular realm was the dining-room, instructed her in the clearing of a table. 'Dervla,' his mother said when the older waitress had led her away with cutlery and plates piled on to her tray. 'Her name is Dervla.' After that she was always in the dining-room at mealtimes.

It was then, too, that she began to come to the hotel on a bicycle, her day longer now, arriving before breakfast, cycling home again in the late evening. Once there was talk about her living there, but nothing had come of that. Christopher didn't know where she did live, had never once noticed Thomas MacDonagh Street in his wanderings about the town. Returning from boarding-school in Dublin, he had taken to going for walks, along the quay of the river where the sawmills were, through the lanes behind Brabazon's Brewery. He preferred to be alone at that time of his growing up, finding the company of his sisters too chattery. The river wound away through fields and sometimes a dog from the lanes or the cottages near the electricity plant would follow him. There was one in particular, a short-tailed terrier, its smooth white coat soiled and uncared for, ears and head flashed with black. There was a mongrel sheepdog also, an animal that ceased its customary cringing as soon as it gained the freedom of the fields. When he returned to the town these animals no longer followed him, but were occasionally involved in fights with other dogs, as though their excursion into the country had turned them into aliens who were no longer to be trusted. He went on alone then, through darkening afternoons or spitting rain, lingering by the shops that sold fruit and confectionery. There'd been a time when he and Margery-Jane and Molly had come to these shops with their pocket-money, for Peggy's Leg or pink bon-bons. More affluent now, he bought *Our Boys* and *Film Fun* and saved up for the *Wide World*.

His sisters had been born in the Royal Hotel, but he— before his father owned the place—in Dublin, where his parents had then lived. He did not remember Dublin: the hotel had become his world. It was a white building, set back a little from the street, pillars and steps prefacing its entrance doors. Its plain façade was decorated with a yellow AA sign and a blue RIAC one; in spring tulips bloomed in window-boxes on the downstairs windowsills. The words *Royal Hotel* were painted in black on this white façade and repeated in smaller letters above the pillared porch. At the back, beyond the yard and the garden, there was a row of garages and an entrance to them from Old Lane. The hotel's four employees came and went this way, Mrs O'Connor the cook, whatever maids there were, and Artie the boots. There was a stone-flagged hallway with doors off it to the kitchen and the larders and the scullery, and one to the passage that led to the back staircase. It was a dim hallway, with moisture sometimes on its grey-distempered walls, a dimness that was repeated in the passage that led to the back staircase and on the staircase itself. Upstairs there was a particular smell, of polish and old soup, with a tang of porter drifting up from the bar. The first-floor landing—a sideboard stretching along one wall, leather armchairs by the windows, occasional tables piled with magazines, a gold-framed mirror above the fire-place—was the heart of the hotel. Off it were the better bedrooms and a billiard-room where the YMCA held a competition every March; above it there was a less impressive landing, little more than a corridor. On the ground floor the dining-room had glass swing-doors, twelve tables with white table-cloths, always set for dinner. The family occupied a corner one between the fire and the dumb waiter, with its array of silver-plated sugar castors and salt and pepper and mustard containers, bottles of Yorkshire Relish, thick and thin, mint sauce in cut-glass jugs, and Worcester sauce, and jam and marmalade.

When Christopher was younger, before he went away to school, he and Margery-Jane and Molly used to play hide and seek in the small, cold bedrooms at the top of the house, skulking in the shadows on the uncarpeted stairs that led to the attics. Occasionally, if a visitor was staying in the hotel, their father would call up to them to make less noise, but this didn't happen often because a visitor was usually only in the hotel at night. They were mainly senior commercial travellers who stayed at the Royal, representatives of Wills or Horton's or Drummond's seeds, once a year the Urney man; younger representatives lodged more modestly. Insurance men stayed at the hotel, and bank inspectors had been known to spend a fortnight or three weeks. Bord na Móna men came and went, and once in a while there was an English couple or a couple from the North, touring or on their honeymoon. When Miss Gilligan, who taught leatherwork at the technical college, first came to the town she spent nearly a month in the Royal before being satisfied with the lodging she was offered. Artie the boots, grey-haired but still in his forties, worked in the garden and the yard, disposed of empty bottles from the bar and often served there. Old Mary served there too, and at a busy time, which only rarely occurred, Mrs O'Connor would come up from the kitchen to assist. Dr Molloy drank at the Royal, and Hogarty the surveyor, and the agent at the Bank of Ireland, Mr Madden, and a few of the other bank men in the town. The bar was a quiet place, though, compared with the town's public houses; voices were never raised.

The main hall of the hotel was quiet also, except for the ticking of the grandfather clock and its chiming. There was the same agreeable smell there, of soup and polish, and porter from the bar. A barometer hung beneath a salmon in a glass case, notices of point-to-point races and the Dublin Spring Show and the Horse Show hung from hooks among coloured prints of Punchestown. The wooden floor was covered almost completely with faded rugs, and the upper half of the door to the bar was composed of frosted glass with a border of shamrocks. There were plants in brass pots on either side of a wide staircase with a greenish carpet, threadbare in parts.

'Your inheritance one day,' Christopher's father said.

*

It was very grand, Dervla considered, to have your initials on a green trunk, and on a wooden box with metal brackets fixed to its edges. These containers stood in the back hall, with a suitcase, at the beginning of each term, before they were taken to the railway station. They stood there again when Christopher returned, before Artie helped him to carry them upstairs.

On his first day back from school there was always a great fuss. His sisters became very excited, a special meal was prepared, Mr Congreve would light cigarette after cigarette, standing in front of the fire on the first-floor landing, listening to Christopher's tale of the long journey from Dublin. He always arrived in the evening, sometimes as late as seven o'clock but usually about half-past five. In the dining-room when the family had supper he would say he was famished and tell his sisters how disgraceful the food at the school was, the turnips only half mashed, the potatoes with bits of clay still clinging to their skins, and a custard pudding called Yellow Peril. His mother, laughing at him, would say he shouldn't exaggerate, and his father would ask him about the rugby he had played, or the cricket. 'Like the game of tennis it would be,' Artie told her when Dervla asked him what cricket was. 'The way they'd wear the same type of clothing for it.' Miss Gillespie, the matron, was a tartar and Mickey the furnace man's assistant told stories that couldn't be repeated. Dervla imagined the big grey house with a curving avenue leading up to it, and bells always ringing, and morning assemblies, and the march through cloisters to the chapel, which so often she had heard described. She imagined the boys in their grey suits kneeling down to say their prayers, and the ice on the inside of the windows on cold days. The chemistry master had blown his hair off, it was reported once in the dining-room, and Dervla thought of Mr Jerety who made up the prescriptions in the Medical Hall. Mr Jerety had no hair either, except for a little at the sides of his head.

Dervla managed the dining-room on her own now. Mary had become too rheumaticky to make the journey at any speed from the kitchen and found it difficult to lift the heavier plates from the table. She helped Mrs O'Connor with the baking instead, kneading dough on the marble slab at the side table in the kitchen, making pastry and preparing vegetables. It took her half a day, Dervla had heard Mr Congreve say, to mount the stairs to her bedroom at the top of the hotel, and the other half to descend it. He was fond of her, and would try to make her rest by the fire on the first-floor landing but she never did. 'Sure, if I sat down there, sir, I'd maybe never get up again.' It was unseemly, Dervla had heard old Mary saying in the kitchen, for an employee to be occupying an armchair in the place where the visitors and the family sat. Mr Congreve was devil-may-care about matters like that, but what would a visitor say if he came out of his bedroom and found a uniformed maid in an armchair? What would Byrne from Horton's say, or Boylan the insurance man?

In the dining-room, when she'd learnt how everything should be, 'the formalities', as Mr Congreve put it, Dervla didn't find her duties difficult. She was swift on her feet, as it was necessary to be, in case the food got cold. She could stack a tray with dishes and plates so economically that two journeys to the kitchen became one. She was careful at listening to what the visitors ordered and without writing anything down was able to relay the message to the kitchen. The family were never given a choice.

*

Often Christopher found himself glancing up from the food Dervla placed in front of him, to follow with his eyes her progress across the dining-room, the movement of her hips beneath her black dress, her legs clad in stockings that were black also. Once he addressed her in the back yard. He spoke softly, just behind her in the yard. It was dark, after seven, an evening in early March when a bitter wind was blowing. 'I'll walk with you, Dervla,' he said.

She wheeled her bicycle in Old Lane and they walked in silence except that once he remarked upon the coldness of the weather and she said she disliked rain more. When they reached the end of the lane he went one way and she the other.

'Hullo, Dervla,' he said one afternoon in the garden. It was late in August. He was lying on a rug among the hydrangeas, reading. She had passed without noticing that he was there; she returned some minutes later with a bunch of parsley. It was then that he addressed her. He smiled, trying to find a different intonation, trying to make his greeting softer, less ordinary than usual. He wanted her to sit down on the brown checked rug, to enjoy the sun for a while, but of course that was impossible. He had wanted to wheel her bicycle for her that evening, as he would have done had she been another girl, Hazel Warren or Annie Warren, the coal merchant's daughters, or a girl he'd never even spoken to, someone's cousin, who used to visit the town every Christmas. But it hadn't seemed natural in any way at all to wheel the bicycle of the dining-room maid, any more than it would have been to ask a kitchen maid at school where she came from or if she had brothers and sisters.

'Hullo,' she said, replying to his greeting in the garden. She passed on with her bunch of parsley, seeming not to be in a hurry, the crisp white strings of her apron bobbing as she walked.

*

In her bedroom in the house in Thomas MacDonagh Street she thought of him every night before she went to sleep. She saw him as he was when he returned from his boarding-school, in his grey long-trousered suit, a green-and-white striped tie knotted into the grey collar of his shirt. When she awoke in the morning she thought of him also, the first person to share the day with. In winter she lay there in the darkness, but in summer the dawn light lit the picture of the Virgin above the door, and when Dervla felt the Virgin's liquid eyes upon her she prayed, asking the Holy Mother for all sorts of things she afterwards felt she shouldn't have because they were trivial. She pleaded that he might smile when he thanked her for the rashers and sausages she put in front of him, that his little finger might accidentally touch her hand as only once it had. She pleaded that Mr Congreve wouldn't engage her in conversation at lunchtime, asking how her father was these days, because somehow—in front of him—it embarrassed her.

There was a nightmare she had, possessing her in varied forms: that he was in the house in Thomas MacDonagh Street and that her mother was on her knees, scrubbing the stone floor of the scullery. Her mother didn't seem to know who he was and would not stand up. Her father and her uncle from Leitrim sat drinking stout by the fire, and when she introduced him they remarked upon his clothes. Sometimes in the nightmare her uncle nudged him with his elbow and asked him if he had a song in him.

'That young Carroll has an eye for you,' her father said once or twice, drawing her attention to Buzzy Carroll who worked in Catigan's hardware. But she didn't want to spend Sunday afternoons walking out on the Ballydrim road with Buzzy Carroll, or to sit with his arms around her in the Excel Cinema. One of the Christian Brothers had first called him Buzzy, something to do with the way his hair fluffed about his head, and after that no one could remember what Buzzy Carroll's real name was. There were others who would have liked to go out with her, on walks or to the pictures, or to the Tara Dance-hall on a Friday night. There was Flynn who worked in Maguire's timber yard, and Chappie Reagan, and Butty Delaney. There was the porter at the auction rooms who had something the matter with his feet, the toes joined together in such a peculiar way that he showed them to people. And there was Streak Dwyer. 'You're nothing only a streak of woe,' the same Christian Brother had years ago pronounced. Streak Dwyer had ever since retained the sobriquet, serving now in Clancy's grocery, sombrely weighing flour and sugar. Dervla had once or twice wondered what walking out on the Ballydrim road with this melancholy shopman would be like and if he would suggest turning into one of the lanes, as Butty Delaney or Buzzy Carroll would have. She wouldn't have cared for it in the Excel Cinema with Streak Dwyer any more than she cared for the idea of being courted by a man who showed people his toes.

*

'Dervla.'

On a wet afternoon, a Tuesday in September, he whispered her name on the first-floor landing. He put his arm around her, and she was frightened in case someone would come.

'I'm fond of you, Dervla.'

He took her hand and led her upstairs to Room 14, a tiny bedroom that was only used when the hotel was full. Both of them were shy, and their shyness evaporated slowly. He kissed her, stroking her hair. He said again he was fond of her. 'I'm fond of you too,' she whispered.

After that first afternoon they met often to embrace in Room 14. They would marry, he said at the end of that holidays; they would live in the hotel, just like his parents. Over and over again in Room 14 the afternoon shadows gathered as sunlight slipped away. They whispered, clinging to one another, the warmth of their bodies becoming a single warmth. She sat huddled on his knee, holding tightly on to him in case they both fell off the rickety bedroom chair. He loved the curve of her neck, he whispered, and her soft fair hair, her lips and her eyes. He loved kissing her eyes.

Often there was silence in the bedroom, broken only by the

faraway cries of Molly and Margery-Jane playing in the garden. Sometimes it became quite dark in the room, and she would have to go then because Mrs O'Connor would be wanting her in the kitchen.

'Not a bad fella at all,' her father said in Thomas Mac-Donagh Street. 'Young Carroll.' She wanted to laugh when her father said that, wondering what on earth he'd say if he knew about Room 14. He would probably say nothing; in silence he would take his belt to her. But the thought of his doing so didn't make her afraid.

'Oh, Dervla, how I wish the time would hurry up and pass!'

Over the years he had come to see the town as little better than a higgledy-piggledy conglomeration of dwellings, an ugly place except for the small bridge at the end of Mill Street. But it was Dervla's town, and it was his own; together they belonged there. He saw himself in middle age walking through its narrow streets, as he had walked during his childhood. He saw himself returning to the hotel and going at once to embrace the wife he loved with a passion that had not changed.

'Oh, Dervla,' he whispered in Room 14. 'Dervla, I'm so fond of you.'

*

'Well, now, I think we must have a little talk,' Mrs Congreve said.

They were alone in the dining-room; Dervla had been laying the tables for dinner. When Mrs Congreve spoke she felt herself reddening; the knives and forks felt suddenly cold in her hands.

'Finish the table, Dervla, and then we'll talk about it.'

She did as she was bidden. Mrs Congreve stood by a window, looking out at people passing on the street. When Dervla had finished she caught a glimpse of herself in the mirror over the fire-place. Her thin, pretty face had a frightened look, and seemed more freckled than usual, perhaps because she had paled. She averted her gaze almost as soon as the mirror reflected it. Mrs Congreve said:

'Mr Congreve and I are disappointed that this has happened. It's most unfortunate.'

Turning from the window, Mrs Congreve smiled a lingering, gracious smile. She was wearing one of her green and blue dresses, a flimsy, delicate garment with tiny blue buttons and a stylishly stiff white collar. Her dark hair was coiled silkily about her head.

'It is perhaps difficult for you to understand, Dervla, and certainly it is unpleasant for me to say. But there are differences between you and Christopher that cannot be overlooked or ignored.' Mrs Congreve paused and again looked out of the window, slightly drawing the net curtain aside. 'Christopher is not of your class, Dervla. He is not of your religion. You are a maid in this hotel. You have betrayed the trust that Mr Congreve and I placed in you. I'm putting it harshly, Dervla, but there's no point in pretending.'

Dervla did not say anything. She felt sick in her stomach. She wished he wasn't away at school. She wished she could run out of the dining-room and find him somewhere, that he would help her in this terrifying conversation.

'Oh, Christopher has done wrong also. I can assure you we are aware of that. We are disappointed in Christopher, but we think it better to close the matter in his absence. He will not be back for another three months almost; we think it best to have everything finished and forgotten by then. Mr Congreve will explain to Christopher.'

Again there was the gracious smile. No note of anger had entered Mrs Congreve's voice, no shadow of displeasure disrupted the beauty of her features. She might have been talking about the annual point-to-point dinner, giving instructions about how the tables should be set.

'We would ask you to write a note now, to Christopher at school. Mr Congreve and I would like to see it, Dervla, before it goes on its way. That, then, would be the end of the matter.'

As she spoke, Mrs Congreve nodded sympathetically, honouring Dervla's unspoken protest: she understood, she said. She did not explain how the truth had come to be discovered, but suggested that in the note she spoke of Dervla should write that she felt in danger of losing her position in the Royal Hotel, that she was upset by what had taken place and would not wish any of it to take place again.

'That is the important aspect of it, Dervla. Neither Mr Congreve nor I wish to dismiss you. If we did, you—and we—would have to explain to your parents, even to Father Mahony, I suppose. If it's possible, Dervla, we would much rather avoid all that.'

But Dervla, crimson-faced, mentioned love. Her voice was weak, without substance and seeming to be without conviction, although this was not so. Mrs Congreve replied that that was penny-fiction talk.

'We want to get married, ma'am.' Dervla closed her eyes beneath the effort of finding the courage to say that. The palms of her hands, chilled a moment ago, were warmly moist now. She could feel pinpricks of perspiration on her forehead.

'That's very silly, Dervla,' Mrs Congreve said in the same calm manner. 'I'm surprised you should be so silly.'

'I love him,' Dervla cried, all convention abruptly shattered. Her voice was shrill in the dining-room, tears ran from her eyes and she felt herself seized by a wildness that made her want to shriek out in fury. 'I love him,' she cried again. 'It isn't just a little thing.'

'Don't you feel you belong in the Royal, Dervla? We have

THE WEDDING IN THE GARDEN

trained you, you know. We have done a lot, Dervla.'

There was a silence then, except for Dervla's sobbing. She found a handkerchief in the pocket of her apron and wiped her eyes and nose with it. In such silly circumstances, Mrs Congreve said, Christopher would not inherit the hotel. The hotel would be sold, and Christopher would inherit nothing. It wasn't right that a little thing like this should ruin Christopher's life. 'So you see, you must go, Dervla. You must take your wages up to the end of the month and go this afternoon.'

The tranquillity of Mrs Congreve's manner was intensified by the sadness in her voice. She was on Dervla's side, her manner insisted; her admonitions were painful for her. Again she offered the alternative:

'Or simply write a few lines to him, and we shall continue in the hotel as though nothing has happened. That is possible, you know. I assure you of that, my dear.'

Miserably, Dervla asked what she could say in a letter. She would have to tell lies. She wouldn't know how to explain.

'No, don't tell lies. Explain the truth: that you realise the friendship must not continue, now that you and he are growing up. You've always been a sensible girl, Dervla. You must realise that what happened between you was for children only.'

Dervla shook her head, but Mrs Congreve didn't acknowledge the gesture.

'I can assure you, Dervla—I can actually promise you—that when Christopher has grown up a little more he will see the impossibility of continuing such a friendship. The hotel, even now, is everything to Christopher. I can actually promise you, also, that you will not be asked to leave. I know you value coming here.'

*

At school, when he received the letter, Christopher was

(276)

astonished. In Dervla's tidy, convent handwriting it said that they must not continue to meet in Room 14 because it was a sin. It would be best to bring everything to an end now, before she was dismissed. They had done wrong, but at least they could avoid the worst if they were sensible now.

It was so chilly a letter, as from a stranger, that Christopher could hardly believe what it so very clearly said. Why did she feel this now, when a few weeks ago they had sworn to love one another for as long as they lived? Were all girls as fickle and as strange? Or had the priests, somehow, got at her, all this stuff about sin?

He could not write back. His handwriting on the envelope would be recognised in the hotel, and he did not know her address since she had not included it in her letter. He had no choice but to wait, and as days and then weeks went by his bewilderment turned to anger. It was stupid that she should suddenly develop these scruples after all they'd said to one another. The love he continued to feel for her became tinged with doubt and with resentment, as though they'd had a quarrel.

*

'Now, I don't want to say anything more about this,' his father said at the beginning of the next holidays. 'But it doesn't do, you know, to go messing about with the maids.'

That was the end of the unfortunateness as far as his father was concerned. It was not something that should be talked about, no good could come of that.

'It wasn't messing about.'

'That girl was very upset, Christopher.'

Three months ago Christopher would have said he wanted to marry Dervla, forced into that admission by what had been discovered. He would have spoken of love. But his father had managed to draw him aside to have this conversation before he'd had an opportunity even to see her, let alone speak to her. He felt confused, and uncertain about his feelings.

'It would be hard on her to dismiss her. We naturally didn't want to do that. We want the girl to remain here, Christopher, since really it's a bit of a storm in a tea-cup.'

His father lit a cigarette and seemed more at ease once he had made that pronouncement. There was a lazier look about his face than there had been a moment ago; a smile drifted over his lips. 'Good term?' he said, and Christopher nodded.

*

'Is it the priests, Dervla?' They stood together in a doorway in Old Lane, her bicycle propped against the kerb. 'Did the priests get at you?'

She shook her head.

'Did my mother speak to you?'

'Your mother only said a few things.'

She went away, wheeling her bicycle for a while before mounting it. He watched her, not feeling as miserable as when her letter had arrived, for during the months that had passed since then he had become reconciled to the loss of their relationship: between the lines of her letter there had been a finality.

He returned to the hotel and Artie helped him to carry his trunk upstairs. He wished that none of it had ever happened.

*

Dervla was glad he made no further effort to talk to her, but standing between courses by the dumb waiter in the dining-room, she often wondered what he was thinking. While the others talked he was at first affected by embarrassment because

at mealtimes in the past there had been the thrill of sur-
reptitious glances and forbidden smiles. But after a week or so
he became less quiet, joining in the family conversation, and
she became the dining-room maid again.

Yet for Dervla the moment of placing his food in front of him
was as poignant as ever it had been, and in her private moments
she permitted herself the luxury of dwelling in the past. In her
bedroom in Thomas MacDonagh Street she closed her eyes
and willed into her consciousness the afternoon sunlight of
Room 14. Once more she was familiar with the quickening of
his heart and the cool touch of his hands. Once more she clung
to him, her body huddled into his on the rickety chair in the
corner, the faraway cries of Molly and Margery-Jane gently
disturbing the silence.

Dervla did not experience bitterness. She was fortunate that
the Congreves had been above the pettiness of dismissing her,
and when she prayed she gave thanks for that. When more time
had gone by she found herself able to confess the sinning that
had been so pleasurable in Room 14, and was duly burdened
with a penance for both the misdemeanours and her long delay
in confessing them. She had feared to lose what there had been
through expiation, but the fear had been groundless: only
reality had been lost. 'Young Carroll was asking for you,' her
father reported in a bewildered way, unable to understand her
reluctance even to consider Buzzy Carroll's interest.

Everything was easier when the green trunk and the box with
the metal brackets stood in the back hall at the beginning of
another term, and when a few more terms had come and gone
he greeted her in the hotel as if all she had confessed to was a
fantasy. Like his parents, she sensed, he was glad her dismissal
had not been necessary, for that would have been unfair. 'Did
my mother speak to you?' The quiet vehemence there had been
in his voice was sweet to remember, but he himself would

naturally wish to forget it now: for him, Room 14 must have come to seem like an adventure in indiscretion, as naturally his parents had seen it.

Two summers after he left school Dervla noticed signs in him that painfully echoed the past. An archdeacon's daughter sometimes had lunch with the family: he couldn't take his eyes off her. Serving the food and in her position by the dumb waiter, Dervla watched him listening while the Archdeacon's daughter talked about how she and her parents had moved from one rectory to another and how the furniture hadn't fitted the new rooms, how there hadn't been enough stair-carpet. The Archdeacon's daughter was very beautiful. Her dark hair was drawn back from a centre parting, her light-blue eyes lit up when she smiled. A dimple came and went in one cheek only; her skin was like the porcelain of a doll's skin. Often in the dining-room she talked about her childhood in the seaside backwater where she had once lived. Every morning in summer and autumn she and her father had gone together to the strand to bathe. They piled their clothes up by a breakwater, putting stones on them if there was a wind, and then they would run down the sand to the edge of the sea. A man sometimes passed by on a horse, a retired lighthouse keeper, a lonely, widowed man. Christopher was entranced.

Dervla cleared away the dishes, expertly disposing of chop bones or bits of left-behind fat. Mary had years ago shown her how to flick the table refuse on to a single plate, a different one from the plate you gathered the used knives and forks on to. Doing so now, she too listened to everything the Archdeacon's daughter said. Once upon a time the Pierrots had performed on the strand in August, and Hewitt's Travelling Fun Fair had come; regularly, June to September, summer visitors filled the promenade boarding-houses, arriving on excursion trains. Garish pictures were painted with coloured powders on the

sand, castles and saints and gardens. 'I loved that place,' the
Archdeacon's daughter said.

Afterwards Dervla watched from an upstairs window, the
window in fact of Room 14. The Archdeacon's daughter sat
with him in the garden, each of them in a deck-chair, laughing
and conversing. They were always laughing: the Archdeacon's
daughter would say something and he would throw his head
back with appreciation and delight. Long before the engagement was announced Dervla knew that this was the girl who
was going to take her place, in his life and in the hotel.

*

The Archdeacon conducted the service in St Peter's, and then
the guests made their way to the garden of the hotel. That the
wedding reception was to be at the hotel was a business
arrangement between the Archdeacon and Mr Congreve, for
the expenses were to be the former's, as convention demanded.
It was a day in June, a Thursday, in the middle of a heatwave.

Dervla and a new maid with spectacles handed round glasses
of champagne. Artie saw to it that people had chairs to sit on if
they wished to sit. The Archdeacon's daughter wore a wedding
dress that had a faint shade of blue in it, and a Limerick lace
veil. She was kissed by people in the garden, she smiled while
helping to cut the wedding cake. Her four bridesmaids, Molly
and Margery-Jane among them, kept saying she looked
marvellous.

Speeches were made in the sunshine. Dr Molloy made one
and so did the best man, Tom Gouvernet, and Mr Congreve.
Dr Molloy remembered the day Christopher was born, and Mr
Congreve remembered the first time he'd set eyes on the
beauty of the Archdeacon's daughter, and Tom Gouvernet
remembered Christopher at school. Other guests remembered
other occasions; Christopher said he was the lucky man and

kissed the Archdeacon's daughter while people clapped their hands with delight. Tom Gouvernet fell backwards off the edge of a raised bed.

There was an excess of emotion in the garden, an excess of smiles and tears and happiness and love. The champagne glasses were held up endlessly, toast after toast. Christopher's mother moved among the guests with the plump wife of the Archdeacon and the Archdeacon himself, who was as frail as a stalk of straw. In his easy-going way Christopher's father delighted in the champagne and the sunshine, and the excitement of a party. Mr Madden, the bank agent, was there, and Hogarty the surveyor, and an insurance man who happened to be staying at the hotel. There was nothing Mr Congreve liked better than standing about talking to these bar-room companions.

'Thanks, Dervla.' Taking a glass from her tray, Christopher smiled at her because for ages that had been possible again.

'It's a lovely wedding, sir.'

'Yes, it is.'

He looked at her eyes, and was aware of the demanding steadiness of her gaze. He sensed what she was wondering and wondered it himself: what would have happened if she'd been asked to leave the hotel? He guessed, as she did: they would have shared the resentment and the anger that both of them had separately experienced; defiantly they would have continued to meet in the town; she would have accompanied him on his walks, out into the country and the fields. There would have been talk in the town and scenes in the hotel, their relationship would again have been proscribed. They would have drawn closer to one another, their outraged feelings becoming an element in the forbidden friendship. In the end, together they would have left the hotel and the town and neither of them would be standing here now. Both their lives would be quite different.

'You'll be getting married yourself one of these days, Dervla.'

'Ah, no no.'

She was still quite pretty. There was a simplicity about her freckled features that was pleasing; her soft fair hair was neat beneath her maid's white cap. But she was not beautiful. Once, not knowing much about it, he had imagined she was. It was something less palpable that distinguished her.

'Oh, surely? Surely, Dervla?'

'I don't see myself giving up the hotel, sir. My future's here, sir.'

He smiled again and passed on. But his smile, which remained while he listened to a story of Tom Gouvernet's about the hazards to be encountered on a honeymoon, was uneasy. An echo of the eyes that had gazed so steadily remained with him, as did the reference she made to her future. That she had not been turned out of the hotel had seemed something to be proud of at the time: a crudity had been avoided. But while Tom Gouvernet's lowered voice continued, he found himself wishing she had been. She would indeed not ever marry, her eyes had stated, she would not wish to.

A hand of his wife's slipped into one of his; the voice of Tom Gouvernet ceased. The hand was as delicate as the petal of a flower, the fingers so tiny that involuntarily he lifted them to his lips. Had Dervla seen? he wondered, and he looked through the crowd for a glimpse of her but could not see her. Hogarty the surveyor was doing a trick with a handkerchief, entertaining the coal merchant's daughters. Mr Madden was telling one of his stories.

'Ah, he's definitely the lucky man,' Tom Gouvernet said, playfully winking at the bride.

It had never occurred to Christopher before that while he

and his parents could successfully bury a part of the past, Dervla could not. It had never occurred to him that because she was the girl she was she did not appreciate that some experiences were best forgotten. Ever since the Congreves had owned the Royal Hotel a way of life had obtained there, but its subtleties had naturally eluded the dining-room maid.

'When you get tired of him,' Tom Gouvernet went on in the same light manner, 'you know who to turn to.'

'Oh, indeed I do, Tom.'

He should have told her about Dervla. If he told her now she would want Dervla to go; any wife would, in perfect reasonableness. An excuse must be found, she would say, even though a promise had been made.

'But I won't become tired of him,' she was saying, smiling at Tom Gouvernet. 'He's actually quite nice, you know.'

In the far distance Dervla appeared, hurrying from the hotel with a freshly laden tray. Christopher watched her, while the banter continued between bride and best man.

'He had the shocking reputation at school,' Tom Gouvernet said.

'Oh? I didn't know that.' She was still smiling; she didn't believe it. It wasn't true.

'A right Lothario you've got yourself hitched to.'

He would not tell her. It was too late for that, it would bewilder her since he had not done so before. It wouldn't be fair to require her not to wish that Dervla, even now, should be asked to go; or to understand that a promise made to a dining-room maid must be honoured because that was the family way.

Across the garden the Archdeacon lifted a glass from Dervla's tray. He was still in the company of his plump wife and Christopher's mother. They, too, took more champagne and then Dervla walked towards where Christopher was standing with his bride and his best man. She moved quickly through the crowd, not offering her tray of glasses to the guests she passed, intent upon her destination.

'Thank you, Dervla,' his wife of an hour said.

'I think Mr Hogarty,' he said himself, 'could do with more champagne.'

He watched her walking away and was left again with the insistence in her eyes. As the dining-room maid, she would become part of another family growing up in the hotel. She would listen to a mother telling her children about the strand where once she'd bathed, where a retired lighthouse keeper had passed by on a horse. For all his life he would daily look upon hers, but no words would ever convey her undramatic revenge because the right to speak, once his gift to her, had been taken away. He had dealt in cruelty and so now did she: her gift to him, held over until his wedding day, was that afternoon shadows would gather for ever in Room 14, while she kept faith.